PRAISE FOR *THIS WON'T END WELL*

"Never has a quirky lead character been so lovable or well drawn as Annie, the lovelorn chemist who carries *This Won't End Well*. Though she pretends to be closed off to the world, in fact she can't stop caring—and that push-pull of who to let into her life, and under what terms, is something we all understand at a soul-deep level. Annie's journey from oblivious in love to aware and empowered had me cheering and turning the pages madly, unable to tear myself away. If you want to laugh and lose yourself in a great read, this is the one for you!"

—Kelly Harms, bestselling author of *The Overdue Life of Amy Byler*

"Witty, wise, and of the moment, *This Won't End Well* is a story of unlikely friendships, calculated risks, and taking a stand—even when it's easier to maintain the status quo. Charmingly flawed and endearingly real characters combine with a unique format to make Camille Pagán's latest page-turner her best book yet."

—Kristy Woodson Harvey, bestselling author of
Slightly South of Simple

"Camille Pagán writes with deep compassion for her characters and for all of us who try so hard to do the right thing by the people we love. Annie, the protagonist at the center of her latest novel, is no exception. Quirky and occasionally clueless, charming and vulnerable, Annie's so real that you'll want to make her your best friend by the time you've reached the last page. *This Won't End Well* is Pagán at her finest—capturing readers with warmth, honesty, and keen observations about keeping love simple in a complicated world."

—Ann Garvin, *USA TODAY* bestselling author of *I Like You Just Fine*
When You're Not Around

THIS
WON'T
END
WELL

OTHER BOOKS BY CAMILLE PAGÁN

THIS WON'T END WELL

Camille Pagán

LAKE UNION
PUBLISHING

Published by Lake Union Publishing, Seattle

www.apub.com

Amazon, the Amazon logo, and Lake Union Publishing are trademarks of Amazon.com, Inc., or its affiliates.

ISBN-13: 9781542014809 (hardcover)
ISBN-10: 1542014808 (hardcover)
ISBN-13: 9781542014823 (paperback)
ISBN-10: 1542014824 (paperback)

Cover design and illustration by David Drummond

Printed in the United States of America

First edition

Dedicated to women in science—especially my inimitable friend Stefanie Galban.

ONE

July 14
TO: Jon Nichols
FROM: Annie Mercer
SUBJECT: What I didn't say

Dear Jon,

Hello seems like such an innocuous word, but it's really a portal to loss. One minute you're exchanging small talk with a green-eyed stranger; the next thing you know, five years have passed, that stranger is now your fiancé, and he's just informed you that he needs time to get his head on straight before marrying you.

While I'm being a bit glib, Jon, I actually understand—I really do. You've been pining for Paris for ages now, and it was shortsighted of me to suggest we go to Quebec instead. What French teacher *wouldn't* want to visit the motherland? I should have surprised you with a trip for two, but it's not too late to plan a Parisian honeymoon. (I hope you're taking notes as you saunter down the Champs-Élysées.) At any rate, I'm truly sorry. You listen to me ramble about graduate school all the time; maybe I haven't been giving your dreams equal attention.

I'm also sorry we fought about having children last week. I thought we were on the same page about the world's overpopulation problem and the inherent risks of creating small humans who share at least some of my parents' genetic material. I'll be the first to admit that I discounted your desire to carry on the Nichols name. I was wrong—but we can talk about this. Well, we could if you were here in Michigan instead of on the other side of the Atlantic, or at the very least had not announced that you intend to be out of touch for a whole month. (Yet you're no doubt checking email multiple times a day as you always do, and because you love me—you told me that yourself when you called to say you were leaving—I trust you'll do me the courtesy of reading this message. I will do my best to make it the only one I send.)

You swore this wasn't cold feet, but if you find yourself reaching for a pair of socks, I forgive you. Certainly you wouldn't be the first groom-to-be stricken with premarital angst, and I do hope these next four weeks prove to be fruitful. Now that I think about it, perhaps my father wouldn't have flown our family coop if he, too, had gone on a personal fact-finding mission before marrying my mother.

I know that it's been just two short days since you and I last spoke. It was only after you were already en route to Charles de Gaulle that I realized there was so much I should have said while I was standing in my mother's driveway, staring at my phone with my mouth hanging open. For example, I'd be remiss not to point out that your timing was less than ideal. Obviously, I'm struggling with the fact that my career was just derailed after Todd groped me in my own lab. (I'm aware that you believe I should've let SCI fire me so that I could at least collect unemployment, if not sue them—but as I pointed out the last time we discussed this, resigning was the only proactive action I could take, now that I know how deceptive and irrational Todd truly is.) But to add insult to injury, Leesa and I are no longer speaking.

Naturally, I called her yesterday to tell her about your leaving, and she rushed right over to comfort me. Instead of words of wisdom, however, she offered to sell me a chunk of rose quartz and a vial of frankincense essential oil, which she claimed was most effective when inhaled through a $131 diffuser ("friends and family discount," my foot!). These products, she said, were best for healing a broken heart. When I explained my heart was not broken, as your absence is temporary, she suggested I consider a piece of lapis lazuli for "truthfulness." At which point I informed Leesa that the truth was that lately, my oldest friend only seems to have time for me when she's trying to peddle a bunch of shiny rocks and scented mineral oil with absolutely no scientific evidence to support their so-called curative properties. I mean, really—has she forgotten I'm a chemist? Anyway, she got all huffy and said that her *other* friends appreciate her entrepreneurial spirit, and she didn't know why I couldn't, too. I'll be honest, Jon; that hurt. Because by "other" friends, she, of course, means the mommy-and-me crowd she took up with after Molly and Ollie were born. Leesa and I have known each other since kindergarten, and like two ions with opposite charges, our differences have always brought us closer together. But now it seems as though just because I don't drive around town in a minivan and count the hours in espresso shots until wine o'clock arrives, she can't relate to me.

Or maybe I can't relate to her. Because if I realized one thing yesterday, it was that Leesa's lost her ability to be objective—and I don't know where that leaves us, let alone what it means for her status as my matron of honor.

At any rate, I still blame myself for your leaving. If I had moved in with you last year when you asked, maybe we would've had more opportunities to work through some of the issues that you're now tackling alone in a foreign country. When you get back, I'll be ready to discuss what's bothering you and find a home together prior to our wedding. Maybe we can look for something with several bedrooms, in case we do decide to have children.

Mostly, though, I'm writing to let you know I already miss you. I'm sure I'm overreacting because of my father—and of course, you'd be the first to say that my predisposition to cynicism leads me to seek out the worst-case scenario until solid data points me in a sunnier direction. But I can't help but worry that now that you're in France, you're going to want to stay there, rather than returning to the woman who loves you.

Please provide evidence to the contrary, Jon. I eagerly await your response.

Love always,
Annie

TWO

July 15

I must have fallen down an existential black hole, because I haven't kept a journal since I was a child and my dear neighbor, Viola, gave me a pink plastic-coated one with a tiny heart-shaped lock. While I continue to question the value of writing to oneself, I do recall the many aha moments I experienced when scribbling my childhood angst on those lined pages. Granted, I'm typing in a word-processing document this time instead of putting a pen to pink paper—but research supports the efficacy of both mediums. Here's hoping I find some clarity yet again, because to be honest, I feel like the events of the past week or so have sapped my greatest strength: the ability to think clearly.

Anyway, I need to do *something* other than overload Jon's inbox. Maybe this will help me stay in a productive headspace in preparation for his return so we can work through—well, whatever it is that's caused him to take such drastic measures. I've been searching the far corners of my mind for days trying to figure out why he did this, and I'm not coming up with anything concrete. Wouldn't there have been signs if he were in the midst of a crisis?

I certainly didn't notice any when we had dinner together last Tuesday. Now, he did wait until my mouth was full of chicken satay to relay Carolyn's "concern" about my twenty-seven-year-old eggs, which she feels are fast approaching their expiration date. And yes, I shut that conversation down as soon as I'd swallowed—as I maintain that Jon's mother has no business weighing in on anything pertaining to my pelvic region. But we made love at his apartment afterward, and while he did seem a bit preoccupied, it's not like there was a packed suitcase beside his bed. And when he kissed me goodbye at the end of the night, I never got the sense it was for a whole month.

Then Thursday afternoon, he called to say he was off to Paris.

Without me.

"I've been so stressed, Annie," he said. "You know that."

Did I? Because last time I checked, he had the entire summer off to decompress. Teaching won't make him rich, as Carolyn and Charles are forever reminding him—but it does come with that perk.

"And it just seems like . . . well, like it's now or never," he added.

"Now or never? You have your whole life ahead of you," I said.

"Roger probably thought that, too," he said.

Yes, there's the issue of his childhood friend dying of cancer. While it was awful, it happened a full year ago. Maybe the anniversary triggered Jon? Or maybe being unable to ask Roger to be in his wedding party reminded him of the fleeting nature of life. I'm speculating, of course, as he didn't fill me in. Worse, he seemed eager to get off the phone.

"Do you want me to come with you?" I asked, already calculating the cost of a last-minute ticket. My steady paycheck has been replaced with a slim stack of small bills from my housecleaning clients, but I do have savings.

"That's the thing. I really want to do this alone—it's the only way I'm going to be able to fully immerse myself in French. Think of it as a Buddhist retreat."

"I don't think they serve Bordeaux and coq au vin at those," I pointed out.

He sighed, which was when I really started to get nervous. "I just need to get my head on straight, Annie. Can you give me a month?"

"Give you *a month*? What does that mean?"

"I've asked my family not to be in touch while I'm away. I'd like it if you'd consider doing the same."

"Okay," I said, staring at my mother's lawn and willing myself not to cry, for fear my mother would notice and begin to ask questions she didn't actually want the answer to. "I understand."

But I don't understand at all. Jon has always been a careful, advance-planning kind of person—just like me. That's one of the many things I love about him. So I'm supposed to accept his spontaneous departure as *normal*?

Maybe it's normal on some continuum I'm unfamiliar with. Because four days later, I'm still shocked and somewhat appalled that he would leave, especially so soon after my career collapsed. (Did I talk about that too much? I know he felt I should have taken action against SCI, but would my decision really have sent him running? It seems improbable.)

Well, I suppose everyone is bound to be selfish from time to time, as some of the people closest to me seem intent on reminding me. I'm determined to allow Jon this sole indulgence so he can get over it, and we can move forward with the life we've planned.

Step one is staying busy. As soon as Viola learned that I was out of a job for the foreseeable future, she asked me to come clean her house again, as I used to when I was in high school. I'm sure some college-educated professionals might have turned their noses up at such a request. But cleaning is honest work, and I like to think of myself as an honest person—if only because I don't harass and assault my coworker, just to cry foul when she pushes me into thousands of dollars' worth of lab equipment. (I wish I could stop replaying that scene in my head over and over. Though I do wish I hadn't behaved so rashly, Todd doesn't deserve a nanometer of my mental space.)

Viola's home is always sparkling clean; she doesn't realize that I'm aware she's really asked for my help because she wants to assist me financially, and since Ned died last year, she could use the company. How could I say no? After my father left, she was the one to swoop in and save seven-year-old me. Now, my mother fed and clothed me, and made sure I saw the doctor when I was ill. She did her best, but my father's leaving was the inciting incident for her depression, and she had very little to offer by way of emotional support, especially for that first year. Viola somehow knew this, because soon she was inviting me over after school for a snack and asking me how my day had gone, and later, letting me set up experiments in her kitchen. Though it took a while for me to warm up to her, it wasn't too long before she became a surrogate parent of sorts. My mother did improve—well, up until her regression two years ago—but it was still Viola who encouraged me to go to college and live out my dreams. I may have had to set my MIT hopes aside (as any person in my situation would have), but I can't stick my nose up at a University of Michigan degree. And while I won't say all's well that ends well, I *did* become a scientist, as I planned to.

Anyway, upon the news that I was in need of work, Viola's old mothering instincts kicked back in, and she called Bess Rogers and Donna Guinness to see if they might need cleaning assistance, too. And just like that, I had three clients instead of one.

Yesterday, I dropped by to bring Viola some oranges—my attempts to get my mother to eat healthfully continue to be less than successful, and I can't go through that much produce on my own—and she mentioned that a couple had recently moved into the area and were looking for a cleaner. She knew this, she explained, through the neighborhood Listserv, and suggested I subscribe to it. "But in the meantime, Annie, would you like me to pass your information on to them?" she asked.

Living with my mother for the past two years has helped me pad my savings, but it won't last forever. So I was about to tell Viola yes when it hit me: Why would I open myself up to new problems?

By problems, of course, I mean people.

I love Jon, naturally, and I'm glad we were seated beside each other on that fated flight to St. Louis. Yet if I'd not made small talk with him, and he hadn't been instantly smitten with me, as he claimed he was when he asked me to dinner that same night, then I wouldn't find myself having to debate whether or not to email *my own fiancé* after he decided to take a month-long sabbatical from his life and—though this went unsaid—from our relationship.

Likewise, if I'd only finished applying to graduate school rather than accepting Todd Bizer's fool's gold of an offer, I would not have wasted my time doing someone else's research, only to find myself banned from the entire field of chemistry for two whole years.

And while I won't fault my kindergarten self for succumbing to Leesa's gift of gab and ending up as her best friend, I *did* have a choice when she introduced me to Simone last year. We were both childless professionals, and Simone seemed intelligent and interesting. But as if it wasn't bad enough that she implied I could "manifest" away the raging rash I got from the essential oils I tested at Leesa's last LITEWEIGHT sales-pitch party, now Simone's been texting me to see if I won't make amends with Leesa, whose "feelings are hurt."

Feelings are not facts. I seemed to have forgotten that over the past few years, but fortunately, that's a fixable problem.

A renewed focus on life's tangible truths isn't the only step I'm taking to create a peaceful, focused mental state. I've sworn off new people—which is why I thanked Viola for her kind offer but told her I would prefer to only clean for neighbors I already knew.

I understand my vow will limit me to the company of a select few, and that one of those few includes my mother, whose hoarding makes Donna Guinness look like the patron saint of sanitation. (I swear,

Donna must apply mud for moisturizer each morning.) But unlike the wildcard behaviors of persons unknown, I know what to expect of my existing relationships and already possess the tools to navigate them.

For example, I know Leesa can talk a blind man into seeing things her way, so I've chosen to avoid communicating with her until she apologizes, lest I get conned into doing the apologizing. That's the sort of nuance that takes years to pick up on, and I simply don't have the bandwidth to exhaust myself learning new strategies for strangers. No—I must save my resources for Jon's return.

—AEM

THREE

July 19
TO: Ann Mercer
FROM: Bethanne Wynn
SUBJECT: Resignation Agreement

Ann Mercer:

The following information has also been sent to you by certified mail via US Postal Service to the address listed in your employment file.

This letter is to confirm that your employment with Sanity Chemical Innovation formally ended July 5 of this year, following your resignation, and to inform you that a two-week investigation into Todd Bizer's claim against you concluded that you engaged in:

> Misconduct against a colleague (superior).

> Contribution to hostile work environment.

These findings are not reversible.

On July 13, you received a final payment for weekly compensation and unused vacation time via direct deposit. Sanity Chemical Innovation owes you no further compensation.

Your health insurance benefits, including vision and dental, have been terminated. However, because you have not been found to have committed an act of gross misconduct during our investigation, you are eligible for COBRA coverage. Attached please find enrollment information. Attached also please find information regarding management options for your retirement account.

Please keep in mind that you have signed a legally binding non-compete agreement (attached) that prevents you from creating any sanitation product for five years or working for any competitor to Sanity Chemical Innovation (see list of qualifying criteria, attached) for two years following the date of your termination. Should you violate this agreement, Sanity Chemical Innovation will take swift legal action against you, and if applicable, against your employer.

If you have any questions about this letter, your compensation, benefits, or other matters regarding your prior employment for Sanity Chemical Innovation, please contact me directly.

Sincerely,
Bethanne Wynn
Senior Human Resources Manager
Sanity Chemical Innovation
[ATTACHMENTS: 4]

July 19
TO: Bethanne Wynn
FROM: Annie Mercer
SUBJECT: Re: Termination Agreement

Bethanne:

I reread your email three times, thinking perhaps my synapses were misfiring and causing me to scramble your meaning or intent. But no—it appears you and your employer have decided to carry on with this ridiculous charade. When I came to you, I tried to explain what had happened with Todd, only to discover he had fabricated a story about my behavior. To review:

- After more than four years of what I regard as a cordial if occasionally strained working relationship, Todd Bizer began sending me a series of inappropriate emails using his personal email account. While I regret that I did not bring these emails to your attention sooner, I was hopeful that my nonresponse and cold shoulder would dissuade Todd without jeopardizing my employment. Clearly, I was mistaken.

  Said emails (see six attachments, below) date from January 12 to June 18. Given this timeline, I believe that Todd's emails began in response to my announcement in January of this year that I was engaged to my fiancé, Jon Nichols. As you will see, these emails included, among other problematic content: references to Todd's unhappiness in his marriage; inquiries as to whether I would be willing to wear skirts instead of pants if the lab were warmer, and whether I wanted to join Todd in his personal box, whatever that is, at a University of Michigan football game this fall; a link to a story on a site called Mansplain.com saying that female scientists who marry and have children are less successful and significantly less happy than those who commit to a "life of science"; and a complete mangling of a *Star Wars* quote in which I believe Todd attempted to say—in reference to my forthcoming nuptials—that marriage is a trap.

- When I approached Todd in March to inform him that my wedding was planned for December 22, and that I would be taking the following three weeks off for my honeymoon—with the specific purpose of giving my colleagues adequate time to continue or conclude all in-process projects prior to my leave—he asked whether I really wanted to do so. Obviously, I said yes. He then told me he was unable to grant me the aforementioned time off, and in fact he would need me to return to the office on December 27, which occurs during SCI's paid holiday break. As you may recall, I then filed a formal vacation request with Human Resources—which is to say you, Bethanne—which you approved, as this courtesy would have been extended to any SCI employee.

- My vacation request prompted an escalation of Todd's behavior. By April, he was routinely touching my arm or shoulder, and at one point (again—I should have documented this, but was still guilelessly hoping I was wrong about his intentions) touched my lower back while I was examining a slide. As someone who created a chemical formula to stop the rapid transmission of fecal bacteria, influenzas A, B, and C, and myriad other pathogens, Todd should know better than to engage in unwanted touching—even if he does have a habit of applying FastDry Sani-Foam* to his hands far more frequently than clinically recommended.

- From July 2–4, SCI employees were given paid vacation leave for the Fourth of July holiday. On July 3, however, Todd called me on my cell phone to ask me to come into the lab to do a safety check on a FastDry Sani-Foam (v. 2) experiment in process. While I felt this was unnecessary—I had followed SOP the prior Friday in preparation for the break—given Todd's position as my supervisor and CEO, I felt obligated to do as he asked.

When I arrived at the lab, I discovered that Todd had already run the additional (unnecessary) safety check himself. When I noted this aloud, Todd immediately began inquiring about my relationship with my fiancé, claiming that he sensed I had some hesitation about my upcoming nuptials.

Before I could respond to this ridiculous statement, Todd Bizer, founder, CEO, and chief scientific officer of Sanity Chemical Innovation, lunged forward and hugged me. During this unsolicited encounter, he let his hand drop to one of my gluteal muscles. I thought perhaps this was unintentional, but then his fingers began to squeeze that muscle. At that point, I dislodged myself from Todd's unwelcome grasp, and before I could consider what I was doing, shoved him away, which caused him to fall onto a lab table and destroy several digital microscopes.

As an avowed pacifist, I concede that my behavior was regrettable. However, for every action there is an equal and opposite reaction (FYI: that's Newton's third law, Bethanne). I would never have touched Todd in any way had he not first acted upon me.

Moreover, just as any scientist worth their atoms would do, I have since conducted additional research. What I have discovered, as outlined in various journal articles in peer-reviewed publications including *Social Sciences Review*, the *Journal of Business Ethics & Management*, *Ethics in Science and Engineering*, and *Employment Rights Legal Review* (see links for full studies), is that such shock-driven self-defense behaviors are well documented in situations of harassment and not grounds for any punitive measure. Todd's claim is baseless.

As to the nondisclosure agreement, I have no intention to disclose SCI's trade secrets, though let's face it—I would need a frontal lobotomy in order to forget everything I learned or did during my ill-advised five-year tenure at SCI. However, as a human rights professional, you should be well aware that the scope of the non-compete criteria detailed in your email is perilously broad and in essence prohibits me from getting another chemistry position for the next two years. I will not give you the satisfaction of knowing the direct impact of this financial impediment on my day-to-day life. However, Bethanne, I must ask you: How do you sleep at night?

Sincerely,
Annie Mercer

*For the record, the recent addition of 1,4-dioxane to the SCI FastDry Sani-Foam formula is extremely troublesome—as animal studies suggest, 1,4-dioxane is linked to kidney and liver problems and may contribute to an increased risk of stillbirth and birth defects. I brought this to Todd's attention two months ago, and he called me "maddeningly naïve." If maddeningly naïve means believing it's my duty to keep a harmful substance out of a product distributed in hospitals and other medical facilities frequented by expectant mothers and infants (and while we're at it, believing I have the right to work in an environment where I won't be harassed), then yes—I am hopelessly, undyingly so. Consider that—as well as the increasingly nefarious behavior of your employer—as you're counting sheep, Bethanne.

[ATTACHMENTS: 6]

FOUR

Dear Jon,

I saw the footage of the World Cup on the news last week. What a thrill it must have been to be in Paris on the very day that the French team captured the title! Were you out in the streets, waving flags and setting off fireworks with the throng? Or perhaps in a café, sipping rosé and chatting to your fellow diners in French? Soccer enthusiast that you are, I find myself wondering if maybe the game was the reason for your sudden departure. Because as you might have gleaned from my emailing again, I'm still struggling to make sense of your leaving. "I just need time to think before we get married" doesn't give me much to go on. Our wedding is six months away, Jon—that's plenty of time to think.

Would you like me to make an appointment for couples counseling? While I don't relish the idea of spilling my innermost thoughts to a stranger, I can't pretend the research on talk therapy isn't compelling. And though I always thought of us as a harmonious and well-suited pair—remember how, when you proposed, you said I was not just the love of your life, but also your best friend?—I'd be willing to give it a go if you are.

Though I was trying not to interrupt your trip a second time, I thought I should let you know that I received a letter from SCI two days ago that included the "findings" of a so-called "investigation" into Todd's claim. I still can't believe he had the nerve to file a complaint against *me*. As CEO and chief scientific officer of SCI, what precedent is he setting? While I do worry about former female colleagues, I suppose it's no longer my concern what precedent is being set at that godforsaken place.

No surprise: said investigation did not include me or my side of the story, but I finally took the opportunity to detail it in a letter to HR. You were right—his behavior *was* escalating, and I should have taken action a long time ago. Unfortunately, I made the mistake of letting a tiny bit of optimism leak into my realism. I should hardly be surprised by the outcome.

Jon, you've been gone for ten days, or a third of your trip. When I first wrote you last week, I cursed my lack of self-control and my inability to honor your request to wait a month to contact you. Did you know that an animal need only be rewarded for a behavior *once* before it continues to replicate that behavior again and again—even if a second reward never arrives? We are all creatures of habit, and while I wish it weren't true, I'm no exception. When I used to email you at work, you always found a way to respond so quickly that I sometimes pictured you in front of the chalkboard, holding up a hand and saying *en français*, "One second, class—I need to write back to Annie."

Well, maybe that conditioning was for the best. Because just this morning, as I was glancing at my computer and trying to decide whether to give in to that old familiar itch, it struck me that our connection has always been fostered by one thing (and no, it's not what you're probably thinking). I'm talking about communication. You said yourself you loved my mind as much as any of my other features, and that you could talk to me for hours and still never grow bored because I always helped you see the world with fresh eyes.

I hope you'll read this email and remember that. And when you're done marinating in Burgundy and are ready to discuss what's on your mind, I'll be here.

Love always,
Annie

FIVE

I'm already reaping the rewards of my resolution to avoid new people. Just this morning, a monstrosity of an SUV pulled up in front of my mother's neighbor's house. The Novaks used to live there, but after Linda died, Bob decided to spend his third act steering a golf cart around Orlando. Their home was always enviably pristine, so I wasn't surprised when a **SALE PENDING** placard was affixed to the sale sign almost immediately after it went on the market. The pool alone—well, let's just say that if I were still making five figures and the Novaks' wasn't directly beside my mother's hoarding hut, I might actually see if Jon wanted to take a look at the place with me. Really, that would have been perfect—we could have our own space, but I could still keep an eye on my mother.

What did surprise me was the woman who poured herself out of the SUV. Initially I thought perhaps she was a Realtor, but I quickly realized how impractical it would be for a working professional to be wearing that bandage of a black dress at ten in the morning. Moreover, the woman's highlighted hair was pulled into a chignon and she was carrying what I initially mistook for a mop head but later identified as a Shih Tzu. All of this suggested to me that her GPS had scrambled its coordinates, accidentally landing her 613 miles west of Manhattan.

Even before my vow, I wouldn't normally have indulged in the prolonged observation of a stranger. But I'll admit, I've grown a bit bored since leaving SCI, and have found myself gravitating toward activities I would normally eschew (e.g., watching the home improvement shows my mother leaves on at all hours of the day). And this particular woman—well, it was like spotting a gazelle galloping through our suburban neighborhood. How could I look away?

At any rate, I was in the middle of cleaning the top of the credenza, which had miraculously replenished its piles of newspapers and circulars overnight, and this location in front of the window gave me a bird's-eye view of my new neighbor. She was using her free hand to block the bit of light that must have snuck in over the rim of her enormous sunglasses, and I wondered if she might be suffering from a migraine. But then she dashed back to her SUV—a feat, considering the heels she was wearing—and grabbed her purse from somewhere in the vehicle.

Now, I expected that she would merely fish for her keys and let herself inside, but I must have forgotten the lesson I learned during childhood, which is that optimistic assumptions are the fastest way to become deeply disillusioned by human nature. Best to anticipate the worst and then enjoy the momentary satisfaction of having your predictions pan out.

Instead, my neighbor retrieved a large phone from her tiny purse and proceeded to take what must have been several dozen photos of herself making peace signs in front of the Novaks' meticulously pruned hedges. Then she unlocked the door and let Moppet (as I've begun mentally referring to her ankle biter) pee on the threshold before wandering inside, and finally, all bee-stung lips and blinding white teeth, pranced into the house herself.

While I do wonder what it must be like to sail through life with so few cares, this journal entry would have ended here were it not for what happened next.

I had just glanced down at the credenza, where I'd found that a flier dated October 1999 had not only *not* been tossed out, but actually found its way to the top of an otherwise current heap of papers, when a car alarm began bleating. Naturally, I peered up to see the woman's vehicle blinking like a disco ball.

That's when I spotted a stiletto-clad foot sticking out the front door of the house.

When it was clear that the foot and the person attached to it were not moving, I quickly decided I could honor my civic-minded instinct without breaking my new vow and ran outside. By the time I reached the front door, the horn had subsided but the woman was still lying there, limbs akimbo. She was clutching her phone in one hand and her key fob in the other. I can't say for certain that her eyes were open, as she was behind her dark glasses, but she must have been regarding me because before I could address her, she said, "Are you okay?"

"Me?" I said. I'm sorry to say that personal care has slipped down my priority list of late, and so I was not wearing a bra beneath my T-shirt and had been planning to shower after decontaminating Larry and Bess Rogers' place. Still, just because I wasn't done up for a photo shoot did not imply I was *not* okay. "I was coming to find out if you were all right," I said. "Did you trip?"

"No," she said, still supine on the tile. It was then I realized her hair was no longer pulled into a neat knot but was instead fanned around her head like a halo. "I'm *terrific*. I've never seen this place in person and I just *adore* it. So I was getting a shot of me falling for my new home. Literally!"

Then she extended a hand into the air. I was so busy staring at her glossy, seashell-pink nails—while simultaneously wondering how it was possible that she was only now seeing the home she owned for the first time—that I didn't realize she was expecting me to help her. "Could you?" she said.

I hoisted her back onto her feet. She had just opened her mouth to introduce herself or make some other comment that might pique my interest when I held up a hand to stop her. "I must be going," I said, and although I could tell she found my behavior odd, I was not about to stick around and explain that civic duties aside, good fences make good neighbors. What Robert Frost did not mention—as his poem is actually a naïve denunciation of healthy human separation—is that fences can also be blackout curtains, cordial waves from one's driveway, the complete absence of small talk, and serious conversations only in actual matters of life and death (i.e., not when my neighbor decides to position herself like a corpse so as to get the exact right shot to post to some social media site I've probably never heard of).

Now I won't have a chance to finish sorting through my mother's papers before heading to the Rogers' to make their carpets and counters appear, however fleetingly, as though they don't own four cats. As it happens, short-haired felines shed more dander and fur than the long-haired variety, which ultimately results in more odor. (This, of course, is the sort of factoid I'd normally share with Jon. When he returns, I'll have to ask him if the cats of France, like the women, smell of perfume.)

At any rate, my interaction with this champagne bubble of a stranger was blessedly brief—and just as well. Had I lingered to chat, it's possible she would have invited me in for coffee or a drink, at which point we might have begun exchanging confidences. Before long, I would have formed an attachment that would threaten the calm existence I'm striving for.

Though I was skeptical, it seems journaling *is* providing some clarity—though I'm still checking my inbox multiple times a day to see if Jon has responded. Of course he hasn't. He's a man of his word, and if his plan is to have a month to himself, then that's what he'll do. I've certainly retreated into myself during difficult times; I didn't leave my room for a solid week after writing MIT to tell them I'd had a change of heart and would be attending U of M instead.

So I do understand Jon's impulse. I just wish I knew what was really troubling him, so I could begin to search for a solution.

—AEM

SIX

July 25
TO: Annie Mercer
FROM: Leesa Sato Liznewski
SUBJECT: Annie!

A—

As you know, I've been trying to call you. I'm so sorry that Jon took off for Paris without you, especially right on the heels of what happened at SCI. (Are you sure you don't want to contact an employment lawyer? I can get some referrals!) I know that must hurt, so I understand why you overreacted when I came over. But it's been almost two weeks, and I still haven't heard from you. Don't you think you're lashing out at the wrong person?

When I brought the LITEWEIGHT™ products over to your mom's place, I was only trying to be helpful. I promise that it was never my intention to make you feel you had to buy them. I'm totally willing to admit that sometimes I forget not everyone connects with my enthusiasm as a brand evangelist—I'm just so passionate about this company and the way it empowers women. As you know, the minute I bought my first LITEWEIGHT™ crystal, my life completely transformed. Now every day, I'm harnessing the power of the understanding that if I can believe it, I can be it. You can't be mad at me for wishing that for you, too, Annie. A twenty-seven-year-old chemist with no kids and practically your whole life ahead of you—you are *so* blessed! This may be impossible for you to visualize now, but in a few months, I bet you'll look back on this unplanned pivot as one big favor from the Universe.

Speaking of LITEWEIGHT™ . . . since I haven't seen you, I haven't had a chance to tell you that Josh, the twins, and I are going to St. Petersburg at the end of October!!! I've had such a successful quarter that the company is putting me up for FREE for a night at the Sandpiper and waiving my fees for our annual wellness sales conference! We'll have to cover flights and a few nights at the hotel, but there's no way we could have afforded a family vacation like this if LITEWEIGHT™ wasn't so incredibly generous. And—knock on rose quartz—I'm pretty sure I may just be the top Southeastern Michigan Sales Rep for a second year in a row (fingers, toes, and chakras crossed)! Be happy for me, Annie. I don't think that's too much to ask for—do you?

Can we please realign? We've been best friends nearly our entire lives. I know I've been a little less present lately, but between the kids and Josh and getting my new business off the ground, I'm doing the best I can. And now that you're free during the day, and the twins are in preschool, it will be easier for us to meet up. If you need a way to make money, I could even tell you more about coming on board as a LITEWEIGHT™ sales rep. Wouldn't it be great to be your own boss for a change?

Simone told me you've stopped responding to her text messages, too, so I know it's not just me. I don't blame you for being completely shell-shocked by Jon's decision—but don't throw your friends out with the bathwater! Come on, Annie. I know you're strong and smart and you can get through this alone. But why would you want to?

I miss you.
xoxo, L

Leesa Sato Liznewski
LITEWEIGHT™ Brand Evangelist
LITEWEIGHT™ Southeastern Michigan Sales Representative of the year!!!
Could your life use a lift? I can help!
Ask me how I got these lashes!

July 25
TO: Leesa Sato Liznewski
FROM: Annie Mercer
SUBJECT: Re: Annie!

Leesa,

Let me begin by saying the photo beneath your email signature is mildly terrifying. Who wants to look as though she has spider legs for eyelashes? Moreover, have you actually researched the mechanism of the product you're selling? (Please don't offer "proprietary formula" by way of an explanation.) According to a cursory literature search, in order to spur hair growth, the hair follicle must be widened and the hair's natural resting phase must be lengthened. This is done by changing the body's hormonal balance. What exactly is *in* the stuff you're dabbing on your lids each night?

If you find out, don't tell me—it's a question I'll never need the answer to.

For the record, I'm not shell-shocked. While no, I didn't know Jon was going until he was on his way to the airport, I've had some time to reflect and have come to the conclusion that a premarital trip to Paris is a perfectly reasonable endeavor for a French teacher who's soon to be married, *non*? Anyway, you're always saying that relationships are hard work—and you're right. Jon is working through some issues right now, but soon he (and we) will emerge stronger and better than ever.

It may be difficult for you to believe, Leesa, but I'm doing quite well. Relying on my own company means any given day holds far fewer unpleasant surprises. And to your claim that I'm now free during the workday, that's not true. In addition to cleaning Viola's home, I have three new clients—two neighbors I've known since I was young, and as of yesterday, our old classmate Seth Williams, who recently moved back to the area and needs some help tidying up. While I didn't intend to set up a cleaning business, you're right: I do like being my own boss. Staying physically active and financially solvent—without being subject to the perverse whims of a megalomaniac—suits me just fine.

I wasn't sure whether to respond to your email, as you never actually apologized for mistaking your oldest friend for a sales prospect, but now I'm glad I did. Because now I can take this opportunity to let you know that I need some space, and will reach out again when I'm ready.

Annie

SEVEN

July 27
TO: Annie Mercer
FROM: Oak Grove Neighborhood Association
SUBJECT: Abridged summary of OakGroveMI-
NeighborhoodAssociation@googlegroups.
com—3 updates in 2 topics

Today's Topic Summary
View all topics

- Free hummus—2 Updates
- Welcome!—1 Update

Free hummus
Pete_Yacob9243@gmail.com 8:44 a.m.
We have half a large tub of gluten-free vegan garlic-
lovers hummus left over from my son's birthday party
last Sunday. I hate to throw it out, and we've had our
fill of legumes for the week. I thought someone in our

'hood might want to use it as a healthful plant-based protein.
Pete

Pete_Yacob9243@gmail.com 9:50 a.m.
The hummus has been claimed.
Pete

Welcome!
MargieSueLinden@aol.com 6:05 p.m.
A warm welcome to our newest Listserv members:
  jossjossjoss82@gmail.com
  ItsHarperBishes@gmail.com
  Mercer_AnnieE@compuquest.com
A friendly reminder to all that we encourage active participation as well as civil discourse—and discourage lurking! New members, please introduce yourselves when you have a chance.
Namaste,
Margie Linden

EIGHT

July 30

Jon still hasn't written me back, nor has he called. Logically, I knew that he wouldn't. Yet his silence is sending my mind into a downward spiral of unsavory possibilities. Did I do or say something terrible without realizing it? What if he likes Paris so much he stays there?

I should stick to the facts; I know that. He told me that he'd be out of touch for a month, and he meant it. He returns in two weeks. I can work with that.

To fill the hours and occupy my mind, I've taken on another client, First Presbyterian Church—as I figure a nonprofit entity isn't really a new person. I joined the neighborhood Listserv, too. While part of me suspects it's a rabbit hole of dysfunction, it *is* proving to be an effective diversion. Anyway, I have no intention of actually interacting with anyone on there.

If only my mother would stop reminding me Jon is gone. Since January, our engagement has become her primary energy source. In fact, when I told her I'd resigned from SCI, she congratulated me, because it meant I'd have more time for wedding planning. (I didn't have it in me to give her the whole sordid story, knowing how it would sink her mood.) "You have your entire life to work—well, until you have children," she said, because she continues to pretend I never told her I'm not sure about starting a family. "But for now, what a wonderful thing you're doing, focusing on your relationship with Jon. Men want dedication. Trust me, this is the kind of decision that's going to lead to a long, happy marriage."

I can't imagine my mother ever suffered from a lack of focus or dedication—those were my father's problems, which is why one morning he woke up and decided an exciting new life was waiting for him on an Alaskan oil rig. This December will mark three years since his death. I'll never forget the terrible guttural noise my mother made when a distant relative called to tell her that for all his freewheeling adventures, my father had died the most mundane way possible: in his sleep.

I know "well" is not a quantifiable measure, but my mother really *had* been doing so well up until that point. She seemed to like working as a receptionist, and she'd been attending church regularly, which had always buoyed her. Though her house was never going to be free of clutter, it was in the best shape it had been since I left for college. She almost never mentioned my father anymore.

Then a twenty-second call wiped out nearly twenty years of gains.

I still question my decision to move out of my apartment and in with her. But she was so despondent that I feared—I feared she might hurt herself, to be honest. And someone had to make sure she was eating something other than sandwich cookies and that the electric bill was paid (as I discovered upon coming home one evening to an eerily dark and quiet house). I may not have known how to make her feel better, but I have a black belt in task execution, and I decided to use it to be of service to the woman to whom I literally owe my life.

Even with antidepressants, she didn't improve all that much, which often made me wonder whether my being there for more than those first few months had somehow extended her depression rather than easing it. But then came a breakthrough—in the form of a glittering lab-simulated diamond on my left ring finger. If I could transform that hunk of carbon into hundreds of happy pills, I would, because my engagement put a light in my mother's eyes that hadn't been there in a very long time. Would I choose a ball gown or a demure ivory sheath? she wanted to know. And while roses are a classic December wedding flower, perhaps gardenias or ranunculus would be a nice choice? Suddenly she was in possession of both a new vocabulary and a more hopeful outlook on life.

Maybe that's why I've been dodging her unanswerable questions.

Just this afternoon, I took her grocery shopping. I was hoping for Trader Joe's, but she wanted to go to the dreadfully dingy ShopMore, and because she hadn't left the house in nearly a week, I decided not to argue. I know how important it is to be out in the world, building strong neural connections through different experiences—in that way, I do understand Jon's desire to escape the humdrum of our life here in Michigan. Really, it's why I decided to clean houses. As much as I miss my lab, I still appreciate the novelty of my current occupation. Will Donna Guinness' trash bin be overflowing onto the linoleum in the kitchen or inexplicably shoved into her powder room? How many times will I have to empty the vacuum canister at the Rogers'? While I can't claim every day is a thrill, it's better than sitting around, skimming the science journals I no longer have any use for.

Anyway, my mother and I were in the freezer aisle, squabbling about whether the broccoli sprinkles in the frozen mac-n-cheese meals she was piling into the cart qualified as a serving of vegetables, when Betty Smithers came zipping down the aisle like a contestant on my mother's old favorite show, *Supermarket Sweep*. A shame no one plays the reruns anymore—now my mother has become a devotee of HGTV, in which every decorator seems to have the same reverence for shiplap and myriad shades of gray.

"Fae? Is that really you?" said Betty, pretending to do a double take. She and my mother have been frenemies since they wore the same dress to their first communions, so I wasn't surprised when Betty immediately homed in on my mother's use of a motorized cart. "Are you *okay*?" she said with wide eyes.

I knew my mother was just tired—depression is more exhausting than most people comprehend, and she's often depleted long before dinner arrives, which is why she ended up retiring early from her job (thank goodness my father had substantial life insurance and left my mother as his beneficiary). But instead of admitting this, she told Betty that her fatigue and aching joints lead her to believe she may have fibromyalgia. It's a serious diagnosis, obviously, and there's been an incredible amount of progress on the diagnostic front, even if treatment options remain wanting. Yet she'd never mentioned aching joints or fibromyalgia to *me* before, and I couldn't help but feel that she was looking for an excuse for being less than her best. That made me as sad as I've been in a long time, which is saying a lot. Because when I opened my eyes this morning and remembered that Jon was still gallivanting around Paris, I considered going right back to bed, just as my mother often does.

Condensation was forming on my bags of vegetables, and I knew I would open the cauliflower later this week and discover it had freezer burn from melting while Betty informed my mother she would add her to the list of "lift ups" at her next prayer circle. Naturally, Betty had to assert that it would be even better if my mother could join her, or even better, come to Saturday evening Mass. My mother got all flustered, because as all three of us were aware, she hasn't been to church in the better part of a year, and it's hard to pretend the action you've been taking month after month is a one-off.

It's not the kill but the chase that truly satisfies, so Betty smiled victoriously at my mother, then began peppering me with questions about the wedding. She eyed my ring, speculating on the carat size, then asked if Jon and I would be married in the church.

"No, we're opting for a nondenominational venue," I said.

"Hmm," she said, with obvious disapproval. "And this lovely man you're going to marry. Does he live in East Haven, too?"

"Ann Arbor, actually," I said.

"So you're in separate cities. How interesting!"

Separate countries, technically, not that Betty needed to know that. By that point, I'd begun blinking like a lizard in a sandstorm and had a newfound understanding of why my mother had just felt compelled to embellish the truth. "Yes, but we'll be moving in together soon," I said. "Possibly before our wedding, even."

Betty frowned down at my mother. "Oh, Fae, that will be so hard for you, won't it? I bet you just *love* having Annie around."

My mother shook her head firmly. "Not at all. I'm excited for Annie to enjoy the true happiness that comes from being loved by one man for the rest of your life."

I couldn't tell if my mother was referring to her own marriage or Betty's annulment. Either way, Betty winced and said she had to get going. I thought that was the end of that until my mother turned to me and said nervously, "Annie, when does Jon get back again? We need to discuss the reception and schedule a cake tasting."

"Mid-August," I said, hoping this was enough to assure her.

Because sometimes when she looks at me, I suspect she's actually eyeing a second chance.

We spent another hour shopping—thankfully, running into Betty just once more in the dairy section—but by the time we got home, I was certain at least a third of the items we had purchased had spent so much time out of a sub-forty-degree environment that they had already begun to spore. I was unloading groceries when who should come waltzing outside but my new neighbor.

She was dressed in skintight leather pants, even though it was nearly ninety out, and was wearing a ripped black tank top printed with a giant tongue. As when I last saw her, much of her face was hidden beneath sunglasses; this time they were gold aviators. I may have to invest in a pair myself, because at some point I realized I had forgotten about my groceries as well as my manners and was staring at her. I couldn't help it, though—something about her made me feel like a child who'd just been instructed not to look directly at the sun. How could such a beautiful thing cause damage, one wonders, even as one's retinas begin to fry?

Within seconds, I was spinning theories out of thin air. I decided the woman had been raised in Los Angeles and was a former child star trying to reestablish her career. Being of the method school of acting, she was studying for her role as a twentysomething Midwesterner with few prospects but who would soon have her heart opened after the sudden appearance of a handsome stranger. Despite her professionalism, the actress was accustomed to having the wide world within her manicured fingertips, and so the adjustment to suburban life was proving to be a bit of a struggle. I found myself wishing I had asked for her name when I had gone over to help her the week before, so I could at least google her and paint my mental picture with a few strokes of reality.

Then I realized what I was doing and willed myself to return to the groceries. I was nearly up the walkway to the house when a terrifying pile of fur came racing at me, teeth bared, as though *I* were intruding on my own property.

"Moppet!" I yelled without thinking.

I'll be damned if the dog didn't stop dead in its tracks and stare up at me like it was waiting for a piece of steak.

"How did you do that?" said my neighbor, ambling over to me on a pair of cork stilts.

"Do what?" I said.

"Get him to stop," she said.

"Him?"

"My dog?" she said, like she wasn't sure if the rabid beast was actually hers. "Was that word you used some kind of secret command?"

I started to laugh, probably because I wasn't sure how else to respond. "Moppet," I said again.

The woman cocked her head. "Is that Mandarin?"

I laughed even harder, which was truly a shame, because the woman's mirror neurons kicked in and she started laughing, too. When we had both collected ourselves, I told her it wasn't Mandarin but she was welcome to try it on her dog. Then I looked down into the abyss of the brown paper bag I was holding, painfully aware that I wouldn't be able to eat the turkey breast I purchased without spending the following six hours wondering whether I was exhibiting symptoms of listeria infection. "Well," I said, "I've got to get going if I want to make sure these groceries don't spoil."

I was nearly to the door when I heard her voice. "Harper."

Now it was my turn to wonder what language we were communicating in as I spun around. "What's that?" I said.

"I'm Harper," she said. "Harper Brearley."

"Oh," I said.

"And you are?"

My mother, bless her, chose that moment to holler for me. "*I* am at the mercy of my mother," I told her. "See you around, Harper." And then I escaped inside, where the one person waiting for me was someone who would disappoint me only in ways I was prepared to deal with.

At dinner tonight, my mother and I sat across from each other eating our separate meals—a chicken Caesar salad for me, and microwave mac-n-cheese for her. As I listened to her prattle on about Betty's prayer circle and whether she could manage Mass next Saturday, it occurred to me that she didn't start out the way she is now. Really, who does? For example, once upon a time, my new neighbor was a young child with certain set characteristics but a malleable range of sociological responses. At some point she must have decided, at least subconsciously, that she would pursue a life of glamour, just as I committed myself to science after realizing the inherent comforts of the quantifiable world.

Likewise, my mother was once a relatively content woman who, while always a bit of a human tornado, threw out cottage cheese containers rather than storing them for—well, I don't know what she's storing them for, as all the leftovers in southeast Michigan couldn't begin to fill the polypropylene in our cupboards. She wanted a good life for herself; I know she did. But then my father left, and while I doubt that desire changed, her possibilities seemed to.

I'm trying hard to remain rational, but I must admit panic is creeping in. My career is on long-term hold. The person I love more than any other chose to run off to his dream destination without me. And instead of being able to share my thoughts with him, as I used to every day, I'm now forced to unload them into a word-processing document.

August 12 can't arrive soon enough.

—AEM

NINE

August 2

I'm embarrassed to admit that I've been increasingly intrigued by my new neighbor. I have little doubt that even with four cleaning clients and my mother's house to tend to (which is the equivalent of three additional clients), I continue to have too much time on my hands. But it's not just an issue of boredom. There's something about the way Harper glides around on four-inch heels that transfixes me. What must it be like to spend the day shopping and talking on your cell phone and splashing in the pool? I don't resent her. If anything, watching her makes me feel like life could be easier—if only I had fewer familial responsibilities and could turn my brain off once in a while. It's almost like I'm nostalgic for a carefree existence I've never actually known.

Or maybe I just miss Leesa. She used to be more like that, back before she had the twins and got wrapped up in a python-oil pyramid scheme.

Up to this point, I've observed Harper in the same detached manner my mother views home improvement TV shows. But late yesterday afternoon, a luxury sedan with tinted windows pulled into the Novaks' driveway. (I suppose I should stop referring to the house as the Novaks' and start calling it Harper's.) I won't feign as though I inadvertently noticed the car; I was done with work for the day, had grown tired of attempting to bring order to the living room chaos, and was more or less staring out the window waiting for something to happen before it was time to make dinner.

Then the car door opened and out emerged a man. He was about my age, maybe thirty at most, and was dressed in a beautifully cut gray suit. I've been doing a bit of reading about France, naturally, and it's my understanding that such finery is typical Gallic attire. But here in the States, I don't see many men wearing tailored garb. Maybe that's why I couldn't return my attention to the circa '83 *Ladies' Home Journals* I had been trying to convince my mother to archive in the recycling bin. As the man strode up the walkway, I found myself wondering if he and Harper had a date—after all, his impeccable suit, coiffed hair, and general air of sophistication were perfectly matched to her style. I had never seen the man before, nor his car, hence my assumption that he was a visitor who was there to court her.

Imagine my surprise when he let himself inside as though he owned the place.

Maybe Harper has the same sort of dust allergy that Viola suffers from, because she had replaced the Novaks' heavy curtains with beautiful Bali blinds (it's nearly impossible not to acquire a decorator's vocabulary when HGTV is the soundtrack of one's waking hours). The blinds were closed, so I couldn't see inside the house—but I'm sorry to say I wasn't finished finding out why a stranger just walked right into Harper's house.

It occurred to me that my mother's lawn was parched. Thanks to *Yard Crashers*, I now know that the ideal time to soak grass is before or after the sun has set. But this was more than a matter of curb appeal, so

I moseyed outside and set up the sprinkler I purchased last month. (My mother is still up in arms; she insists that her rusted old sprinklers—one of which no longer oscillates, another of which only shoots water from a few holes, and yet another that has a bent hose attachment, rendering it utterly useless—were sufficient. If that were true, her yard would not resemble the Kalahari Desert.) I was about to turn on the sprinkler when I heard a caterwauling sound.

It was distant at first, then a little louder. Initially, I wondered if maybe one of the Rogers' "fur babies" had escaped and had been dragged into the sewer by a raccoon. Sometimes it takes the ears a moment to process—or maybe it's that the brain needs time to interpret the signals coming in across the auditory nerves—and after a few seconds, I realized it was not a cat at all, but rather a human crying. The crying began to sound like yelling, and it occurred to me that I was actually hearing two people, a woman and a man.

All of this clamor was coming from next door.

Hand still on the spigot, I froze. My heart was racing; I knew something wasn't right. But I thought the same thing the last time I attempted to intervene in what I believed to be a dangerous situation, only to find Harper shooting photos of herself. Reminding myself that I've vowed not to get entangled in the affairs of persons unknown, I decided to take a watch-and-wait approach vis-à-vis the conflict.

I turned on the water, praising myself for having the good sense to buy a relatively quiet sprinkler, and listened. The hollering grew dim and then subsided, but I sat on the bench beside the front door and continued to steal westward glances, wondering if the finely dressed fellow and/or my neighbor would appear. I pretended to be entranced by the grass and studied the creeping ivy while awaiting a sign I should take a proactive but distanced measure to help without landing myself in the eye of someone else's hurricane.

The yard was saturated by the time the man came strolling out the door. He looked every bit as unruffled as he'd been when he arrived. So did Harper when she appeared seconds later. She was wearing white jeans, a fuchsia tunic, and heels that looked as though they had been designed for the specific purpose of impaling someone. She had on another pair of large black sunglasses, which may have been why she didn't appear to notice me. I suppose I could have flagged her down or called out to ask her if she was okay, but by all accounts, she appeared unharmed.

The man walked over to Harper's SUV in the driveway. He opened the driver's-side door for her, though not the way a valet would—it seemed more of a romantic gesture. But she didn't look at him lovingly as she hoisted herself into the vehicle and yanked the door closed. Then the man got in his sedan. Harper in the lead, the pair zipped down the road at a speed that was sure to prompt one of our fellow neighbors to snap a photo of their license plates and post them on the neighborhood Listserv.

Point being, I did not insert myself in the situation. In fact, by this morning I had nearly forgotten all about it.

But shortly before ten, I had just set out for Donna Guinness' when who should I see but Harper, clad in a printed purple caftan that would have made me look like a Golden Girl, but rendered her impossibly chic. Moppet was yapping at her heels, and I was tempted to warn her about walking the beast without a leash—if the neighborhood Listserv is to be believed (and I'm not sure that it is), a vicious Labradoodle escaped and attacked an unleashed puggle two blocks over a few days ago. Then I remembered that making small talk would threaten my interpersonal embargo.

However, I do believe one can be courteous while remaining closed off to friendship, so I glanced her way and said plainly, "Hello."

"Hi!" she said. "Where are *you* headed?"

I was hauling my steam mop in one hand and a large plastic organizer full of cleaning supplies in the other. "I run a cleaning business," I explained. "I clean homes for some of our neighbors."

"You do?!"

She seemed oddly excited about my line of work and was staring at me intently, which was when I realized she wasn't wearing sunglasses for a change. Her twinkling eyes were an unusual shade of bright gray; I wouldn't be surprised if she had been referred to as bewitching at least a few times in her life. But what was even more unusual was her right eye, which was circled by a reddish-blue bruise.

I immediately thought of Todd. Though I've been berating myself for shoving him, maybe I should have given myself over to impulse entirely and let my fist make an emergency landing in his eye socket—after all, the end result would have been the same. The thought quickly flew out of my mind, because Harper was still regarding me expectantly. I could see that she had attempted to cover her bruise with makeup, but she didn't seem self-conscious about it, which eased my fears. If the man who I'd seen yesterday had struck her, wouldn't she be wearing the sunglasses that were perched atop her head? Surely she had a secret clumsy side, the way movie ingénues so often do, and had opened a champagne bottle too close to her face.

"I desperately need someone to clean my place," she said. "Are you taking on new clients?"

The word *yes* was on the tip of my tongue; I forced myself to swallow it. No matter how curious I may be about Harper Golightly, a promise is a promise—even when it's only made to oneself. "I'm so sorry, but I'm booked solid at the moment," I lied.

My gaze must have flitted to her right eye, because her face suddenly flooded with panic. "Oh!" she said, appearing to realize for the first time that her sunglasses were still nestled in her hair. She turned away from me and yanked them down. This pair was enormous and rectangular and looked an awful lot like the glasses Viola wore for weeks after her cataract surgery, if clearly more expensive. "Sorry," she said, not nearly as spritely as before. "I'm not quite camera-ready yet."

I'm never camera-ready these days, but I'm sure Harper figured that out the first time we met. "No need to apologize," I said, my voice stiff with self-consciousness. Which struck me as ridiculous—one can only be self-conscious if one actually cares, and I have no reason to care what a virtual stranger thinks of me. Yet I could tell that Harper was aware that I knew that something was amiss. She might have even seen me watering the lawn the day before and deduced that I had been a partial observer to what I now hypothesize was assault.

She bit her bottom lip. "So you're really a housekeeper?"

"Cleaning professional."

"Got it. What did you say your name was?"

There was no *again* to it—I didn't introduce myself the last time we met. I still didn't want to, but she seemed so simultaneously vulnerable and hopeful that I couldn't help myself. "Annie," I said.

"Annie! That's a great name."

"Thank you. It suits me." I've always thought my given name, Ann, was a better fit for someone who crosses her legs at the ankles and throws a great party (which is to say the kind of daughter-in-law Carolyn wishes she was getting). But an Annie—well, she's too busy with the periodic table to set the dinner table. She's a woman who doesn't need society, or her soon-to-be mother-in-law, to tell her how to be useful. My nickname is the only good thing my father left me.

She cocked her head and regarded me from behind her opaque lenses. "Annie, you were outside yesterday, right?"

I nodded.

"Did you see anyone stop by?"

"Stop by where?" I asked, because if there's anything I've learned from science, it's that it's best to ask more questions when you're unsure how to proceed.

"My house."

"Your house?" I asked.

She stared at me curiously. "I thought so. I have a tiny favor to ask."

"And what's that?"

"Can you please pretend you weren't there?" she said in the manner of someone used to trapping flies with honey.

In seconds I had concocted multiple scenarios involving missing persons, meth labs, and the exotic-animal trade. I quickly reminded myself that even if any one of those was true—and objectively, I know they're not—it didn't have anything to do with me. "Sure," I said. "I saw nothing."

She squeezed my arm lightly and gave me the kind of smile that makes you feel like the sun's shining directly on you. "God, you're the best. Thank you."

"No problem," I said.

Moppet was frenetically circling a tree and barking its head off at a squirrel. Harper looked at the dog for a split second, then turned back to me. "Will you let me know if you hear of another cleaner who's looking for work? Particularly someone who isn't nosy and uses green cleaning products."

I'll admit, hearing that she had a preference for nontoxic cleaners was like finding out we had a mutual friend in common. "Green cleaners are hard to come by," I told her. "I think I'm the only one in this neighborhood."

"Then I'll have to keep my fingers crossed that someone on this block croaks sometime soon so you can swing by my place!" She bent to pick up Moppet, at which point her glasses slid down on her nose, again revealing her black eye. If anything, it looked even worse than I had initially observed. Still crouched and oblivious to my distress, she lifted her head and flashed me the peace sign. I wasn't sure if I was supposed to respond in kind, but I was still holding all my cleaning products so I suppose it didn't matter.

"Well, Harper, hope you have a good rest of your day," I said.

She stood and gave me yet another smile, but this one wasn't like the others. It was genuine but also uncertain, and made her look like a small child. For the first time I wondered how old she actually is. I've been thinking mid- to late-twenties, but now I peg her as just over the legal drinking age.

How does someone that young buy an entire house? And why?

I strongly suspect something next door is amiss. Based on Harper's shiner, I can even reasonably speculate that she's in danger. I did some reading earlier. As it turns out, most mental health professionals and women's rights advocates say the best way to be an ally to someone who may be the victim of abuse is to observe and, when possible, take notes (I suppose this journal serves that purpose), and call the police the minute you actually witness an act of violence.

But Harper asked me to pretend I hadn't seen or heard what happened yesterday. And for reasons that completely escape me, I agreed. In doing so, I essentially confirmed that I'll stay out of her affairs. Which is exactly what I've already vowed to do.

So . . . why do I feel so bad about that?

Obviously I'll contact the authorities if I see her being harmed. But in the meantime, am I really supposed to just wait? I can't befriend her. But neither can I unsee what I saw nor erase the sound of her crying and arguing with that man.

My hope is that he simply won't come around more than once, and the situation will resolve itself. But "once" is perhaps the most misused word in the English language—as the incident with Todd recently reminded me, almost every behavior and thought is soon revealed to be part of a pattern.

I only pray that Jon's French exit proves to be the exception to that rule.

—AEM

TEN

August 4
TO: Jon Nichols
FROM: Annie Mercer
SUBJECT: Sabbatical

Dear Jon,

I promise this will be my last letter until you return. In fact, I would not have written at all—well, other than to find out when your flight gets in—were it not for an unsettling encounter I had at Community Cup this morning.

I was feeling a bit sluggish and had an hour to kill before I was due at Seth Williams' (an old classmate of mine, for whom I'm now cleaning house—my business is rapidly expanding), so I decided to treat myself to a cup of coffee. I'd just ordered my usual when a man came charging at me with an enormous smile on his face. "Annie Mercer, I thought that was you!" He thrust his hand out at me before I could place him. "Ben Farber. I work with Jon at County Day."

"Oh, of course," I said, because by that point I had remembered that he was the math teacher with the perma-grin.

"Surprised you're not in Paris with Jon," he said jovially.

"Yes, well, that makes two of us." I retrieved my coffee from the bar, hoping that would be the end of it. (I'm not unhappy for you, but it's hard for me to go about my day knowing you're on the other side of the Atlantic having a blast without me.)

Alas. "What a lucky guy he is to be on a trip like that. Meanwhile, I'm teaching summer school. Melinda's due with number four in October. Our next vacation will be eighteen years from now," he said, chuckling at himself.

"Congratulations."

"Thanks! It's finally a girl."

"That's great."

He was still smiling at me like a sociopath. "So are the rumors true?"

"Rumors?" I said blankly. My first thought was that he somehow knew I'd left SCI, but it quickly occurred to me that he's probably never heard of SCI and had no idea that the T-shirt and sweatpants I was wearing weren't my normal work attire.

"So you two aren't planning a move to France?"

"Uh, no," I said.

"That's what I told everyone," he said, bringing his hand down on the bar. I jumped, but he didn't seem to notice he'd surprised me. "But when we saw the post about a long-term French substitute teacher go up, a lot of us were worried. No one wants Madame LeBlanc to come back," he said, pretending to shudder.

"Maybe they're looking for another teacher to expand the language program," I supplied.

He shook his head. "Budget cuts, budget cuts, budget cuts. They're talking about getting rid of German altogether, and forget raises. Anyway, I don't want to bore you when Jon's probably told you all this. It was nice seeing you, Annie," he said.

"Yeah, you, too," I mumbled. "Good luck with the baby."

"We've got it down to a science by this point," he said, and though I knew he wasn't being literal, it was perhaps the most compelling argument for childbirth I've yet to hear. "Tell Jon I said hi and that I'm relieved he'll be back in September. It's not every day a teacher like him comes along."

"No, it's not," I agreed, because I know how hard you've worked to make French a living language for your students, Jon.

Which is why I'm wondering why a substitute position has been posted for your job. While I trusted Ben was telling me what he knew to be the truth, I still verified it as soon as I got home from Seth's. Sure enough: a three-second web search led me directly to the listing for a position that looks identical to yours—at County Day.

As I hope you are aware, the beginning of the school year is four brief weeks away. It took you six months to decide to move from St. Louis to Michigan, and you can spend half an hour staring at a menu before making up your mind. Believe me, that's a compliment—I've always loved your analytical approach to the world. So I'm trying to believe that there's some other logical explanation for what I discovered today.

Please write back at your earliest possible convenience.

Love,
Annie

ELEVEN

August 7

I was not doing particularly well when I set out for Viola's house this morning. Because the run-in with Ben and Jon's continued silence have illuminated something quite unfortunate: the life I've carefully crafted appears to be crumbling faster than I've allowed myself to admit.

At one point, I must have been a relatively worry-free child—I don't remember all that much before my father left. What I do remember is that after he took off and my mother fell into the hole of her own emotions, I quickly realized the safest way to navigate the wider world was to stick to the facts.

Fact: Leesa was my friend regardless of arbitrary factors (e.g., whether I wore brand-name clothes or hung out with the popular kids—neither of which I ever did, obviously). She never took advantage of me (e.g., trying to get me to help her cheat on tests). She accepted me for the person I am, and though she's always been a social butterfly, she still made time for me. I could count on her.

Fact: Science allows for possibilities within a defined set of rules. While there's often no such thing as a "correct" answer, every outcome is measurable, and in many cases can be predicted in advance. I know how to operate and excel within those confines. I can count on science.

Fact: Jon and I both enjoy road trips within the continental US, long tangents, and clean, modern spaces. We share the same visceral aversion to the sound of food being slurped, and neither of us wants children, or so I was led to believe. We look forward to moving somewhere other than Michigan (Cambridge, perhaps?) in the next five to ten years. We are perfectly suited for each other. I can count on Jon and our relationship.

Except now my friendship with Leesa has new requirements. I'm not just supposed to hold my tongue over her peddling "wellness" products that purport to have properties that are completely unsupported by science, let alone rational thought. No, she actually expects me to be *enthusiastic* about her ill-advised venture.

And science is no longer my safe space. I loved waking up every morning, putting on my lab coat, and running the data on my latest experiments. The days flew by so quickly that I didn't even feel bad that I'd put graduate school on hold. Then Todd popped that bubble. Even if I had not shoved him, I couldn't have stayed at SCI knowing my own supervisor felt my body was his property.

But Jon . . . as completely out of character as his hopping on a plane to France was, I believed it was an anomaly. And most anomalies are soon revealed to be the result of a systematic error or faulty interpretation, at which point they can be corrected. Whatever Jon is going through, I expected him to get over this.

Now I'm not so sure.

Though a few tears escaped this morning when I checked my inbox and found it empty, I managed to arrive at Viola's with a brave face. "Annie, my girl! You're a sight for sore eyes," she said, wrapping her thin arms around me. She's one of the few people I actually enjoy hugging, but today her embrace only made me feel sadder.

"Thanks, Viola," I said, trying to ignore the saltwater tingle at the back of my throat. "Did you send your letter about Line 5 to the governor?"

Viola and I have spent hours upon hours discussing the oil pipeline that runs through the Mackinac Straits. The Great Lakes are already teeming with bioaccumulative toxins and can't afford another oil spill, but based on probability alone, we agree the pipeline is guaranteed to leak.

"Yesterday, in fact," she said, passing me a spray bottle full of white vinegar. (Viola is the only client of mine who doesn't complain about the smell, which quickly dissipates. Her mother had the cleanest house in all of greater Detroit, she says, and she only used vinegar and baking soda.)

I followed her into the living room. "I'm glad. How are you feeling?" She looks frailer every time I see her. I suppose that's not a surprise for an eighty-two-year-old woman, but it still concerns me.

"I've been having a little gut trouble," she said, patting her midsection with the feather duster she just picked up. "Is there a supplement I could take? I don't want a prescription."

"Hmm, I'm not sure," I told her. Viola is constantly forgetting that being a chemist does not qualify me to dispense health advice. Then again, Leesa has a degree in American Studies and runs around telling people to swap their flu shots for oregano oil. I lifted a jade Foo dog on the mantel so I could wipe off the invisible dirt beneath it—from the state of Viola's floors alone when I arrived, I knew she had been cleaning for hours this morning, and probably last night as well. Sometimes I wonder if Viola's influence is the real reason I'm a neatnik. "You may want to ask your doctor about probiotic supplementation. The research is promising."

She beamed at me. "You're such a smart girl, Annie."

I thanked her, because even though I think intelligence is mostly a construct made of curiosity, opportunity, and plain old hard work, sometimes it *is* the thought that counts.

"And how are *you?*" she said, readjusting the Foo dog sculpture. "How are you holding up?"

"Oh, you know," I said, waving my microfiber cloth in her direction. "Happy to be keeping busy. I'm up to four cleaning clients now."

"I'm glad. But surely you're thinking about your next step."

Aside from the wedding, I haven't been thinking about next steps, because doing so causes me immense stress. Even if there weren't the matter of the non-compete clause, who would hire me? I certainly can't use SCI as a reference. "Not yet, but I will soon."

"I should hope so. Graduating at the very top of your class and then getting a big job at a chemical company—surely this current juncture is a blip, and soon you'll be off to even better adventures."

Better adventures have to be put on hold until I'm sure my mother won't relapse, which is why Jon and I weren't planning to leave the state for several years. "I'm not unhappy," I told Viola.

She sat on the edge of the sofa, looking a bit winded. "Not unhappy is not the same thing as being happy, you know."

"Right," I said. What I didn't say is that happiness has never really been my concern. Or at least not happiness as it's colloquially defined. I don't need birds chirping in my window; predictability is what brings me true pleasure. Most people don't understand that, but Jon always did. Or at least he used to.

She pointed a finger at the light fixture hanging in the foyer. "Can you do something about the cobwebs up there, love? Try as I might, I just can't seem to rid this old house of spiders."

"The Rogers swear their cats eat all the spiders and millipedes," I said. It's possible they're correct about that. For all the fur tumbleweeds, I can't recall ever seeing a single bug in their home. "Maybe you could get a cat."

Viola looked at me as though I'd just suggested she adopt a wild boar. "Filthy," she said with a little shudder.

"Right," I said.

"And, Annie," she said as I wielded my duster like a magic wand, zapping nonexistent web silk, "how is Jon?"

Viola's always had an uncanny ability to work her way into my thoughts.

"I don't mean to shine a floodlight on the elephant in the room," she said, "but you've barely mentioned him lately. Are you two having trouble?"

"Not trouble, per se," I said, polishing the banister like my life depended on it. "It's just that he's in France."

"France!"

I nodded. "He's been gone for almost a month."

"My goodness. Why didn't you say so?"

"Because it upsets me," I admitted. "He didn't tell me he was going until he was on his way to the airport. And . . ." I hesitated, unsure of whether to continue. It was as though saying it out loud made it sound even worse than it was. "He asked to be left alone while he was away. I haven't talked to him once."

Viola's eyes were wide. "That seems *very* unlike Jon."

"I know," I said, relieved that she thought so, too.

"Well, you tell him to come home right this minute," she said firmly.

"I can't," I said. "He needs this time to get his head on straight before we get married."

She stared at me. "My dear girl. You haven't asked for a single thing in your God-given life. Now would be a good time to start."

"I've asked for plenty of things," I said (a bit weakly, I'll admit). "I requested a raise at SCI last quarter."

"After how many years of accepting the same pay?" she said, raising her eyebrows. "And then after what that terrible man did to you . . ."

"I didn't want to prolong the process any longer than necessary," I reminded her. Viola and I have already discussed this, and I made it perfectly clear why I arrived at the decision I did.

"Oh Annie. I'm not trying to upset you, and I'm certainly not saying you're a pushover. But you are entirely too skilled at putting other people's needs ahead of your own."

"Maybe," I said, because I felt uncomfortable pointing out to a childless widow that putting others' needs first is often the byproduct of having loved ones. What's the alternative—become a recluse? Truth be told, that's starting to sound more and more appealing. Forget new people. Maybe I should just avoid people, period.

"I have no doubt Jon loves you and will do the right thing," said Viola. "And I know Fae counts on you for a lot. I just pray that you're thinking about *your* next step, Annie, not someone else's. As much as I'll hate to have to use one of those generic cleaning services again, a gal like you . . ." She looked at me so adoringly that I wondered if her cataracts were back, because I was in an MIT T-shirt and leggings, which were relatively clean but happened to have a hole in the knee from where they caught on a nail while I was attempting to degrime Donna Guinness' linoleum. Moreover, I was beaded with sweat; Viola keeps the house at seventy-five degrees, even in August. And as my mother pointed out just this morning, I've let myself go a bit. But I plan to address my own mess prior to Jon's return.

"You've got great things ahead of you," Viola continued, "and I have a feeling none of them are to be found on Willow Lane. Have you thought about applying to graduate school again?"

"I want to apply soon. Possibly as early as next year," I said. This hadn't actually been my plan, but it made sense as I said it, and now I'm thinking it might just be a good idea. Maybe after Jon comes home and we get through the archaic, overpriced party that is to be our wedding, my mother will be doing well enough that I can consider making the leap.

"Good," she said, nodding. "Why don't you go see about the upstairs bathroom?"

"I'll do that," I said, knowing she had made the suggestion to give me a little privacy. While there's certainly room for two in the bathroom—which boasts his-and-hers sinks and has a short wall separating the toilet from the rest of the space for privacy purposes—it's the one place Viola doesn't follow me when I'm cleaning.

I closed the door behind me and had just lifted the blinds to spray the windowpane with vinegar when what should I see through the glass but the inside of the Novaks'.

I can't say for certain which room Viola's bathroom gave me a direct view into, but it was possibly Harper's bedroom (I saw an empty bookshelf and some sort of wardrobe, though no bed). Regardless, her blinds were up and her window was open.

I should have looked away. But Harper was singing at the top of her lungs—or at least her mouth was wide open in a way that suggested actual vocalization rather than lip-synching. In fact, she looked so natural doing it—she even had a pair of round John Lennon–style sunglasses on, though it occurs to me now that maybe this was to cover her shiner—that I'm wondering if she's a singer rather than an actress. At any rate, even with Viola's window sealed shut, I could hear that she was singing along to "The Weight."

And suddenly I was on the cold tile floor, sniffling into my filthy T-shirt.

When I was young, my mother used to turn it up loud when that song came on the radio, and she and my father would swing me in their arms as they sang, *"Take a load off, Annie! Take a load for free!"* It's one of the few memories I have of the three of us together, and it's a good one.

I was in college when Leesa overheard me belting it out with Joe Cocker (whose cover happens to be my favorite) and asked me, very quietly, if I was aware that the actual lyrics were "Take a load off, Fanny."

In fact, I hadn't been aware of that at all. Long after my father left, I continued to hear "Annie," regardless of whether the Band or Aretha Franklin or Joe Cocker was singing. Because that is what my parents sang, and I had attached meaning to it. And that meaning-filled mis-belief canceled my ability to be objective.

The music from Harper's house had stopped, so I dried my face, pulled myself off the floor, and finished cleaning. But as I made my way through the rest of Viola's house, I kept returning to one thought.

What if I've attached so much meaning to my relationship to Jon that I've missed some crucial detail indicating that he's the kind of man who would walk out the door on the woman he claims to love?

—AEM

TWELVE

August 10
TO: Annie Mercer
FROM: Jon Nichols
SUBJECT: Update

Dear Annie,

    Last night, I opened my inbox for the first time and read through all your emails. Gosh, Annie—I'm so sorry my trip has stressed you out. That wasn't my intention at all. You sounded so understanding when I called you that I guess I thought you understood. I'm kicking myself, but I didn't even think about your dad leaving and how that might feel the same for you. I'm really, really sorry.

    I know it was nuts for me to pick up and go with no warning. I still don't even know how to explain it, except that I kept thinking about how I'm turning thirty in November and how Roger never got to see thirty, and now we're getting married, and . . .

I won't say I freaked out, but this feeling of *now or never* came over me, and I knew I had to act on it.

You know I felt strangled growing up in Frontenac, and my undergrad years at Mizzou weren't a whole lot better. Things improved at Tufts, but I realize now I was a total idiot not to take my graduate advisor's advice and move to France before getting locked into teaching. I was so worried my dad would die after his heart attack, and then you and I met, and as they say, the rest is history.

I know you've never been keen on the idea of Paris, but it's magical here, Annie—you have to see it. And there's so much to do. No one thinks less of you if you spend the morning wandering around a museum and then go have a glass of wine for lunch and stare at all the people walking past your café, because everyone else is doing the same thing. That said, I'm not being a total slouch. I've been tutoring English on the side, which isn't half as fun as chatting with the guy I buy chocolate bread from every morning.

See, that's the thing: People here speak to me *in French*. Apparently, I sound just un-American enough to pass. And every time I hear myself (I know this makes me sound like my marbles have rolled out of my head and down the street, but hear me out) it's a sign that all those years of studying and that miserable semester I spent in Montreal weren't for nothing. They actually paid off.

I feel like myself here, Annie. I think that's why I needed to do this alone—to see who I was when no one else was around, if that makes any sense.

And I'm not ready to give it up just yet.

I'm sure you're assuming the worst right now, but keep reading. I'm not suggesting we put our wedding on hold, or that we call off our engagement. And this has nothing to do with our conversation about having kids (which we should revisit, but again—this isn't about that).

But I would like to extend my trip by a few weeks. The couple I'm renting my apartment from are staying in Morocco longer than they originally planned to and asked if I wanted to stay on another six weeks.

If I'm honest with myself, I do. This is the opportunity of a lifetime, and I'd be a fool not to take it.

As you deduced from your conversation with Ben, I asked County Day for a leave of absence, which they've graciously agreed to. I'll return in January after we're back from our honeymoon, so the timing will work out perfectly.

Which brings me to my most important point:

Come to Paris.

There's so much I can't explain in an email, or even over the phone. So let me show you in person. The timing is crap, I know—well, except for the fact that you're finally not tied to your lab. What happened was rotten, but now that it's over, why not take advantage of it? Between your mom and mine, they should be able to handle any wedding-related tasks that need to be taken care of. (As we both admitted when we nixed the idea of eloping, the wedding is really for them, anyway.) And as you said, we've got time.

I've made arrangements with Air France—all you have to do is call them, give the code below, and let them know when you'd like to fly.

I love you,
Jon

>>>
AIR FRANCE
TRAVEL CONFIRMATION NUMBER
R76W335757670

August 10
TO: Jon Nichols
FROM: Annie Mercer
SUBJECT: Re: Update

Dear Jon,

I was so relieved to hear from you . . . until I actually read the entirety of your message. Six weeks is not "a few." But it's not even the duration of your stay that concerns me. One data point does not constitute a pattern, but two rash decisions, Jon—that means something.

Do you even plan to return to Michigan?

Remember the way you chatted me up the entire duration of that first flight, then asked if you could see me again as soon as possible as the plane touched down in St. Louis? Do you recall our first date at the French bistro the following night, when you kissed me under the stars on the rooftop bar? You said you didn't believe in love at first sight until I sat down in 11B. You moved across two states to be with me. You asked me to spend the rest of my life with you, Jon. Only one of us is good at math, so let me break it down for you: the sum of that equation is *not* your continuing your personal pilgrimage.

And while I'm glad you've finally decided to invite me to join you, you know I can't just leave my mother here. Maybe I could convince my uncle Lou to come up from Tennessee to stay with her— but that would require advance planning, rather than the whimsy that suddenly seems to be your new MO.

Likewise, I may have lost my job at SCI, but my cleaning business is going well, and I'm not about to sabotage that. It takes money to live, and I don't have a trust fund to fall back on. (I know you've told me repeatedly that what's yours is mine, but if I've learned anything from years of watching my mother check the mailbox for child support payments, it's that a woman must have money of her own in order to feel at peace.)

You say, "I would like to extend my trip," but you're not actually asking me—you're telling me. If you've secured a leave of absence from your job, it's been a done deal for some time now.

Do you know what Viola pointed out to me the other day? She said I haven't asked for a single thing in my life. Initially I scoffed at this, but I've since come to realize that while it's obviously hyperbole, there's a kernel of truth in it, too.

Well, no more. I am asking you to come home.

Not in six weeks. In two days, just like you told me you were going to. Go take a selfie in front of the *Mona Lisa*, then pack your bags. Upon your return, I believe you'll be surprised to find your conscience waiting here in this provincial place we call home—right beside the woman who you asked to be your wife.

Love,
Annie

August 10
TO: Annie Mercer
FROM: Jon Nichols
SUBJECT: Re: Update

Annie, please. Don't make me choose, when both things are possible. Your mother isn't an invalid—you said yourself that she's been doing so much better, and you're moving out at the end of the year anyway. Wouldn't now be the perfect time for a test run? You'll love Paris. Trust me.

Jon

August 10
TO: Jon Nichols
FROM: Annie Mercer
SUBJECT: Re: Update

Jon,

I'm not making you choose anything. It's clear that you've already chosen, and expect me to be on board with your plan.

Well, I'm not the same person you left behind in July. You say "trust me," but every time I trust someone, it backfires and even more trouble comes flying my way. I'm done being a sitting duck, Jon.

To be clear, I am *not* coming to Paris.

Since you are opting not to honor my direct request for you to come home, I have another to make—and this one is nonnegotiable.

Remember how you asked me not to contact you during the month you were supposed to be away? Granted, I didn't quite manage to follow through, but it didn't matter, since you weren't reading my emails anyway.

Now it's my turn. I don't want to hear from you during the six weeks you're gone. And if you try to get in touch, know that your email/text/voicemail will be ignored.

That's right—I'm telling you to stay in Paris. Because it's clear you're not done finding yourself, and if we're going to get married at the end of

December, I'd like both of us to know who you are before we do.

I'll be in touch,

Annie

August 10

TO: Annie Mercer

FROM: Jon Nichols

SUBJECT: Re: Update

Annie,

    Can we please talk about this? Let me call you.

Jon

August 10

TO: Jon Nichols

FROM: Annie Mercer

SUBJECT: Automatic response: Update

To whom it may concern:

    I am away from email until September 23 and will respond when I return.

Sincerely,

Annie Mercer

THIRTEEN

August 12
TO: Annie Mercer
FROM: Oak Grove Neighborhood Association
SUBJECT: Abridged summary of OakGroveMI-NeighborhoodAssociation@googlegroups.com—8 updates in 4 topics

Today's Topic Summary
View all topics

- New neighbors—help!—3 Updates
- Recycling pickup—3 Updates
- Unsubscribe me—1 Update
- Suspicious activity on Willow Lane—1 Update

New neighbors—help!
LarryNBessRogers@yahoo.com 10:43 a.m.

Friends,

It appears we have some new neighbors! At least two large groundhogs have taken up residence in our backyard. They're cute as can be, but they've chewed through our green beans, zucchini, and even our basil, which I thought for sure they wouldn't be interested in. Worse, they've dug a hole under our garage, and Larry is concerned they'll damage the foundation. As many of you know, we're the fur parents to four cats, and as animal lovers and advocates, we want to make sure we're doing right by these creatures. Any recommendations for humane traps or pest control services that can help?

Smiles,
Bess

Pete_Yacob9243@gmail.com 1:33 p.m.
Larry and Bess,

If you're truly animal lovers, skip the traps. Groundhog traps regularly trap other unwitting animals (like cats!). More often than not, these animals end up imprisoned for days and die of dehydration. Also, despite what Pe$t Control companies may tell you, trapping is *NOT* an ethical way to treat groundhogs, a.k.a. woodchucks, a.k.a. land beavers, who happen to be among the most peaceful of all rodents. (See links below for additional information.) Imagine someone picked you up from work one day, blindfolded you, and dropped you in the middle of an unknown land? (Exactly.) To relocate an animal is to sentence it to death—period.

I urge you to reconsider. A few missing vegetables and a hole under your garage is a small price to pay for sharing this earth with the species who were here first.

Pete
https://www.peta.org/issues/wildlife/cruel-wildlife-control/cruel-wildlife-trapping/
http://www.humanesociety.org/news/magazines/2015/01-02/strangers-in-a-strange-land-why-you-shouldnt-trap-and-relocate-wildlife.html
https://blog.nationalgeographic.org/2014/01/31/9-things-you-didnot-know-about-groundhogs-2/

LarryNBessRogers@yahoo.com 8:43 p.m.
Thanks for this information, Pete. Larry and I will consider it.

Smiles,
Bess

Recycling pickup
jossjossjoss82@gmail.com 3:37 p.m.
Greetings, gang. Does anyone know when recycling gets picked up?

Cheers,
Joss

NFlynn782@gmail.com 1:20 p.m.
Joss:

The information you're seeking is on the front page of the city's website.

Regards,
Nathan Flynn
442 Oak Grove Lane

jossjossjoss82@gmail.com
Nathan,

Touché!

Cheers,
Joss

Unsubscribe me
DieHardTigersFan4EVR@gmail.com 5:01 p.m.

To whoever manages this email list, please unsubscribe me. I clicked the unsubscribe link at the bottom of the email three times but I'm still getting daily updates. —Mike

Suspicious activity on Willow Lane
MargieSueLinden@aol.com 6:43 p.m.

Warning! A twentysomething Middle Eastern man in a battered silver hatchback was parked in front of our house for nearly an hour this afternoon. I was afraid to go outside to jot down his license plate number, but I did call the police. The officer I spoke with said that loitering on a public street isn't technically illegal, but leaving an engine idling violates a city ordinance. (Sidebar: Can we revisit the possibility of installing no-standing signs in the neighborhood, and possibly speed bumps as well?) The officer encouraged me to call again if the man returns.

Stay vigilant, folks! If you see something, say something. For reference, the non-emergency line is 722-SAFE, and as ever, you can always do what I did and dial 911.

Namaste,
Margie

FOURTEEN

August 13

A few months ago, Jon and I were driving out of a state park after a long hike. I spotted an overflowing dumpster at the park's entrance, and remarked that I'd recently read that trash, especially the plastic variety, will be one of the primary reasons humans go extinct in the next three generations.

Jon, who was at the wheel, turned to me briefly with the bemused expression he sometimes gets when I've pointed out something unappealingly logical. "Come on, Annie. Even if that's true, isn't it more fun to look on the bright side? At least we won't be here to find out how it ends."

I wanted to tell him that I already knew it would end badly—there's really no other kind of ending, if you think about it. But I just said, "I can see your point," because I was at least trying to.

Never again. Because come to find out, the bright side is blinding. And I have been lying to myself for far too long.

Here I've been thinking of myself as a realist (Jon would call me a pessimist, and I suppose one could make the argument for those being the same thing). In reality, I've been expecting the best in spite of all evidence to the contrary—including an unshakable feeling that my so-called fiancé would not be coming home tomorrow as he claimed.

And I was wrong.

It's not that I don't have theories as to why Jon did what he did. His parents' unmeetable expectations have weighed heavily on him his entire life. Bad enough that Charles and Carolyn clearly would have preferred a more conventional wife for their beloved eldest son. But when he told them he wasn't planning to produce two perfect children, they must have been beside themselves (though Jon's second thoughts about our having children suggest the guilt may have gotten to him, after all). If he didn't procreate, what would ever spur him to finally come to his senses and get a job in finance?

And yet his flight across the Atlantic was an act of free will. It was entirely his decision to cut off contact while he went and "found himself," or whatever new-age excuse he's using as justification for having abandoned me.

Because that's what he's done, even if he hasn't realized it yet. Deep down, I knew it the moment he said, "Annie, I'm at the airport." Yet fool that I was, I kept hoping I was mistaken. I wrote him like everything was fine and allowed myself to get excited when I saw his name in my inbox yesterday. I even let myself think that his email was a sign he'd woken up and realized the error of his ways.

Then I kept reading.

Instead of crying, as I did at Viola's, I had to resist the urge to throw my laptop across my bedroom. (Thankfully, I remembered that I couldn't afford a new one before I hurled it at the wall.) The dum-dum is under the impression he's actually going to make it back to the States and marry me. As one of my professors liked to say, "What happens twice, happens thrice." Or in the case of my father, what happens once is permanent. He told me he'd come back, too. I remember seeing him haul his army-green duffel bag to the door and asking him where he was going. "Dad's off on a little adventure, Annie," he said, tousling my hair. "But don't you worry, I'll be back."

"He'll be back," my mother agreed, but I still remember that she was standing in front of the door, almost like she was trying to block him.

My father's idea of "back" was sending postcards and the occasional birthday check and calling on the day of my high school graduation (not that I spoke with him—if he couldn't show up to hear me give my valedictorian speech, I was not about to let him congratulate me).

What a rude awakening it will be when Jon realizes his long, strange trip has been a neon sign that it's not just his teaching job he wants to leave behind. It's his whole life.

As with the end of the world, I'm glad I won't be there to witness it.

I'm not calling the wedding off just yet. For starters, I don't think it's fair for me to look like the villain in this scenario. Of course, now he can tell everyone that he invited me to France, albeit belatedly, and that I said no.

It was a fundamentally unfair request. No, my mother's *not* an invalid, as Jon rudely pointed out. Aside from her depression, she's a stunningly healthy fifty-nine-year-old woman. But how is she going to react if I do the same thing Jon just did to me and surprise her by telling her I'm taking off?

In the meantime, I have to figure out how to explain to her that Jon's still abroad, and that I don't actually anticipate him coming back . . . ever. Just this afternoon, she suggested having him over for dinner next week.

"He should be home any day now, shouldn't he?" she added.

She looked so hopeful that I just couldn't bring myself to tell her the truth. "I'm not sure," I said, hoping my cheeks weren't burning.

Thank Einstein that as I was debating if and when to tell her about Jon's email, my phone started buzzing on the kitchen counter. It was Donna Guinness, calling to ask if I could possibly spare an extra hour on Thursday. I could, though I'm afraid to find out why Donna's abode requires more than four hours of my time.

As I was hanging up the phone, I happened to look beyond the hedges separating our yard from Harper's (I've finally managed to stop calling her home the Novaks'). I couldn't see much, but I could tell someone was lounging near the pool. I wish my mother's house wasn't a ranch—though a second floor would provide more space for her odds and ends to multiply like rabbits in the spring, it would also give me a better vantage point to inconspicuously check on Harper and make sure that bad man hasn't returned to hurt her. Since this wasn't an option, I had to resort to my yard-work trick.

It took me a while to find the pruning shears, which were on top of the fridge, wedged between a pack of stale mini-muffins and a bag of dog treats (for whose dog, I'm not sure; we've never owned one).

"Where are you going with *those*?" my mother said, frowning at the shears.

"I told you the other day, I'm trying to work on this place's curb appeal," I told her. "You're welcome."

"But the curb is in the other direction!" she squawked as I let myself out the back door.

I'm not sure the hedges have been pruned since I was a child; they're technically ours, so the Novaks let them grow. Now they're higher than my head and so dense that it was hard to see much other than a blur of blue water through them. I suppose I could have fetched a ladder from the garage and made a show of trimming the top of the laurels while I was spying, but I'm not sure my mother's ladder is to be trusted. Anyway, if Harper spotted me, we would then have to engage in small talk, and all I wanted to do was make sure she was okay.

But lo and behold, there was a curious hole in the hedges near the far end of the yard, perhaps the work of a hungry deer or a wayward meteorite. The opening was approximately the size of a soccer ball, perhaps three feet off the ground, and it gave me a near-perfect view of

Harper, who was floating on a large inflatable raft in the center of her pool. She was wearing a bright yellow bikini, which covered so little that I couldn't help but notice that she was very thin, and even tanner than she had been when she arrived. No surprise—August has been oppressively hot. She was wearing sunglasses, the aviators again this time, so I couldn't tell if her eye was still bruised (I assume so).

The Novaks did a beautiful job on the pool. Instead of a typical concrete border, bright blue and yellow Spanish-style tiles line the perimeter, and there's a small, mosaic-tiled water fountain in the deep end. I wonder if they would have had the pool installed if they'd known Linda would have less than two years to enjoy it.

At any rate, Harper was alone. This was a relief. Late last night, shortly after midnight, I heard a car door slam and a vehicle skid out of the driveway, so I knew there was a possibility the man had returned. It would have been conspicuous to leave my head in the hole for too long, so I quickly glanced around, mostly to see if she had company. After all, if I saw something, then it was my duty to say something.

But as I began to retreat, I spotted something scurrying just beyond the pool.

It was a groundhog, squat and sleek. Though it appeared to be in a hurry, it abruptly stopped at the pool's halfway point and cocked its head to look at Harper; apparently I'm not the only one who finds her enthralling. Then it pushed through the hedges at the back of her yard and disappeared into the Rogers' garden.

Bess spent nearly half an hour on Monday telling me how a pair of groundhogs were destroying her crops, and she feared it wouldn't be long before an entire colony popped up under their garage, setting the stage for a sinkhole that would suck Larry out of his workshop and right into the earth. I decided it was better to skip a brief tutorial about the conditions in which sinkholes form, and instead impart upon Bess that groundhogs are solitary creatures. Their mating season, as my own has turned out to be, is quite brief. Then they return to their pleasant, self-sufficient existence. The young, I assured Bess, stay with their parents but a few months before setting off on their own. (On that count, groundhogs and I differ.) Not that I said this to Bess, but provided their garage isn't sitting on top of a mile of eroded limestone or, say, Line 5, Larry is safe for now.

Or is he? I was about to return to my pruning when I heard a rustling behind me. While Harper's house abuts the Rogers' backyard, my mother's house backs into a trail leading into County Park. There's a waist-high stone wall separating the trail from the yard. My mother claims my father built the crumbling wall, which always does remind me of that foolish Frost poem, shortly before he set out for Alaska. Beyond the wall are a bevy of holly bushes, punctuated by a smattering of oaks and evergreens. It was among these trees that I saw something out of the corner of my eye. And whatever this something was, it was definitely larger than a groundhog. On another day I might have taken the darting figure for a doe, but I had just read Margie Linden's post on the neighborhood Listserv (note to self: consider unsubscribing). So my first thought was that it was a human—maybe even someone casing the joint.

Now, on the one hand, I welcome whomever would like to rob my mother's house to do so—the treasure is so deeply buried among the trash that I daresay even *American Pickers* would run screaming in the opposite direction. On the other hand, the idea that I was being watched gave me goose bumps.

But my fear was more than a sign I'd contracted a mild case of mass hysteria (Margie, naturally, being patient zero). Because the flash I saw was dark, possibly black, rather than fawn colored. What's more, I saw—I'm almost certain of it—the back of a man's head.

Except I can't remember if his hair was black or brown. Nor do I know how tall he was. Was *he* even a he at all? I know too much about recall bias to let my mind fill in memory gaps with details that match my already-established beliefs. The only truly important thing is that the incident rattled me profusely.

I was tempted to walk over to Harper's and knock on the door like a normal person and let her know I had concerns about someone potentially spying on her. Then I thought better of it. In addition to the fact that I have no concrete proof anything dangerous or illegal had happened, I really don't want to interact with anyone other than my mother, Viola, and my other cleaning clients (who are usually gone when I'm there anyway, thank goodness).

Fact: People are the cause of most pain.

Fact: I cannot handle any more pain right now.

So I will continue to surreptitiously check in on Harper. I wish she had arrived in our neighborhood with less baggage. But if a little intrigue—albeit from a distance—distracts me from my own troubles, who am I to mind my own business?

—AEM

FIFTEEN

August 15
TO: undisclosed-recipients
BCC: Annie Mercer
FROM: Leesa Sato Liznewski
SUBJECT: FALL into a Whole New YOU!

Ladies!

Could your life use a lift? (You know what I'm going to say next, right?!)

LITEWEIGHT™ can help!

Please join me on September 1, 6:30 p.m., at my house, for a big reveal:

The LITEWEIGHT™ Transformative Collection™!

Without giving too much away, I can tell you that in addition to LITEWEIGHT™ signature products like *CashLash*™ and *LifeMadeLite*™, I'll be unveiling:

*The crystal with the power to put the va-va-voom back in your bedroom!

*The essential oil that adds a spring to your step AND melts belly fat!

*The herbal-infused lotion-oil (yes, there is such a thing—just wait until you try it!) that completely eliminates the need for lasers and injections. Ladies, this product ZAPPED my wrinkles in less than two weeks—saving me potentially thousands of dollars in invasive cosmetic procedures!

*And so much more!

As always, wine and Lite apps (pun totally intended!) will be served. Space is limited, so please claim your spot by RSVPing here. *Psst*: If you're one of the first five women to register, you'll get $5 off your order!

xoxo,
Leesa

Leesa Sato Liznewski
LiteWeight™ Brand Evangelist
LiteWeight™ Southeastern Michigan Sales Representative of the year!!!

August 15
TO: Leesa Sato Liznewski
FROM: Annie Mercer
SUBJECT: Re: FALL into a Whole New YOU!

Leesa,
When I said I needed space, that *definitely* meant I don't want to receive sales pitches. However, since you sent this to me anyway, I feel obligated to point out a few things:

- You know a crystal can't actually change anyone's libido, right? At best, there may be a placebo effect at play.

- Ditto for essential oils. Also, you can't target fat loss in one specific area . . . and even if you could, would you really want to? Fat makes it easier to get through long Michigan winters, and for women who are so inclined, ups the odds of bearing children.

- While I would argue that the best way to stop worrying about wrinkles is to reject societal norms that dictate women should avoid signs of aging at all costs (while men with gray hair and laugh lines are considered sexy—what's that about?), the fact remains that you're 27 years old—i.e., a little young for crow's-feet. And you've always had amazing skin, just like your mom. Remember how you told me that Japanese women just don't age the way other women do? While I'm not sure whether that's true, there's no doubt you owe a great deal to genetics—not a lotion-oil, whatever that is.

At any rate, for the love of Marie Curie, please unsubscribe me from this mailing list.

Annie

August 15
TO: Annie Mercer
FROM: Leesa Sato Liznewski
SUBJECT: Re: Re: FALL into a Whole New YOU!

Annie,

I'm SO sorry you got my LITEWEIGHT™ letter—
that was a mailing list glitch. I've unsubscribed you
and it shouldn't happen again.

But I have to ask: What is going on with you? I
don't say this meanly—I'm legit worried. I know you
asked for space, which is why I haven't been emailing or calling, but it's been a MONTH, Annie. We
have literally never gone a month without speaking, even when I was studying abroad in Florence.
Also, I'd really like to start planning your bridal
shower soon!

Is this about your job? Or Jon? (Is he home
yet?) I wish you would tell me so I could help you.

When you're ready to talk, I'm here.

xxxx x 1,000,
L

Leesa Sato Liznewski
LITEWEIGHT™ Brand Evangelist
LITEWEIGHT™ Southeastern Michigan Sales Repre-
sentative of the year!!!

August 15
TO: Leesa Sato Liznewski

FROM: Annie Mercer
SUBJECT: Re: Re: Re: FALL into a Whole New YOU!

Leesa,

I appreciate your concern, and your unsub-scribing me. I'll be fine. Tell Molly and Ollie I say hi, and please don't worry about the bridal shower. I'll be in touch later.

Annie

SIXTEEN

Aristotle said that nature abhors a vacuum. While there's some debate as to the scientific validity of his statement, it certainly applies to my life. Aside from a brief email exchange with Leesa (which I shouldn't have done—while I wasn't flat-out rude, my anger toward Jon does seem to be spilling over into other areas), I've mostly managed to clear the deck of my own problems. So other people's have managed to find me.

I guess drama from a distance is better than reading Jon's emails over and over, as I'm embarrassed to admit I've been doing. It's an exercise in self-flagellation—what's done is done, and I'm certainly not going to Paris. But I just keep thinking . . . was his request some kind of test? Am I supposed to prove to him that I love him so much I'm willing to ditch everything and fly to Paris? If so, he's mistaken me for someone else. I gave him four weeks, even though one should not need a vacation from the person one intends to spend the rest of one's natural life with. That was nothing if not an act of love, and if he can't see that . . . well, as much as I hate to admit it, it makes me wonder if he really loves *me*.

Anyway. As previously noted, I've been keeping a watchful eye on Harper when possible, worried that what I may or may not have witnessed last month will happen again. The mystery man hasn't come back around—at least not that I've seen, as Harper keeps such odd hours (a funny thing for me to say, I suppose, given that I'm as likely to be spotted at seven in the morning lugging a vacuum down the street as at seven at night). Just yesterday she came teetering out of the house wearing a pair of wedge sandals, those cataract sunglasses, and a long, tight dress. She was holding a flute of sparkling wine, which would have been less peculiar if it hadn't been two o'clock on a Wednesday afternoon. Then a blue sedan pulled up in front of her house and she ducked into the backseat, glass still in hand, not to return until nearly midnight. Watching her, sometimes, I get the sense I'm doing it all wrong—and I'm not even talking about waiting too long to close my life to new applicants.

Anyway, this evening I heard splashing coming from Harper's pool, and I wanted to confirm that said splashing was not actually the sound of, I don't know—someone drowning, perhaps? I decided to take advantage of the late August sunlight and went out back to prune the bushes. I was still conscious of the darting figure I saw in the trees earlier this week and considered slipping a small pruning knife in my back pocket for protection. After some debate, I decided I was more likely to injure myself than another person, and left the back door cracked so I could call for my mother if I were attacked.

I made my way to the hole in the hedges, but a woman wearing a large sun hat, who I assume was Harper, was floating on a lounger in the pool. Unfortunately, she was facing the hole. Hoping for a less obvious vantage point, I crept over to the low stone wall, moving slowly to avoid attracting attention. When I reached the wall, I was pleased to see that if I climbed it and positioned myself behind the large oak at the corner of Harper's yard, I could get a good view of the pool and avoid being seen.

I can hardly be described as athletic, but there are certain advantages to being tall, so I got on top of the wall with little effort. I was just inching toward the oak tree when I heard the same sort of rustling I'd heard the other day.

The sound must have startled me, because one second I was wondering whether a deer could make that much noise; the next, I was on my back on the ground on the other side of the wall.

Except . . . I wasn't on the ground. I'd landed on something cushioned yet firm.

And that thing was a man.

I'm pretty sure you're supposed to scream in such situations, but I'm sorry to admit that I made this terrible squawking noise as I rolled off him. I looked around for my pruning shears to defend myself, only to realize I'd abandoned the shears in the yard. (Good thing—otherwise I might have impaled myself.) Then I jumped up and scrambled for the wall. But before I tried to climb over, I couldn't help turning to get another look at the person I'd fallen on.

He was a few inches shorter than me, with black curls, brown eyes, and tan skin. He looked to be in his midtwenties, though it might have just been the black T-shirt and cargo shorts he was wearing. "Shhh," he said, lifting a finger to his lips.

"No, I won't *shhh!*" I hissed. "You're trespassing!"

"This is city property," he whispered, gesturing to the bushes behind him. "It's part of the County Park trail."

I shouldn't have kept talking to him, but he looked . . . tremendously unthreatening, to be honest. Now, I'm painfully aware that I'm not in a position to be making judgment calls about other people (see also: my fiancé). Still, his expression told me he was just as surprised as I was that I had landed on him.

"That may be true, but you were lurking behind *my* wall, weren't you?" I said in a low voice.

He nodded.

"I should call the police," I said.

He held up both hands, palms facing out, like he was a crime suspect. This was not reassuring. "Please don't," he said. "I'm doing the exact same thing you are."

"And what's that?"

He lowered his hands. "You first. Why did you climb the wall? I thought you were perfectly happy spying on your neighbor from the comfort of your own backyard."

I could feel my cheeks grow warm (I really should see a dermatologist about my eczema). "I was not *spying*," I told him. "I was minding my business in my bushes and simply needed to get higher to trim a certain part of the laurel."

"Which is why you left your scissors in the grass," he said, grinning. Feeling guilty for smiling back at him, I reminded myself that human emotion is contagious. Then I pushed my lips back into an even line, because I didn't want to give him the impression his behavior was acceptable.

"They're pruning shears," I informed him. "And anyway, what I'm doing should be of no interest to you."

"If that's true, then what I'm doing should be of little interest to *you*. By the way, you're welcome. You could have broken something if you'd fallen flat on your back."

"I'm supposed to thank *you* for creeping around my backyard?" I narrowed my eyes. "Was it you parked in a silver sedan on the other end of the block earlier this week?"

"I'm not at liberty to say," he said, but then he laughed. "I'm just kidding. Yeah, it was me." He reached into his back pocket.

Afraid he was going to pull out a weapon, I started for the wall again. Then I heard Harper call out, "Hello? Hello? Is someone back there?"

We ducked. After we were crouched low to the ground, he looked over at me. He had a wide, welcoming face, though it's possible that was said of Charles Manson.

He passed me a small rectangular card. It said, *Mo Beydoun, Private Investigator.*

"If this is true," I said, examining the card, "then aren't you supposed to be incognito?"

"Well, you already spotted me. I don't want you to think I'm trying to break into your house or something."

"So you're a detective?" I whispered, slipping the card into the pocket of my shorts. "Does anyone even do that anymore?"

"PI, technically. And you're looking at someone who does."

"If you're an investigator, why are you afraid of the police?"

The question didn't seem to faze him. "A couple months ago, I was thrown off a plane for speaking to an old woman in Arabic because someone who couldn't understand us was still absolutely positive I was discussing the bomb I planned to detonate in the middle of the flight. Last week, a man called me a terrorist in Walmart, right in front of a security officer, and the officer got in *my* face about it." He shrugged. "I believe most people are good at heart, but given the choice, I'd rather not take a gamble on dudes in power. You know?"

"Oh," I said because I didn't really know, or at least not in the concrete, everyday way he knew. "Sorry."

"Yeah," he said. "Me, too. But it could be worse."

"That could be said of every situation until the moment of one's death. And possibly even after that, though I somehow doubt it."

He chuckled. "Aren't you a ray of sunshine."

"I get that a lot," I said. Obviously, I was kidding, but it made me realize that the only thing I get a lot of these days is compliments about my cleaning. As Viola likes to say, no one knows their way around grout like I do.

We were still crouched down, and my calves were starting to burn. Why hadn't I addressed Harper when she called out? I could have at least offered some lame excuse for why I was back there. Since I had nothing to hide—not really—I wasn't sure. And yet I stayed low to the ground.

It was quiet for a while. Finally, the man, who I suppose I should refer to as Mo, peered over the wall. "The coast is clear," he said, standing.

I stood, too. "You're looking for her boyfriend, aren't you?"

A look of confusion came over his face. "Boyfriend?"

"Well-dressed guy, good-looking, prone to yelling? Looks kind of French?"

"French how?" asked Mo, pulling his phone out of one of the pockets of his cargo shorts. I glanced at the screen and saw that he was opening some kind of app with a microphone logo.

"Are you recording me?" I asked.

"Taking notes."

"By recording me."

He shrugged.

"Absolutely not," I said.

"Fine, fine," he said, turning the phone off and slipping it back in his pocket. "So you were saying, the man you saw looks French."

"Well, I don't know for sure. He just dresses like a European." Or at least he did according to what I'd read. Stranger or not, I didn't want to tell Mo that the farthest I've been abroad is Windsor, Canada—I've always been wary of being more than a short flight from my mother. Last year I returned from a four-day chemistry conference in San Antonio to find every spare inch of her house covered with tchotchkes and papers. The fridge was empty, and the bowl on the counter was filled with moldy fruit. She claims she's doing fine, but the evidence hardly supports that.

"Interesting," said Mo. "This is the first I'm hearing of a European-looking boyfriend."

"Then who are you investigating?"

He paused. Then he tilted his head in the direction of the pool. "Her."

"Harper?"

"Harper," he repeated.

"Harper Brearley? The woman who moved in next door to me in August?" I said, feeling impatient. "Isn't that who you just said you're investigating?"

"Yep."

I narrowed my eyes at him. "Wait a minute. Are you sure you're not stalking her? I don't want to get tangled up as an accomplice in someone else's crime." Or get tangled up in someone else's life—period, I reminded myself.

"Stalking requires an element of harassment, unwanted contact, or intimidation, none of which I would ever engage in. You watch a lot of TV, huh?"

"Actually, no," I said, because I wasn't about to confess that *House Hunters International* is often the last thing I hear before I fall asleep. Last night I dreamed I was searching for an apartment in Italy and couldn't find one near a train line that traveled to France. When I awoke, I was sitting straight up in bed, coated in a cold sweat. To think that just a month ago it was Todd who was the stuff of my nightmares.

"I showed you my card. I'm legit."

"Are you licensed?" I asked. I had no idea whether Michigan requires licensure, but it seemed like a valid guess.

"Almost," he said.

"Uh-huh." I glanced at the back door to my mother's house, wondering if she would ask me why I'd been out so long.

"No, I am. I've been running my own agency for more than three years, and I've met the education requirements."

"So what's the holdup?"

He looked sheepish. "You have to be twenty-five."

"Good heavens," I said, but then I cringed because I sounded just like my mother. "How old are you, exactly?"

"Twenty-four. I'm twenty-five at the end of October."

"So even if this *is* public property," I said, "you're breaking the law by spying on my neighbor."

"I'm just doing surveillance—"

"You're surveilling a person who doesn't know you're doing so. That's spying."

I expected him to be upset, but this just elicited another smile. "Clever. To answer your question, no—it's not against the law to be an investigator without being licensed. It's illegal to pass yourself off as a licensed PI when you're not, and as you can see on my card, I didn't include the word *licensed*. When I'm ready, I'm going to have new cards made, with a custom logo and everything."

I'll admit, he at least sounded like he knew what he was talking about. Then again, I could have memorized the same couple of lines and used them myself if I got caught hunting some unwitting individual.

But what does it matter? I can't get overinvested in something that has nothing to do with me. It's one thing to be on alert for the well-dressed fellow. It's entirely another to devote more than a dozen brain cells to the almost-legitimate investigator keeping tabs on my neighbor.

"I've got to get going," I told him.

"Oh," said Mo.

"Don't take this personally, but if I were you, I really wouldn't hang around this neighborhood."

"And why's that?"

"Because I don't think all of my neighbors would be as generous as me if they saw you creeping around Harper's house."

"Good tip," he said noncommittally. "By the way, I didn't catch your name."

"That's because I didn't give it to you."

"Right," he said, frowning for the first time.

He looked so disappointed that I couldn't help it. "Annie," I said, sighing. "My name is Annie."

His face lit back up. "Pleased to meet you, Annie."

"Yes. Well. I'd better go."

"You'd better," he agreed.

"Listen, if you do end up around here again—and I'm not saying you should—watch out for that French guy, okay? I think he's dangerous."

Mo saluted me. "Will do."

"Good."

I began to climb back over the wall, but I could feel him watching me, which made me nervous and I ended up tumbling into my yard.

"Annie, are you okay," said Mo in a singsong whisper. "You okay, you okay, Annie?"

"I'm fine, and you're a little young for Michael Jackson," I mumbled.

He grinned at me. "So are you."

"So long, smooth criminal," I said. Then I brushed the dirt off my knees and headed back to the house.

When I reached the house, I turned back to look for him, but he was long gone.

"Now, where were you?" said my mother as I walked into the kitchen. She had a smudge of chocolate on her face, probably from the Mallomars that I know she hides behind the expired canned goods she stocked up on in preparation for Y2K. I wiped my lip, hoping she would unconsciously mimic me, but she had more pressing matters on her mind.

"Doing yard work," I said.

"The yard can wait. Have you thought about wedding favors?" She held up a finger, then ran into the living room. She returned with a stack of rumpled sheets that had been torn from magazines. "I found a few ideas."

"Thanks, Ma," I said, accepting them from her. "I'll take a look at these."

"Have you scheduled your dress fitting yet? You know that takes months."

It wouldn't have taken months if I'd chosen something other than the taffeta confection that made her shed tears of maternal pride when I was trying dresses on. I'd wanted a simple off-white, tweed skirt suit. But in the greater scheme of things, if it took twelve hundred dollars of the money my mother had earmarked from my father's life insurance to make her happy, I was willing to make the sacrifice. "No, but I will," I told her. "Anyway, it'll probably fit fine as is."

"I disagree. Regardless, we should get moving on the cake tasting. Can you find out when Jon's available?"

I sighed. "Can we put that off awhile, at least?"

"Annie Mercer," she said, eyeing me suspiciously. "You're awfully unenthusiastic about your wedding these days. Did you and Jon have an argument?"

At the sound of his name, the lip I had just wiped began to quiver. I clamped down on it with my teeth, trying to figure out what to tell her. I decided to settle somewhere between the truth and what she wanted to hear. "It's not that. It's just that . . . well, he's staying in France for a little while longer."

"He's what!"

She looked so alarmed that I half expected her to faint. "I know it sounds bad, but he'll be back before you know it. He's just working through some issues," I said, hoping to reassure her. Because while I don't actually believe that, I don't want to deprive her of her primary source of pleasure. Not yet.

"Aren't we all?" she spat.

Now, this surprised me. My mother has always been Jon's biggest cheerleader. When I told her that he'd asked me to marry him, she acted like I'd just won the lottery. "You just don't find a good, dependable man like that anymore!" she said, crying into my shirt as she hugged me.

No, you really don't. I realize that now.

"I'm very sorry, Annie," said my mother, shaking her head. "After what your father did, I shouldn't be surprised. But people have a way of disappointing me sometimes."

"I know, Ma." I was suddenly very, very tired. "I feel the same way."

She met my eyes. "If you're going to cancel the wedding, you should do it sooner than later. People will be making their travel reservations soon."

I frowned. "How did we go from delaying the cake tasting to canceling the wedding?"

"I'm just saying." She patted me on the shoulder, and then, as if on second thought, pulled me in for a hug. "Whatever you decide, I understand."

That makes one of us. Because every time I think I'm starting to get my footing, the ground shifts beneath me again.

—AEM

SEVENTEEN

August 20

When I let myself into the Rogers' this morning, only Brat Kitt, the tabby with the temper, and Maria Catlas, the howler, were there to greet me. Opurrah and Puma Thurman were hidden elsewhere in the house, and Bess and Larry had left my payment on the table along with a note saying they were volunteering at the shelter and probably wouldn't be back before I was done.

The silence was soothing, at least for the first half hour or so. But by the time I had cleaned out the fridge and degreased the stove, unpleasant thoughts began to echo in all that nothingness. What was Jon doing in France right that very minute? Strolling along the Seine, perhaps? Tutoring a coed who made bangs and striped boatneck shirts look chic, the way only Frenchwomen can? Was he thinking about me and wondering if his decision was worth it? Or was he under the impression that when he returns, all will be forgiven?

Because even if he does come home—and I remain deeply skeptical about that—every day that passes is one in which I feel less inclined to forgive him.

Unfortunately, the longer I let myself mosey on down this mental path, the heavier my limbs became, to the point that I was tempted to lie down on the Rogers' clawed-up sofa and take a nap. That wasn't an option, but drowning out my thoughts with the vacuum was.

When cleaning anyone else's house, I bring along my beloved Bissell. When I clean the Rogers', however, I drag their aging canister vacuum out of the basement, because I don't want to clog up my own machine with cat hair. Though their machine is cumbersome, it doesn't ruin the meditative nature of vacuuming—between the physical exertion it requires, the whir of the motor, and the repetition of going across the carpet in the crosshatch pattern that most effectively removes dirt and dander, it's hard to really devote the mind to much else. And so, after half an hour of this, my mood had greatly improved.

But just as I reached the Rogers' bedroom, the vacuum began to sputter, then shook violently and gave up the ghost. This has happened several times before, but unplugging the vacuum, emptying the canister, and waiting ten to fifteen minutes usually revives it. Hoping that this would again do the trick, I toted the machine outside and shook the canister into the garbage bin on the side of the Rogers' house. I was about to pull out the filter when I spotted a silver car parked at the end of the street.

I left the vacuum on the driveway and made my way to the sidewalk to see if I was seeing what I thought I was seeing. Sure enough—as I approached the car, I saw that a man was slouched low in the driver's seat. He was wearing a baseball cap and sunglasses, so I wasn't sure if it was really him. But the window was cracked, so I said, "Mo?"

Instead of looking my way, he pulled the lever so his seat reclined as far back as it could. He was no longer visible to a passerby, but I could see most of his face now and was able to confirm that it was for certain the person I landed on last week.

"I still see you," I said.

He reached for a button on the door, and the glass between us lowered. "Shhh," he said. "If you want to talk, get in."

"So you can drive off to a wooded lot and murder me?"

He lifted his head to look at me through the open window. "That's lame. If I was going to off you, which I'm not, I'd come up with something way less generic."

"Yeah, that definitely makes me want to get in your car."

"You know my name and my business. You have my address."

"Plenty of men are violent toward women who know and trust them," I said, thinking of Harper. "Not that I know or trust you."

"Good point," he said cheerfully.

"So," I said. I peered into his car, which was curiously clean for an aging vehicle that belonged to a man in his early twenties. "What are you doing? I told you it's not a good idea to hang out around here."

"You did tell me that. I took it into consideration and decided that while it's solid advice, I have a job to do."

I was about to retort that his use of the word "job" was questionable when I spotted Margie Linden looking out her front door. She stared in our direction for a moment, then stepped out of the bungalow and began down her walkway. She was wearing what I was pretty sure was a silk kimono.

"You have a look on your face," said Mo. "What is it?"

"The woman headed toward us? She called the cops on you last week."

He reached for a lever and his seat shot forward, putting him in an upright position. "Would you mind getting in the car now? Pretty please?"

I had no real reason not to—well, other than the fact that it went against my vow of interpersonal abstinence. However, if Margie's paranoid post was any indication, I knew things might get ugly if I pretended not to know Mo. I went around the car and let myself in the passenger's side.

"Thank you," he said as I closed the door.

"Don't thank me yet," I said.

Seconds later, Margie's head appeared outside my window. I waved at her weakly, suddenly cognizant of the fact that my T-shirt was covered in cat hair. (At least I put on a bra this morning.) My response must have been insufficient for her, because she knocked on the glass with her knuckles.

"Hello, Margie," I said when I rolled the window down. "Funny seeing you here."

She stuck half her head into the car. "You know this man?" she said, but she was looking at me instead of Mo.

The way she said *this man* irritated me. "No, and I'm afraid he's about to kidnap me," I deadpanned.

Her eyes, which already protrude in the manner of someone with an undiagnosed thyroid condition, bulged further. She yanked her head out of the car and took a step back, indicating that if I were about to be harmed, she did not intend to join me.

"It's a joke, Margie," I said.

"So you *do* know him?" she said.

I glanced at Mo, who was watching us. He was so quiet, so motionless, that he almost appeared to be holding his breath. Maybe he was. I turned back to Margie. "Of course I do," I said. "He's . . ."

"Her friend," supplied Mo. He flashed her a winning smile.

"Oh," she said. "Well. If I had known that earlier . . ."

"Maybe you wouldn't have called the police on him last week?" I said.

"He was loitering in front of my house," said Margie, but she sounded markedly less sure of herself. "And now he's doing it again."

"His engine is off, and he's waiting for me to finish work. The kitchen was twice as dirty as I had expected, so I got held up," I said, marveling at the way the lie rolled off my tongue. I didn't feel bad, though. Since she charged Mo's car like the cavalry, only to retreat at the first sign of danger, it's safe to assume Margie can't handle the truth.

Then again, maybe Jon feels that way about me.

"I see. Well, I've got to get to work. Say hello to your mother, Annie," said Margie, and then she rushed off, her silk garment fluttering behind her.

"Thanks," said Mo once she was gone.

"You're welcome. But just so you know, we're not actually friends."

"Of course not," he said with mock seriousness. "You wouldn't want to be friends with someone like me."

"That's not at all what I meant. It's just that I don't know you."

"Sure you do. Not well, but we're not strangers anymore."

"We are so."

"Fine. Strangers on first-name basis—right, Annie?" he said, grinning again.

I almost laughed, though my depleted willpower isn't actually funny. "You want to tell me what you're doing hanging around here? I know I warned you about this neighborhood, and now that you've met crazy Margie, you know why."

He shrugged.

"Oh, come on," I said. "I already know you're spying on Harper."

"Ashley," he said.

"Come again?"

"Your neighbor's name isn't actually Harper Brearley. It's Ashley Sarah Jones. I can't tell you anything more than that." He was so chipper, he might as well have been a waiter reciting the daily specials. Not that I've been to a restaurant since Jon left.

"That's strange. Are you sure you have the right person?"

He chuckled, but I hadn't been joking. Then he pulled off his sunglasses and met my eyes. "Please don't share that with anyone."

"I have no one to tell, unless you count Puma Thurman."

He did a double take. "Who?"

"She's one of my neighbors' cats. There are four of them, but I really only get along with Puma. She can be testy with strangers, but to me she's very sweet," I said, thinking of the way she plays in the sink while I'm attempting to decontaminate the kitchen. "Point being, I don't have many people in my life—by design."

"You have your neighbors, who you clean house for."

I narrowed my eyes. "How did you know that?"

"I installed a spy cam in your phone."

I must have looked panicked because he laughed and said, "I'm kidding, Annie. I just saw you emptying out a vacuum at a house that isn't yours, and you're covered in dirt."

I glanced down at myself and saw that my MIT T-shirt was in even worse shape than usual.

"If I couldn't figure out why that is, I have no business being a PI," said Mo.

"Oh."

"Using my observations to make logical guesses is half my job," he said, somewhat apologetically.

"What's the other half?"

He pursed his lips together, considering my question. After a moment he said, "I'd say online research, for the most part. Combing through databases and official records, looking at people's social media accounts and their dating profiles. Sometimes that information tells me what I need to know. Sometimes it tells me what I don't know, and then I try to figure that out using surveillance and the like."

A glance at his dashboard reminded me that I had to get back to work if I was going to get out of the Rogers' place before they returned home. "I've got to go, but out of curiosity, do you think Harper is stealing someone's identity?"

"Not necessarily. I can't find records for a Harper Brearley, which makes me believe it's just a name that Ashley made up—or an identity someone else created for her. But it's kind of weird," he said.

"Why's that?"

"Well, usually when a person is trying to become someone else, they choose a generic name, like Michael or Jennifer Smith. Harper Brearley is the opposite of that. For starters, it's really modern—Harper has only become a popular name for girls born in the US over the past six years, and Ashley is twenty-three," said Mo.

She was slightly older than I'd thought, which made me feel better—the thought of someone barely legal rattling around in a big house by herself didn't sit well with me. "And Brearley sounds sort of upper-crust. It's the name of a fancy school for girls in New York," I added. I knew about this because my coworker (er, former coworker), Nicole, had attended a similar school in Manhattan that she claimed was superior to Brearley.

He looked at me with surprise. "Nice catch."

"Thanks," I said, feeling unduly flattered.

"If you think about it, it's a name that's asking to be noticed," he said. "But Ashley Jones wouldn't move to East Haven, Michigan, to be noticed."

"Where'd she move from? And who hired you to investigate her, anyway?"

Mo looked out the window. "I can't say."

"Really? You just told me all of that other information."

"Right, but telling you who hired me breaks PI-client privilege."

"That's not a real thing."

"Is so," he said, turning back to me. "It may not provide legal protection, but it's a major part of the trust between me and the person who hired me."

"Fine." I glanced at Margie's house to see if she was watching us. I could only imagine what she would say to my mother if they bumped into each other at ShopMore. "Well, I have to get going. I assume I'll catch you around, now that my nosy neighbor thinks you're my friend."

Mo grinned at me. "Thanks again for that. By the way, do you have plans on Thursday?"

"Plans?" I said. The word struck me as archaic, probably because I haven't used it in such a long time. "I'm cleaning Donna Guinness' house."

"All day?"

"Of course not," I said, though the truth is, I could in fact clean for a full twenty-four hours and still find nooks and crannies to degrime. "Why?"

"Want to go join me on a job?"

I had already opened the car door, but I paused. "What kind of job?"

"A surveillance mission," he said vaguely.

"Where? And how long?"

"So many questions!"

"Yes, well, the thing is, I've kind of sequestered myself from anyone I don't already know."

"Kind of," he said, sounding unconvinced.

"If you're going to be literal about it, I've absolutely sworn off all new people."

"I'm not new anymore, am I, Annie?" He gave me one of his glowing smiles. "So can I pick you up at the entrance to County Park at five?"

I stared at him for a second. Then, for reasons I still have yet to identify, I nodded.

"Great! I'll see you Thursday," he said.

"See you Thursday," I repeated, sounding almost as stunned as I felt.

I lugged the Rogers' vacuum back inside, locked the door behind me, and put a hand to my forehead as I wondered what on Galileo's round earth came over me. Had I inadvertently been exposed to an excess of 1,4-dioxane during my last few months at SCI? Had too many hours with Puma Thurman, et al., exposed me to Toxoplasma gondii?

Because my agreeing to do a "job" with Mo—whatever that means—shows that when you have nothing going on in your own life, it's entirely too easy to become wrapped up in the details of someone else's. At this rate, it won't be long before I've traded *Scientific American* for the *National Enquirer*.

Yet if I'm honest . . . I'm kind of lonely. And it was nice to have a conversation with someone roughly close to my own age who wanted to talk about something other than using lemon rinds to deodorize a garbage disposal.

That's the thing about Jon—even more than his lovely green eyes or his elegant if lanky frame, his ability to hold a conversation has always been his most attractive feature. I knew from the moment he asked about the documentary I was watching on that flight and listened intently to my answers that *this*—this was a man I could spend a lot of time with.

Now I've agreed to spend time with a man I just met. Which seems like further evidence that I'm not thinking straight. Well, I'll see Mo on Thursday as planned, because I'm a person of my word. But good conversation or not, that's where it will have to end.

—AEM

EIGHTEEN

August 23

Mo pulled up to the entrance to County Park at five sharp this evening. While I applaud his punctuality—Jon is always running five to ten minutes late, and that's if I'm being charitable—I wasn't actually ready. Donna Guinness' house had been especially filthy, even by her standards, and I had stayed an extra twenty minutes before informing her that there was nothing more I could do for her baseboards until my next visit.

"I'm sorry it took me so long," I said to Mo as I rushed up to his car, hoping my mother wasn't watching me out the window. She had been napping when I returned from Donna's, but she could roll out of bed at any minute. And if she saw me getting into a vehicle with another man . . . I'm not sure what she'd say, but I don't really want to find out.

"No worries," said Mo. "You're not late."

"It's three minutes after five," I pointed out.

He cocked his head and looked at me. All at once I felt self-conscious, and not just because I was in a car with a man I didn't know. What was I thinking, agreeing to do this?

That's right—I wasn't.

"I didn't really have time to pull myself together," I said. I had thrown on a button-down and a pair of work slacks, which were so loose that I had been forced to secure them with a belt. Leesa would have called this a good problem to have. To me, though, it seemed like another sign the person I believe myself to be is fading fast.

"No, no, it's not that. How would you feel about wearing this?" he said, pulling a black wig from the backseat.

I eyed it. It was a bob cut in a nice shade and didn't look synthetic—but still. "Is this because I didn't brush my hair?"

He laughed. "You look great. Seriously. But if I'm going to a public place, I like to look like someone else. I figured you might, too."

I suppose I didn't really want it to get back to Jon that I was having dinner with another man if I ran into someone we knew. Then again, does it even matter?

"Oh yeah? Then what's your disguise?" I said, eyeing his tan Carhartt baseball cap and Tigers T-shirt.

"You're looking at it."

"You're kidding."

"I even shaved my beard," he said, frowning slightly, and I saw that his stubble had been removed. "Don't I look more like an average white dude than I did before?"

I had no choice but to admit that he did. Then I took the wig from him and pulled it on over my head. It was itchy, but when I looked in the visor mirror, it was kind of nice to see someone else staring back.

"I think I like your usual brown better, but black suits you," said Mo.

"Thanks, I think," I said. "Where are we going?"

"José's."

"The Mexican place off State Street?"

"You don't like Mexican?"

I happen to like Mexican quite a bit, as I told him. But I wasn't sure what it had to do with his job, as I couldn't picture Harper/Ashley dining at a hole-in-the-wall.

"Oh, this is a totally different job," he said. "I'll tell you more later."

(In retrospect, I'm not sure why it didn't occur to me to ask him why he'd invited me along if we weren't investigating Harper. The longer I'm out of the lab, the less sharp my analytical edge seems to be.)

We didn't say anything else on the short drive, but I was surprised to find that it was a comfortable silence. When we got to the restaurant, Mo retrieved a bulky canvas messenger bag from the backseat. He reached into it and pulled out a pair of horn-rimmed glasses, which he handed to me. "Just to be on the safe side," he explained. "We're not that far from your house, and I'm not sure the wig was enough." Then he slung the overstuffed bag over his shoulder.

"That's awfully full," I noted, squinting at him. The glasses weren't prescription, but it was still strange to view the world through a set of frames. "Wouldn't a backpack be a better choice?"

He looked at me like I'd just suggested we try our hand at nuclear fusion. "Can you think of anything that draws more attention than a young Lebanese guy wearing a backpack?"

"But the trucker hat."

"Every element has to work or the whole disguise fails."

"So you're saying I shouldn't glue on a mustache."

He laughed as though I were actually funny, which made me feel kind of funny inside. But then I reminded myself I was on a "job."

"What have I gotten myself into?" I wondered aloud.

"A free dinner," he said. We had just reached the restaurant's entrance, and he held the door open for me. "Which happens to include the best tortilla chips, and the worst margaritas, in all of southeast Michigan."

"Exciting," I told him, though it almost was.

At Mo's request, we were seated in a booth at the back of the restaurant. After making sure I didn't mind facing the wall, he took the seat looking out at the dining room.

"Want a margarita?" he asked when our waiter arrived.

"I thought—"

"Sometimes bad can be good," he said.

"So you say."

He smiled beatifically at me, then told the waiter we would have two margaritas and a basket of chips.

He wasn't kidding about the chips. Or the drink—when I took a sip, I sputtered a little. Mo seemed concerned, but I explained that I rarely imbibed.

"Now you know why," he said, and took a long drink of his neon-green cocktail, which had been poured into a stemmed bowl rimmed with bright orange salt.

"So, if we're not here about Harper, who are we checking out?"

"Shhh," he whispered, glancing around the room. "This is a straightforward job."

"And what's that?" I said, more quietly this time.

"I'm following someone who's cheating on their spouse. That's roughly eighty to ninety percent of the work I get as a PI."

"Sounds uplifting."

"It can be rewarding, actually. What's amazing is how obvious most people are. Men, women—doesn't matter. They think they're being so sneaky, and maybe they are for the first couple weeks. But then they get tired of being sneaky and can't help but parade around in public with the person they're fooling around with. Sometimes they don't even wait, because the danger is too much of a thrill for them to resist. Then—bam!" he said, hitting the table with his hand.

I laughed, and he did, too.

"I get carried away sometimes," he said with a grin. "Anyway, that's when I catch them in the act. People always leave a digital trail, but most of the time I don't even need it because I get the pictures first. And yeah, it usually splits couples up. The way I look at it, though, I'm giving the partner who gets shafted a fresh start on a better life."

Maybe it was the margarita, but I was suddenly blinking back tears.

"Hey," said Mo, leaning across the table to touch my arm lightly. He meant well, but his fingers on my skin reminded me of how very long it had been since anyone other than my mother or Viola had touched me, and the tears kept coming. After I pulled myself together, I explained that my fiancé probably wasn't my fiancé anymore, even if he still had his head in the sand about that, and had just extended his Parisian walkabout another six weeks.

For a man who spends his workday investigating love's dark side, Mo looked stunned. "Oh man, Annie," he said, shaking his head. "What a massive douchenozzle."

"Douchenozzle isn't a word," I said, sniffing, but saying it made me laugh.

"Is so." He was laughing, too, but then his eyes flicked past me toward the restaurant entrance.

"What is it?" I said, spinning around.

"False alarm. But, Annie," he said in a singsong tone, "rule number one of top-secret spying is not to make any sudden moves."

"Says the man poking around my backyard with the stealth of a charging rhinoceros," I said. But as soon as these words had left my mouth, I pivoted and slunk down in my seat—because I had just seen Todd saunter in with Bethanne trailing behind him like a puppy.

"Mind if I ask who *you're* hiding from?" Mo said from behind his menu.

"My boss," I whispered, still slouched down. "Ex-boss. And the woman who was supposed to support me but ended up siding with him. I'm a chemist, and that guy you just saw owns the company I worked for. I didn't exactly leave on good terms, which tends to happen when a supervisor decides his employee's body is company property."

"Tweedledee and Tweedle Douchenozzle have been identified," said Mo in an official-sounding voice.

I had to bite my lip from laughing, but I suppose that was better than crying.

"You'll be happy to know that Tweedle Douchenozzle has been seated on the other side of the restaurant. But I'll remind you that you *are* wearing a wig and glasses, so even if he were right behind us, you didn't have to hide in that *totally* not-obvious spot under the table."

"I'd like to remind you that you're the one who brought me on your job," I said, sliding back into my seat. "Are you investigating my ex-boss?"

"Nope, though sounds like maybe I should. Why are you afraid of him?"

"I'm not afraid. I just . . ." It took me a minute to find the words. "He brought out the worst side of me. I mean, I've never pushed someone before, even on the playground!"

"You've probably never been assaulted by your supervisor before."

"Good point. Still, he ruined one of the most important parts of my life, and I can't even find another job in chemistry for two years because of a stupid agreement that I naïvely signed years ago. I don't ever want to be face-to-face with him again."

"Man, you're *surrounded* by douchenozzles," said Mo. Before I could respond, he said, "My target just entered the restaurant." He reached into his bag and retrieved a little black point-and-shoot camera, which he aimed at me. "Would you mind smiling?"

"I'm not photogenic," I said.

"That's debatable, but not to worry—you'll barely be in the photo. I'm just going to make it seem like I'm shooting you. Say cheese!" he said.

In spite of myself, I managed to flash him my teeth.

"Thank you," he said, putting the camera beside him on his seat. "Now, since I know you're dying to know who I just snapped a photo of, count to ten, then look behind you. But don't be obvious about it, okay? Pretend you're looking for our waiter."

I nodded and began counting.

"When you turn, you'll see a woman seated three booths back. She's wearing a blue dress and sitting across from a bald man. He's her lover."

I turned as instructed and spotted the woman. She was maybe fifty; the man she was with was at least a decade older. "Just because she's having dinner with a man doesn't mean she's sleeping with him," I said when I turned back to Mo.

"No, it doesn't." He clicked a button on his camera and handed it to me. "But you could say this might."

The screen was lit with a photo. In it, the couple was about to be seated, and the man had his hand on the woman's backside. While I wanted to be appalled by their brazen act of infidelity . . . I felt oddly jealous. Jon and I had a fairly satisfying sex life—or at least I thought it was, and he had never complained. But I couldn't remember a single time when he just *had* to touch me in public. Was that one of the reasons he found it so easy to leave?

I handed Mo the camera. "Don't you feel your line of work is ethically sticky?"

He put the camera on his lap, took another sip of his drink, and then said, "Don't you think it's ethically sticky to cheat on your spouse? In broad daylight? After telling your husband you're going out with one of your female coworkers?"

"Then the husband's the one who tipped you off about them being here."

He nodded. "Apparently this is their usual place."

Maybe it was Bethanne and Todd's usual place, too. What were they doing there together, anyway?

I slowly swiveled in my seat so I could see them. Todd was yapping away while Bethanne leaned forward, her bosom hovering precariously over the bowl of salsa. Perhaps he was telling her how he was mere months away from bringing his new, 70 percent less safe but 17 percent cheaper-to-manufacture hand sanitizer to the market. (I do wish I could blow the whistle on SCI, but the fact remains that 1,4-dioxane, however harmful, remains a legal additive. And given that young adults can purchase cigarettes long before alcohol—even though the government is well aware that those cancer sticks kill—I'm not particularly hopeful that I can do anything for the millions of people who will soon be slathering their mitts with FastDry Sani-Foam.)

Or maybe Todd had just taken Bethanne to dinner so he could convince her that he really was a good guy.

We ordered, and a suspiciously short time later our dinner arrived. That said, my enchiladas were superior to anything I would have made at home, even if my dining out meant my mother inevitably had a bag of potato chips for dinner. And Mo was good company, only pausing twice during our meal to snap more photos of the illicit couple.

As we ate, I learned that Mo's parents had immigrated during the Lebanese Civil War and, after a brief time in Pittsburgh, settled in a flourishing Arab-American community in Dearborn. They spoke to Mo and his sister in English but expected their children to address them in Arabic, "so that we all ended up bilingual," he explained. He was close to them but moved out at eighteen, to his mother's dismay, and then moved to our town a few years ago. When I asked why he left—he had just described Dearborn as the safest place in the US for someone like him—he shrugged. "Well, there was more work in East Haven," he said. "But also, I wanted a life that was different from what I had always known. I needed to see what else was out there, and I'm pretty sure this is just the tip of the iceberg. What about you, Annie?"

Why *do* I live in Michigan? I mumbled something about enjoying all four seasons, then changed the subject. I'd had my heart set on attending MIT as an undergraduate, but couldn't bring myself to leave my mother alone. Anyway, the forty-minute drive from the University of Michigan to our house meant I could live on campus and yet still visit her frequently. I told myself I would apply to graduate school at MIT.

But just as I was finishing my applications, I received the recruitment email from SCI, and then Todd's generous offer, and my mother was so excited about my staying in the Detroit area that I decided to delay my dream for a year.

Then, of course, I met Jon, and between my new job and his eagerness to swap Missouri for Michigan to be with me, I nearly forgot all about Massachusetts (Jon had gotten his master's at Tufts, and claimed Cambridge wasn't all that great a place to live). And maybe that was for the best, because after my uncle Lou moved away, my mother really and truly didn't have anyone else to make sure she hadn't buried herself in a shallow grave of newspapers and collectibles (though I'm loath to use the latter word, as a person like my mother could call a shoebox full of outdated coupons a collection if she were so inclined—and indeed, she is inclined).

I was worried my paltry excuse wouldn't be enough for Mo, but I needn't have. Todd and Bethanne got up to leave, and Mo decided to snap a few photos of them on their way out, "because you never know when a picture will come in handy," he said. Then, even though I argued that we should split it, he paid our bill.

"Thank you," I said when he dropped me off. "That wasn't so bad."

"Thanks . . . I think," said Mo, but he didn't sound offended. He had gotten out of the car to open my door for me, though I had already let myself out and was on the sidewalk before he reached me.

He looked at me again, smiling. "Want to keep the wig and glasses?"

I touched my head self-consciously. "I'd better not."

"Keep the wig, at least. It looks good on you."

I don't know why, but I agreed. Then I handed him the glasses, but he kept standing there smiling at me.

"You know," I told him, "smiling all the time isn't very sneaky."

"You're not the first one to point that out, but I'd argue walking around looking like someone died is twice as suspicious."

That's probably how I look these days, but unlike Mo, I don't have to care what other people think of me. A privilege, I know. Nonetheless, it is so. "Well," I said, "thanks again for dinner. See you around."

"That's your favorite line, isn't it?" He had taken the trucker hat off and his curls were in every direction. That, coupled with his clean-shaven face, made him look even younger than Harper.

"Is there another way you'd prefer I say goodbye?"

"How about, *Mo, this was really fun. Want to hang out again sometime?*"

"Oh. Um."

His face fell.

"It's nothing personal," I said quickly. "It's just that—"

"I know—no new people," he said, holding up his hands. "I get it."

I opened my mouth, but nothing came out.

He got back in his car, and I walked down the street and let myself into the house. When I looked through the door, he was driving away.

I'm hesitant to admit it, but maybe this "no people" thing isn't all it's cracked up to be. Humans are inherently social creatures, aren't they? If I can manage to keep Mo at arm's length instead of letting him get too close, I might actually be able to have a friend—without getting hurt yet again.

—AEM

NINETEEN

August 25
TO: Annie Mercer
FROM: Oak Grove Neighborhood Association
SUBJECT: Abridged summary of OakGroveMIN-
eighborhoodAssociation@googlegroups.com—6
updates in 4 topics

Today's Topic Summary
View all topics

- Friendly reminder regarding East Haven's noise ordinance—1 Update
- Dog waste—3 Updates
- UPDATED: Suspicious activity on Willow Lane—1 Update
- Seriously, unsubscribe me—1 Update

Friendly reminder regarding East Haven's noise ordinance
MargieSueLinden@aol.com 6:45 a.m.

Like many of you, I'm sure, the Linden family had a VERY tough time getting to sleep last night—even our trusty Asian Spa Sounds machine couldn't drown out what I'm fairly certain was rap music containing lyrics that aren't suitable for my son (or me, to be honest).

While I don't want to rain on anyone's party, I have pasted the city's noise ordinance (most relevant text highlighted) below as a reminder to be courteous to your fellow neighbors when hosting a get-together.

Namaste,
Margie

>> Noise Ordinance
If any music or noise can be heard beyond your property line or the physical space of your property between the hours of 10 p.m. and 7 a.m., you are violating the City of East Haven noise regulations. The maximum penalty for each offense is $400. All parties found by the East Haven Police Department to be in violation of this regulation are subject to penalties.

Dog waste
arlen.fletcher3rd@microsoft.net 9:23 a.m.
Neighbors,

Last night, a young woman in a black dress walking a small dog let said dog defecate into the lavender plants on our lawn extension. While the woman—who I did not recognize—did remove the waste from my yard, she then walked right up to our fence and placed it in our trash can.

I really do not want our trash can to smell like feces, and would like to encourage all residents of the greater Oak Grove neighborhood to carry their pets' waste home and dispose of it in their *own* trash.

Best,
Arlen Fletcher on Aspen Drive

HerselfTheElf92@aol.com 7:10 p.m.

When I owned a dog, I wore a fanny pack whenever I took my dog out for a walk. After putting the waste in a small bag, I then put the bag into my fanny pack for convenient storage until I got home. This negated the need for me to ever have to use another person's trash bin.

Stacy

ItsHarperBishes@gmail.com 11:11 p.m.

Stacy,

That is disturbing.

—Harper (who dropped her dog poop in someone else's trash can yesterday—sorry not sorry—and who would literally not be caught dead wearing a fanny pack)

Oh, and Margie, if you're reading this, the music you heard the other night was reggaeton. If you're fluent in Spanish, you probably picked up on some cursing, in which case—sorry. But FYI, my one-woman party was over way before 10 p.m.

UPDATED: Suspicious activity on Willow Lane

Me again. I forgot to mention that the owner of the silver hatchback has been identified as the friend of Annie Mercer (daughter of Fae Mercer, both of whom live at the end of Willow Lane at Birch Street). I'm sorry to have caused any alarm—but crime is on the rise and our economy is *not*, so it bears repeating: Stay vigilant!

Namaste,
Margie

Seriously, unsubscribe me
DieHardTigersFan4EVR@gmail.com 2:01 p.m.

Whoever manages this email list, PLEASE unsubscribe me. Every time I click the link at the bottom of the email that says "unsubscribe me," I get a notice saying I can't unsubscribe because I'm not a member of the group. This is absurd. —Mike

TWENTY

August 26
TO: Mo Beydoun, PI
FROM: Annie Mercer
SUBJECT: Information that may be of interest to you

Mo,

Thank you again for dinner the other night. First, I want to apologize to you about the whole "no new people" issue. As you pointed out, you're no longer new to me. Moreover, I had a really nice time, which is rare for me these days, and I didn't mean to give you the impression that I hadn't.

I also wanted to let you know that I have new information on Harper/Ashley. Specifically, she emailed our neighborhood Listserv yesterday. Though I've since realized she joined at the same time I did, until she commented on a thread, I didn't know that she knew it existed (though my mother tells me that Margie Linden—the woman who came rushing over to your car, who manages the Listserv—provides new neighbors with an information sheet and neighborhood directory).

Not only is Harper subscribed to the Listserv, she took the time to respond to two messages. One was regarding her use of a neighbor's trash bin to dispose of her dog's waste. The other was a complaint from Margie herself, who claimed Harper was throwing a party and playing music too loud Friday night (Harper refutes this, and I must agree; I was home that evening and didn't hear a thing).

Regardless, I wanted to pass along her email address in case you don't already have it: ItsHarperBishes@gmail.com.

Hope your week is going well.

All the best,
Annie

August 26
TO: Annie Mercer
FROM: Mo Beydoun, PI
SUBJECT: Re: Information that may be of interest to you

Hey, Annie,

No need to apologize. I know you're going through a lot right now. Thanks for the email address—I didn't have it. There have been some new developments regarding the case. If you really have broken your vow of solitude, maybe we could discuss over a cup of coffee sometime (or tea, if you prefer)?

Either way, I'm doing well—thanks for asking. Hope you're hanging in there.

Mo

August 26
TO: Mo Beydoun, PI
FROM: Annie Mercer
SUBJECT: Re: Information that may be of interest to you

Mo,

I'm hanging. And coffee sounds great. When and where?

All best,
Annie

August 27
TO: Annie Mercer
FROM: Mo Beydoun, PI
SUBJECT: Re: Information that may be of interest to you

Great! Tuesday? Say, 3 or 4 at Community Cup?

Mo

August 27
TO: Mo Beydoun, PI
FROM: Annie Mercer
**SUBJECT: Re: Information that may be of inter-
est to you**

Mo,

4 is good—see you then.

Looking forward,
Annie

TWENTY-ONE

August 29

On the walk back from Seth Williams' house, I passed a woman pushing a double stroller. My ovaries have never gotten all tingly at the sight of an infant, but the babies *did* make me think of Leesa's twins. Which made me kind of sad. They're the only children I've ever really liked, and I hadn't seen them in a while.

Now, I know the human mind is built to seek out and ascribe meaning to patterns, and that probability, too, often explains what many of us call coincidence. None of this eased the uncanny feeling I had when I opened the door to my mother's house and found Leesa, Molly, and Ollie standing among the wreckage.

Ollie was hidden behind Leesa's leg (which really has too little surface area to be much of a hiding place). But the minute I dropped my vacuum and bucket of supplies, Molly charged me. "Aunt Annie!" she said.

"Hey, kiddo," I said, hugging her. Then I looked up at Leesa. She had a large blue rock hanging from her neck—lapis lazuli, no doubt; I remember her regurgitating LITEWEIGHT verbiage about its honesty and relationship-healing properties—and was smiling at me like everything was fine. I smiled back at her.

Then I remembered that she still hasn't apologized.

"Hi, Leesa," I said. "I wasn't expecting you."

"The twins wanted to see you, so I thought I'd take a chance and stop by." She was unfazed by the state of the living room, though it was even messier than she was used to seeing it. Then again, Leesa's the kind of person who goes out of her way to make others comfortable; she'd never let on if she planned to slather herself and the kids in hand sanitizer the minute they got back in her minivan.

My mother appeared in the doorway between the living room and kitchen. She was wearing a pair of gray sweatpants and a sweatshirt in a similar shade, and though her hair looked as though it had been brushed with a freshly inflated balloon, she'd applied blush. "Annie, it's so nice to see Leesa and her beautiful twins, of course, but if I had known you were going to have company, I would have cleaned up," she said.

Even if she'd tried, it wouldn't have made a difference; the living room and hallway alone would take a solid week to declutter. I love my mother, but for someone who's tired all the time, sometimes it seems as though every minute I'm out tidying and scrubbing other people's homes, she's turning hers into a fire hazard. I knew what I was getting into when I moved in with her, of course, but I clearly had unrealistic expectations about what I would be able to accomplish here. I am Sisyphus, pushing the same pile of bric-a-brac across the floor, day after day after day.

"I didn't know they were coming, either," I said, giving Leesa a pointed look.

"What's this?" said Molly, holding up what had once been a back scratcher but was now a wooden shiv with a tiny hand for a handle.

"Let *me* see it!" cried Ollie, attempting to grab it from Molly.

Molly screeched and, demonstrating the evolution-honed art of tool identification, began stabbing at Ollie.

"Molly, give that to Aunt Annie right now," I said calmly, though I was panicking inside: if one of them impaled the other, I would have no choice but to make restitution via a lifetime order for *CashLash* and crystals. Molly did as I asked, then immediately made a mad dash for an open bag of fertilizer in the corner (which my mother must have dragged in from the back porch; why she did so is anyone's guess, as the only plant in the living room is the corpse of an orchid that she insists is dormant). I managed to intercept and redirect Molly toward the front door.

"Would anyone like anything to eat or drink?" said my mother. She looked especially animated—though maybe it was just the blush.

"No, Ma, we're fine," I told her, gesturing for Leesa and Ollie to follow me and Molly. "Really. We're going to get some fresh air."

Outside, the twins began chasing each other around the yard. I watched them for a moment, feeling nostalgic for the fleeting moments of gleeful oblivion I had enjoyed during my childhood. Then I turned to Leesa. "Are you really here because the twins wanted to see me?"

Her brown eyes looked even larger brimming with tears. "Yes. And I thought maybe we would have an easier time realigning our energy if we were in the same space," she said, sniffing.

She never used to speak like that. Maybe the LiteWeight onboarding process involves memorizing and regurgitating pages of meaningless verbiage. "When you say, 'realigning our energy,'" I said, "do you mean you want to apologize?"

She wiped her eyes. "Well do you? I know you have a problem getting close to people—"

My head shot up. "What's *that* supposed to mean?"

"Exactly what it sounds like," she said. "You never went on a third date with anyone in college, and it's not like you weren't asked."

"There was no one worth dating," I said, recalling the blank stares and awkward small talk.

"You overreacted when Simone made a comment about my essential oils."

"Because she made it sound as though I could mind-control my eczema," I pointed out.

She continued. "And you're not exactly nice to Cherie and Kimmy, when all they want to do is be your friend."

Cherie and Kimmy, who Leesa introduced me to a few years ago, want to be my friend because I'm Leesa's friend—not because I'm me. That's evident every time they try to engage me in conversation about the comings and goings of the other ladies in their wine club or the classes at the gym where they appear to spend inordinate amounts of time. God forbid I should talk about my work. Well, what used to be my work.

"I'm sorry," I told Leesa. "I tried; I really have. But I have nothing in common with either of them."

She crossed her arms. "It's like you seriously can't remember that not everyone is as smart as you."

I sighed. "Leesa, I wish you would stop acting like I'm the only person around here with the ability to employ logic and knowledge to examine the wider world. You're every bit as capable as me."

"See, that's what I mean!"

I ignored her outburst. "Anyway, you have dozens of friends. In fact, until I told you I needed space, it seemed like you were constantly making time for them instead of me."

Now she looked more angry than upset. "This again?"

"Yes, this. When was the last time you asked me to hang out that didn't involve your mom friends or a LiteWeight event?"

She said nothing. Of course she said nothing—we both knew the truth of the situation, but only one of us was willing to admit it out loud. I had Jon, but it was Leesa who managed to help me learn to be enthusiastic about the overattended, ridiculously expensive party that was to be my wedding—when all I wanted was a justice of the peace with Jon at my side. And it was her who I called at the end of a bad day at SCI. She always managed to make me laugh, and somehow I managed to make her laugh, too.

But her bottomless sales pitch was anything but funny. The Leesa I used to know would never believe shiny rocks were the antidote to the miseries of everyday life.

"I'm not sorry that I'm running a business that helps me support my family," she said after a moment. "LiteWeight actually makes it possible for me to work and help others and still be a good mom to the twins."

"Well, I think you could be doing much more with yourself. You have a way with people," I said. "You could be heading up an HR or sales department for a big company."

"Spoken like someone who has no idea what it's like to have two four-year-olds and a husband who works ten hours a day. Use your logic and knowledge and tell me what kind of job a woman with a degree in American Studies can get that will earn enough money to justify paying for full-time preschool for two kids—which, for the record, is a cool twenty-four hundred dollars a month, and that's not even for the 'good' school," she said, making air quotes. "And don't forget to add aftercare and babysitters, because all of the jobs I've looked at say you have to be available after five and sometimes on weekends, too. I have to do something, though. Josh's and my student loans are basically a second mortgage payment."

"Why didn't you just say that?" I asked.

She looked at me. "Because for once, Annie, I wanted to fix my problems on my own. I'm always asking you for advice on everything. I felt like I should be able to figure this out. And I did."

Suddenly Molly and Ollie began to scream in tandem. It's curious how the sounds of joy and terror overlap—and come to think of it, pain and pleasure, too. The first time Jon and I made love, I was so certain he was in the throes of cardiac arrest that I threw him off me to begin chest compressions.

My adrenaline kicked in, and I ran over to the large oak where Molly and Ollie had been playing, expecting to see one of them holding the conch over the other's bleeding body, *Lord of the Flies*–style. But when I got there, both kids were crouched over a fat rodent.

I was going to yell out about rabies—I could just see Leesa dabbing oregano oil on their tiny frothing mouths—when I realized the rodent was Moppet.

"Puppy!" Molly and Ollie were squealing and pawing at Moppet, but amazingly, the dog didn't seem to mind at all. Just the opposite, really. It was pushing its furry little head into their palms and licking their chubby fingers.

There was movement in my peripheral vision, and I turned and saw Harper sauntering out of her house. She was wearing a scrap of a tank top that revealed a sports bra with what seemed to be a dozen different straps, a pair of shiny black leggings with cutouts all the way up to her hips, and sneakers with two-inch soles. The aviators were back, but I sneaked a peek around the side of her face and was relieved to see she was unbruised. "Sassy dog!" she scolded Moppet. "Leave those poor kids alone."

"Poor kids?" I said. "They love it."

She frowned. "So weird. He's usually not friendly, especially with rug rats." She eyed me. "Did you speak Mandarin to him again? Shih Tzus *are* from China, you know, so it makes sense that he would respond to that."

Now it was my turn to look at her questioningly. "You got your dog from a local breeder, right?" I asked.

She frowned. "Is California local?"

So she *had* spent time in California, as I'd speculated when she first moved in. I made a mental note to mention this to Mo when I saw him for coffee. "Domestic," I said. "Was the breeder Chinese?"

"Maybe? It's kind hard for me to tell . . ."

I cringed, because Leesa, who was now standing behind me, was often asked if she was Chinese. She always replied politely, but behind closed doors she liked to say that anyone with one glass eye should be able to tell that most people of Chinese and Japanese ancestry have different characteristics.

"It's safe to hypothesize that your dog wouldn't know Mandarin from Greek," I told Harper.

She put a hand on her hip and examined Moppet, unconvinced. "You never know. Who's to say his ancestors didn't listen to Mandarin for so many centuries that his cells perk up when he hears it?"

"Epigenetics. Very interesting," I said.

Her bright white teeth glinted in the sunlight. "Thanks, Annie."

Not too long ago I read that a person's brain shoots off neural fireworks when they hear someone else say their name. At the time I thought it was ridiculous, but I could not deny that I experienced a gratifying sensation when Harper personally addressed me. However, it also occurred to me that while she and I were now on a first-name basis, I had no idea what to call her pet. "What's your dog's name, anyway?" I asked.

"Oh, Dog doesn't have a name," she said. "Well, unless you count Dog."

"Very *Breakfast at Tiffany's* of you," said Leesa.

Harper smiled at her. "Exactly!"

Then she bent down next to the kids and showed them how the dog liked to be touched. I had never seen her look more normal, or—well, more genuinely happy.

Leesa looked at her phone. "Kids, we need to get to soccer, and Mommy has a sales call after that. Say goodbye to Aunt Annie."

I stared at her. Yes, I hadn't planned on seeing her, but now that she *was* here, it seemed odd that she would leave so suddenly. "That's it?" I said.

She shrugged. "I told you that the twins wanted to say hi."

Harper stood and stuck her hands on her hips. "Ladies, I sense you have much to talk about, so I'm going to jet." She cocked her head. "Annie, want to swing by for a glass of wine sometime?"

I could feel Leesa's eyes on me. And at once I had a sudden (and admittedly ridiculous) need to show her that I was fine. Better than fine, really—as demonstrated by the fact that I would soon engage in that time-tested female bonding ritual of sipping fermented grape juice from a goblet while swapping confessions I would later regret or forget. Leesa wasn't the only one who had other friends.

"You know, that sounds great," I told Harper. "When and where?"

"Friday?" she said. "Let's say eightish?"

I wasn't sure if by eightish she meant 8:05 or nine or Saturday afternoon, but we could work out the particulars later. "Great," I said again. "I'll bring wine."

"Perf!" said Harper. "Can't wait."

Leesa, who had been loading the twins into her van, looked over her shoulder. "Can we talk about your wedding shower soon?"

"Um . . ." I turned my attention to Molly and Ollie, who were waving to me from their car seats. "It was good to see you two," I called. "I've missed you!"

"Bye, Aunt Annie!" they called as Leesa closed the sliding door.

Leesa looked at me. "Call me, okay?"

"Sure," I said.

But I don't want to call her, and not just because she still (still!) hasn't apologized. If I do, then I have to tell her that Jon remains in Paris, and I have no idea what that means for our relationship. Maybe she'll tell me she's sorry and ask for the play-by-play like she used to. Or maybe she'll tell me to heal my wounded heart with a piece of rhodochrosite, not stopping to ask herself how a mineral mined by small children in a third-world country could possibly have "good vibes."

And yet I'm tempted to call her, which makes me wonder if I have a self-protective bone left in my body. Because as that urge and my wine date with Harper demonstrate—say nothing of the breakdown in resolve that prompted me to email Mo and then agree to see him for coffee tomorrow—the spirit is willing. But the flesh is so very, very weak.

—AEM

TWENTY-TWO

August 30

When I arrived at Community Cup, Mo was seated at a café table near the window. He stood when he saw me. I wasn't sure if he was going to lean in for a hug, so I stuck out my hand, which he looked at quizzically, then shook.

He was wearing a T-shirt with two men on it—one in a cowboy hat, the other a baseball cap. Both stood with their legs spread wide, thumbs hooked in their belt loops. "In costume?" I asked, but as I sat down across from him, I took in the stubble that had repopulated his jaw and saw that his black curls were in every which direction. The shirt wasn't a disguise.

I was worried I might have offended him, but he just laughed. "No, I actually like Florida Georgia Line."

"Which is . . . a country band."

"We need to get you out of the house more."

"I get out of the house every single day," I informed him.

"It's just an expression, Annie," he said, grinning at me. "Want a coffee?"

I thought: *Why not?*

See, this is what happens when one swaps scientific rigor for a loosey-goosey civilian approach to life. The correct question to ask myself would have been: *To what end?* Because letting Mo buy my drink after he had already treated me to dinner implied something other than an arm's-length friendship. But my mouth hadn't yet connected with my mind, so I said, "Sure, that would be great."

"Cappuccino? Moccachino? Latte?"

"Just plain coffee with a little room for cream."

He grinned again and lifted his coffee cup to me. "Great minds think alike."

As it happens, most great minds think independently, and die long before the rest of the world comes around to their brilliance. "Great minds," I said.

A few minutes later, he returned with a large to-go cup and a pitcher of cream.

"Thank you. You didn't have to," I said, accepting both from him.

"I'm happy to," he said. He waited as I poured the cream. Then I handed the pitcher to him and watched as he jogged it back to the coffee station. He was on the short side, and kind of stocky, like a former soccer player who now expended his energy at the gym. I could see how that would appeal to some people. "So, how's your week been so far?" he said when he sat down across from me.

Where to even start? I thought. But I must be spending too much time muttering to myself while cleaning, because it turns out I said this aloud.

"Start from the beginning," he said.

"Um, okay," I said, mortified that my private thoughts were leaking into public places. "Sunday, I took my mother grocery shopping."

Which had taken two hours, because she wanted to examine every single item in every single aisle except, of course, the produce section. At least this time we didn't run into Betty Smithers—my mother still hasn't managed to make it to Mass.

"You live with her," he said.

I nodded. "For the past two years. It's a temporary arrangement."

"Got it," he said. "So Sunday was grocery shopping. What about Monday?"

I like that Mo seems to know when to move on. Jon does, too. Though now I wonder if maybe he should have lingered on the tough stuff, like my decision not to move in with him at the beginning of this year. I knew he was unhappy about it, but he let it go—so I did, too. That was a mistake; I see that now. I wonder what else we've been glossing over, and if it even matters anymore.

"Monday, I was at the Rogers' again," I told Mo.

"They're the ones with the cats?"

"Yes. It was a pretty straightforward day, in that I didn't run into any spies who wanted to use me as an alibi to escape crazy Margie's questioning."

"Bummer," said Mo, and we both laughed.

"Tuesday was Viola Moore—she's my neighbor, but kind of like a surrogate mom to me, too," I explained. This week Viola didn't ask about Jon, which was a relief. I know when she finds out he's stayed on in Paris she'll have a few choice words for him.

"Yesterday I cleaned for Seth Williams, a single guy who works at the bank. He's a devotee of that organizing guru who says you should get rid of everything except items that spark joy. He has very little to clean, so it's fast and easy." Cleaning Seth's spartan home is my idea of meditating. Or at least it was until I discovered that Seth's joy is sparked by hard-core pornography, which he keeps in several clear storage bins under his bed. I've known Seth since we were kids, but I can't look him in the eye anymore.

"That's the guy who always wears starched blue button-downs, even on the weekends?" said Mo. I must have looked surprised, because he said, "I wouldn't be a decent PI if I ignored everyone except my client. More often than not people's lives are interconnected, even when they don't realize it."

"I can see your point," I said, thinking of how we'd run into Todd and Bethanne at the restaurant. "Anyway, when I got home yesterday, my best friend had dropped by with her four-year-old twins."

"You don't sound super happy about that."

"We're going through a little rough patch," I admitted. "She sells crystals and essential oils and claims they can heal people."

"And you're a chemist, so . . ." He finished his sentence with a shrug.

I nodded. "Yeah. But I was willing to not say anything until she tried to sell me some of the stuff after I told her Jon had left unexpectedly."

He let out a low whistle. "That was a mistake."

"On both of our parts," I admitted. "I'm just hurt because . . . it's not like her."

"People make mistakes. Sometimes you just need to stay hopeful and give it time." He said something in Arabic, then added in English, "My mother always says that. It means, 'What is coming is better than what has gone.'"

A woman in her sixties had been walking past our table, but she paused for a second and brazenly looked Mo up and down.

"What was *that* about?" I asked.

"That?" he said, watching her stalk off. "Not my problem."

"It's your problem when someone kicks you off a flight, no?"

He lifted a shoulder and screwed up his face as if to say, "What can I do?"

"Don't you think working as a private investigator is twice as dangerous for you compared to, say, someone who . . ."

"Doesn't look Arab?" he supplied. "Probably. But why would I let someone else's fear dictate what I do with my life?"

I smiled. "Good point."

"Thanks."

"What's the new development with Harper? I mean Ashley."

"I know who you mean." His eyes darted around the coffee shop. Then he leaned in toward me. "That guy you saw?"

"Yeah?"

"He's not European."

"Really? Who is he, then?" I'll admit, my mind was already formulating a hypothesis, which isn't suitable for even this private document. (Let's just say it rhymes with *cumin graphicing*.)

"I'm pretty sure it's her brother, David. He wrote a Facebook post about going to visit her."

I let out a breath I didn't know I was holding. "And he's hurting her?"

"What do you mean?"

"I heard yelling when he was over."

"Right . . ."

"And then the next time I saw her, she had a black eye."

He looked startled. "You didn't say anything about a black eye."

I suppose I hadn't, though that's probably because he and I were really and truly strangers when I'd seen it, and then I'd forgotten. I explained this, and told him what I had observed.

"That's not good." He shook his head. "Though maybe it's not what we think it is."

"Don't tell me she walked into a door," I said.

He shrugged. "I try not to jump to any conclusions."

"As a scientist, I commend you. As a human with two eyes and a functioning frontal lobe, I've observed that what most people call a *worst-case scenario* is actually reality, and they just haven't accepted it yet."

He laughed, though I wasn't kidding.

"Did you know she lived in California?" I asked.

He nodded.

"I guess that shouldn't surprise me. But if you just found out that guy was her brother, someone other than Harper's family hired you. Otherwise you would have already known that."

He glanced down at his coffee.

"I know, I know," I told him. "You're not at liberty to say."

When he looked up at me, his warm brown eyes reminded me an awful lot of Leesa's. "Sorry," he said. "You're right—I probably shouldn't have told you about this case. But for some reason I trust you. Is that stupid?"

Heaven help me, I almost said: *I trust you, too.* This is the problem with making a habit of a person: all of the neural pathways he has carved remain long after he's gone. Fool that I am, I've assumed the grooves would close themselves, even as my subconscious mind has been attempting to fill them with individuals who are, for all intents and purposes, not suitable for the space. "You barely know me," I told Mo. "Even if I assure you I can be trusted, all you can do is wait to see whether I'm lying."

"What about intuition?" he said.

"How often does your intuition fail you?"

He leaned back in his chair and crossed his legs. "Almost never."

"Almost never means sometimes," I said.

"Man, if you were any brighter, I'd need sunblock." Mo laughs with his whole body—torso shaking, head bobbing, eyes tearing up. It's viral, that kind of laughter, and I had to try hard not to join him.

"Laugh now," I warned. "But only one of us will be surprised when things go wrong later."

"If you say so," he said, wiping the corners of his eyes.

"That's precisely what I say. By the way, I'm going to Harper's on Friday."

Mo's eyebrows shot up. "Loosening up on the 'no new people' thing, huh?"

"Oh, that's still very much in effect," I said. "Just yesterday I told Seth Williams I couldn't clean for his friends who live in Oak Hills."

"Ritzy neighborhood—you'd stand to make some serious cash over there." He eyed me. "But you won't do it because you don't know them, right?"

"Right, but I already sort of know Harper."

"Good for you," said Mo. "You can never have too many friends."

"I don't know about that," I said, thinking of Leesa. It struck me, then, just how small my circle has grown. There's my mother and Viola, neither of whom is anywhere near my age. I counted my former lab mate, Nicole Radzinksi, as a friend—we often had lunch together and sometimes went to the movies. She even cried when she learned I was leaving. She's (extremely) pregnant with her first child, so a couple weeks ago I emailed her a literature review on 1,4-dioxane to make sure she knew about my concerns, which I should have mentioned to her earlier. I didn't hear back from her after that, which makes me wonder if she wasn't thrilled to receive unsolicited information about the ill effects of her career on her unborn child. I was sad about that, but I wouldn't be able to live with myself if I learned a preventable problem had befallen her or her baby because I signed a non-disparagement clause that requires me to stay silent. Maybe this is my purpose—to blow the FastDry Sani-Foam whistle at a few select individuals, and pray social contagion takes it from there.

"Well, now you have at least one more friend," said Mo. His eyes were actually twinkling—I think it's the first time I've observed that phenomenon in another person—and I had to pretend to be distracted by the barista, who had broken into show tunes.

"I do," I said after a minute. "And at least our friendship is in service of the greater good."

"Which is?"

"To keep Harper safe," I said firmly. "Whatever's going on with her, it isn't right. I won't say my gut says there's danger, because I don't believe in that woo-woo stuff. But I *do* believe in data, and the data certainly points in that direction."

"Well." He drained his coffee. "I think that's a good plan, and if that's your mission, it makes sense to see her on Friday."

"Thank you," I said, because hearing him say this made me feel less ridiculous for my spur-of-the-moment, stick-it-to-Leesa decision.

"Don't worry—I won't ask you to report back on what you two talked about. To quote you, that feels ethically sticky. But I hope you have fun."

"Thanks."

We both stood to leave. This time Mo didn't move in for a hug. He just gave me a broad smile and said goodbye.

I was starting for the door when I turned back to him. "You don't really believe that thing you said, do you?"

"Which one?"

"'What is coming is better than what has gone.'"

I guess I expected him to flash his dimples. Instead, he looked at me with an expression so raw that he might as well have been standing there naked. (I'm blushing as I write this. See what I mean about neural pathways? I'm not even attracted to him and yet here I am, having untoward thoughts.) "Of course I do," he said. "Even if I'm wrong, I don't want to go through life thinking the worst is yet to come."

I nodded in response, though I don't agree at all. Really, poor Mo. For someone who makes a living digging up dirt, he seems incredibly decent and trusting. While I do admire those traits, he might as well pin a target on his back and run around handing out arrows.

"Well, see you around, Annie," he said.

"Isn't that my line?" I said.

Now he smiled at me, though wistfully. "You know how to reach me."

I do. And I understand that he was telling me that the proverbial ball is in my court. The problem is, I have to figure out whether it's worth it to keep it in motion.

—AEM

TWENTY-THREE

August 31

After cleaning First Presbyterian this afternoon, I dropped off my supplies at home and drove to the liquor store to buy wine. I don't have a firm grasp on what most people find palatable, and the man behind the counter was no help in that he tried to sell me a frosted bottle of what purported to be a "skinny" malt-liquor beverage. When I asked why he was under the impression I needed diet alcohol, he apologized and rushed me over to a row of bottles with dessert-oriented names—then added that I would find a well-stocked ice cream freezer at the back of the store. There are days, many in fact, when I remain convinced that women cannot win. We ask for equal pay and a seat at the table, and instead we're handed control-top pantyhose and pink wine with cupcakes on the label.

The latter of which, sadly, is precisely what I walked out of the liquor store holding. This is not on account of successful marketing, but rather because Todd's doppelgänger entered the store seconds after the clerk disappeared, and I panicked and grabbed the first thing within reach. By the time I had paid for my lady libation, I'd already spotted the man again and realized he had far too much hair to be Todd—but

I couldn't shake my apprehension and wanted to get out of there as quickly as possible.

Here I am, complaining about the gender-role status quo—yet when it came time to get dressed and ready to go to Harper's, I found myself wishing for a reference book (say, *Grooming Rituals of the Female Homo Sapiens* or *How Not to Look Ridiculous*). As I rummaged through my closet, it occurred to me that I possess but two types of clothing: business casual, for which I no longer have any use, and glorified pajamas. Since Jon's departure, I have occasionally worn the same yoga pants and T-shirts for up to seventy-two hours, transitioning from day to night with alarming ease. I could drag myself to the mall, of course, but I have no doubt that I would spend a month's worth of what is admittedly meager pay on items that were inevitably identical to the ones I already own.

A somewhat confusing internet search educated me on the "high/low" principle espoused by so-called style gurus, and so I opted for a pair of wool work slacks and a plain navy T-shirt. Leesa helped me choose a concealer earlier in the year, though I never did tell her I was buying it because Todd kept insisting I looked exhausted and needed a night in a hotel. I dabbed a bit of that under my eyes, applied lip balm, and decided that was that.

After some internal debate about when I should show up, I decided I would to mine own self be true and arrived at Harper's at eight on the dot. I rang the doorbell and waited, and though I heard noise coming from within, she did not answer. I had just begun walking back to my house when I heard her squeal, "*Annie!*"

When I spun around, she was standing in the doorway, waving like we hadn't seen each other since before the war. She was dressed in skintight leggings and a T-shirt, albeit a very fancy one made of tissue-thin fabric. I couldn't help but feel disappointed that I had chosen to change out of my yoga pants.

"Oooh, I love rosé!" she said as I handed her the wine. Her feet were bare, and when she leaned in and hugged me, her head only came to my shoulder. High heels must serve their intended purpose, as until that moment I had never realized how petite she truly is. "Thank you!"

"Sure," I mumbled, trying to conceal my discomfort over close contact with a near stranger. "Should I take off my shoes?"

"If you want to. Come on, I'll give you the tour," she said, waving me in.

I'd seen her vestibule the day she moved to the neighborhood. Yet I was still surprised to find that the house looked markedly different from when the Novaks lived there. The walls, once shades of tan and brown, were now a dazzling white that accentuated the dark wood beams spanning the living room ceiling. Harper had hung framed vintage movie posters and arranged two overstuffed leather sofas on either side of a glass coffee table not far from the fireplace.

"You've done a lot with the place," I said, even as I wondered how a twenty-three-year-old could afford leather furniture and a lifetime supply of throw pillows. Family money is the logical answer, but the man who Mo claims is Harper's brother is the only family of hers I've seen. Maybe she's an heiress, or starred in some Disney show for tweens and is now sitting on a pterodactyl-sized nest egg.

"This is my favorite room," said Harper as I followed her into the kitchen. "I didn't have to do a thing to it after I moved in."

"It's great," I said, because it is. The Novaks did a terrific job on the space, even if its lack of pigment stands in contrast to the colorful Spanish tiles they chose for the pool—the granite counters, cupboards, and tile backsplash are white, while the floor is gray slate. I have a feeling they, like my mother, watched a lot of home improvement shows.

Harper retrieved a wine opener and two goblets, then perched on a barstool at the kitchen island. I sat across from her. Through the wide glass double doors behind her, the pool glowed with the reflection of the sun setting.

She poured us each a glass of wine, then lifted hers to me. "To new friends."

"To new friends," I said, my ears aflame as I brought the edge of my glass to hers. Her face was unbruised; she seemed healthy and unharmed. Why, exactly, had I decided to accept her invitation, when she was clearly fine?

She had placed two white bowls in the middle of the island prior to my arrival. One was filled with M&M's; the other, crispy strips of an indeterminate origin. Harper saw me looking at them and said, "Pork rinds, in case you're keto-ing."

I took this to mean the diet Leesa had tried in an attempt to drop into the double digits. After having to be revived with a packet of gummy bears in the middle of one of the twins' playdates, she confessed that perhaps completely eliminating an entire macronutrient wasn't as healthful as she had been led to believe. Here I've been so sure she'll die on her LiteWeight hill—but her dalliance with ketosis reminds me that there's a slim but statistically significant chance she'll convert to science one day.

I smiled at Harper and said, "I love carbohydrates. They're brain fuel."

"Oh, me, *too!*" she said, popping an M&M in her mouth. "Put a breadbasket in front of me and I'll absolutely destroy it. That is, if Dog doesn't beat me to it."

"Speaking of Moppet, where is it?" I asked, glancing around.

As if on command, the beast appeared at my feet. Harper laughed. Her laugh was high and breathy—I could easily imagine her starring in a film about a young woman who briefly loses her way, then finds her purpose volunteering at a soup kitchen run by a hot, humble hero who was finally ready for his happily ever after. "That dog is wild for you!" she said.

"Or just wild," I said as it sank its tiny teeth into my toes.

Oblivious to her canine's attempt to gnaw off my digits, she said, "So what's your story, Annie?"

I am hard-pressed to think of a question I welcome less at this current juncture in life. "I don't have much of a story, I'm afraid," I said, splashing my wine as I shook Moppet from my foot. "I recently left my job in chemistry—"

"I *knew* you were something other than a housekeeper!" she exclaimed.

"I'll always be a scientist," I told her, and in fact hearing myself say these words proved to be a comfort to me. "I happen to not be actively employed in the field for the time being. But I'm happy to help others enjoy clean and pleasing living spaces." If only I were among those savoring the fruit of my labor. But perhaps it's time to admit defeat and accept that my mother's house is, and always will be, a well-furnished storage space.

Harper took a sip of her wine, then said, "Is that why you live with your mom?"

"No, I . . ." I couldn't figure out what to say, and when I finally had an inkling, I wasn't sure how to say it. "She went through a major bout of depression a couple years ago, and I was so worried about her that I moved in with her and ended up staying. I plan to move out by the end of the year."

"That's nice of you. You must love her a lot."

"I do," I said. In fact, though the mess gets me down from time to time, I have to admit that it's been kind of nice spending this time with my mother. We've talked more in the past year than we had in ages, even if most of our conversation has revolved around my wedding. "But what about you, Harper?" I asked, wondering if her pseudonym sounded strange to her, or if she had fully embraced her new moniker. "What brought you to East Haven, of all places?"

"It's kind of a long story."

I glanced down at my wine. "We've got at least another seven minutes."

She laughed again. "You're hilarious. The short version is, I grew up in California and went to college in New York. Now I'm in Michigan to get a fresh start."

A fresh start from what, she did not say. I didn't want to push, so I asked, "Do you work?"

She wrinkled her nose. I assumed this was her response to the plebeian endeavor of exerting effort to complete a task until she said, "I wish. Right now, I'm supposed to be focusing on wellness."

My eyes flitted to her wineglass.

"I'm not in recovery or anything like that," she said.

"Oh. Well. That's good."

"As you might have guessed," said Harper, with a smile that was at once funny and sad, "I just recently got out of a long relationship."

"Ohhh," I said. "What happened?"

She frowned. "I'm really not supposed to talk about it."

"Says who?" I asked, remembering how she'd told me to pretend I hadn't seen the man who'd been at her house. Had her brother been there to warn her?

"Says Wells."

"Who's Wells?"

She leaned in conspiratorially. "My ex."

"Why is he a secret?"

"My family thinks he's bad for me."

"I see," I said, though the truth was, I still had so many questions. Did her family think he was bad because he hurt her? Was that how she'd ended up in Michigan? Or was her brother the one who was really the problem?

Harper seemed to have understood that I had just bitten my tongue on her behalf, because she said, "Thank you. The problem is, Wells *agrees* with my family. He thinks we need to be apart for a while—that's

how I ended up in East Egypt, Michigan, no offense—and buy ourselves time before we make our next move. But I think my brother may
have talked him into the whole thing."

"That sounds terrible," I said, though I was relieved that I was now
allowed to admit I knew she had a brother. "But *was* he bad for you?
Wells, I mean?"

"Wells?" she said, incredulous. "No way. He saved my life."

I hoped she didn't mean he had *spared* her life by only hitting her
in the face, but I reminded myself that she and I didn't have the kind
of relationship that gave me permission to try to dig deeper.

"I miss him so much," she added. "I've been taking yoga and Pilates
and I'm even learning to cook. And obviously I'm looking at my time
in the Midwest as an opportunity to expand my brand."

"Your brand?"

"On social media?" she said, like I should have known this. "I'm a
fashion influencer."

Of course she was. Harper had refilled my glass at some point,
though I'm not sure when. I took a long swig of my pink wine, which
was too sweet but tasted nothing like cupcakes. After I swallowed, I
said, "Being apart from someone you love is hard."

She gave me a knowing look. "Then the cutie in the junky car isn't
your guy?"

"Pardon?"

"That guy I've seen around. Dark hair, beard, drives an old silver car."

This confirmed my suspicion that Mo is the least incognito private
investigator in the greater Midwest. "Oh, *that* guy," I said. "No, he's
just a . . . he's, well, a . . ."

"Friend with benefits?" she said, winking at me. (I can only hope
that her preternaturally long lashes are owing to mascara and not Leesa's
secret serum.)

For some reason, I felt like my heart had just skipped a beat.
"Nothing like that," I said quickly. "I'm engaged."

She looked at my naked hand with disbelief.

"I don't wear my ring all that much," I admitted. Then, for reasons still completely unbeknownst to me, I opened my mouth and told her everything—how Jon had left me without warning, then decided to extend his stay; how I had decided not to go see him, and didn't really know where we stood. I even told her about what had happened at SCI and how lousy Jon's timing was.

Suddenly she was on the other side of the kitchen island, hugging me tight. "Oh, Annie," she said. "How *terrible* for you. This isn't your fault. You know that, right?"

"I know I didn't cause any of it to happen, but I feel like I was too optimistic. I think of myself as a realistic person, yet I was so busy believing life would stay on track that I missed major warning signs about how far off the rails it was all about to go," I admitted.

"You can't expect yourself to be perfect, Annie. My therapist reminds me of that all the time."

I was about to thank her—it's a nice sentiment, at least—when I realized she was staring at me with her big gray eyes. "OMG! You know what you need?"

I shook my head, though I do know exactly what I need—and that is several things I will never have.

"A makeover!"

"I most certainly do not."

She stuck out her hand. "Phone, please. Let me see your Instagram."

"I don't have an Instagram."

"What?" she asked, horrified.

Now it was my turn to laugh. "I have reservations about allowing a commercial entity to data mine my personal information for profit."

"You're ridic!" she said, but she was smiling.

"That's me. Ridic," I repeated.

"It's a *compliment*, silly. You're super strange and I *love* it. So, seriously—a little blush, we'll work some magic on those brows . . ."

She frowned and moved her face uncomfortably close to mine. Then she backed up, eyes narrowed, and said, "Clothes that fit, obviously—don't worry, I know how to find great stuff cheap—and a haircut, for real. Not too much, some layering to give you more body. I wouldn't cut it myself, of course. I just tried someone new in town and he's not half-bad." She smiled at me. "You're so pretty, Annie."

"I'm not."

"You could be, though," she conceded. "Right now, it's almost like you don't want anyone to notice you. Which is kind of funny—I'm the one who's supposed to be keeping a low profile."

Spoken like someone who didn't really know me. "Says who? And isn't a low profile at odds with being a social media influencer?"

Rather than answer me directly, she put her hands on her hips, kicked a perfect, pedicured foot up in the air, and gave me a dazzling smile. "Can't help who I am, can I?"

Though I was dying to know who'd told her to keep a low profile, I managed to smile. "Whether nature or nurture, you are certainly exactly who you are. But the thing is, I'm not really in the mood for change right now."

She pursed her lips. "Well, when you're ready. This fiancé of yours—Jon, right?"

I nodded.

"I've dated lots of men like him."

The idea of her having dated "lots" of men like Jon at age twenty-three is a little alarming, but maybe that's just because I'm protective of her—try as I might, I can't erase the image of her black eye.

"No French teachers, though," she said, winking again. "What I'm trying to say is that men like Jon?"

"Yes?"

"They *always* come running back." She drained her wine, then looked at me. "So when that happens, what will you do?"

I was going to tell her that I didn't need to worry about what I would do, as it was never going to happen. Then a vision flashed through my mind. I was striding through the airport in France, looking chic and holding my head high. In the crowd, Jon was waiting for me with tears in his eyes and clutching a bouquet of roses, even though he's never been one to buy me flowers. And then we kissed and . . . well, I know it was a fantasy, because after we kissed it was like everything was normal again—only even better.

"I don't know," I told Harper. "But if you're right, I may just let you play Beauty Shop Barbie with me."

—AEM

TWENTY-FOUR

September 2
TO: Annie Mercer
FROM: Jon Nichols
SUBJECT: Please read this

Dear Annie,

I know you asked me not to email you. Now I realize why you emailed me when I asked you that same thing. Turns out it's a lot easier to be out of touch when you're the one who's decided it's going to be that way. What can I say? I'm an idiot. I hope you'll forgive me.

I'm writing because I owe you an explanation and an apology—and I don't want you to wait another four weeks to hear either. I'm really, really sorry. I lost my way for a while, and I was afraid to admit that to you. You always seem to know the right thing to do, and I was embarrassed for you to find out how much I was floundering, especially with our wedding coming up.

The thing is, as much as I love *speaking* French, I don't really want to teach it anymore. I've known that for more than a year but have been terrified to tell anyone, including myself. Because then what? I don't want to go into finance and work with my father. And I felt stupid telling you, because you have this one thing you've always wanted to do— that you were *born* to do—and I don't have that. Even though your career has been taken away from you, I have no doubt you'll dive back in two years from now, if not sooner (knowing you, Annie, you'll find a way). It seems like everyone else has it figured out, too. My old roommate Dom has known he wanted to be a TV producer since he was a kid, and sure enough—that's what he's doing. And Mikey (star of my parents' eyes, even if they try to hide it) always wanted to have a gorgeous wife and a gaggle of kids. He's younger than I am and has already made it happen.

I had a panic attack the week before I left for France. I didn't know what it was at the time, but I was in my car outside of County Day, where I was supposed to be dropping off some paperwork, and suddenly I just couldn't breathe. When I finally stopped gasping for air and shaking, I knew something had to change. So I made up my mind to go to Paris as soon as possible. For some reason, it seemed like I would find answers there—answers I couldn't find at home.

And you know what? I have. I've gotten lost on the Métro and ended up in the wrong neighborhood at the wrong time. I've mangled words—for all my studying, there are some things you can only learn by living through them—and missed social cues that even French toddlers seem to be aware of. Yet I've been able to figure it out. Which tells me that even though I'm not sure what my future will look like, I can figure that out, too.

I don't want to do it alone, though, Annie. I miss you so much it's like one of my limbs has been cut off. I know you probably think that's overly dramatic, and maybe it is. It's still true. I know you don't sleep over at my place all that much, and yet when I wake up in the morning here, I often reach for you beside me in bed. Then I remember that you're not here, and that's because of me.

I want to show you that I'm a new man. Or at least a better man. I really wish you would come here so you can see that for yourself and understand why I did what I did; it'll never make sense from Michigan. I know it was wrong—*I* was wrong. I still believe it was one of the best choices I've ever made. Before, I wasn't ready to be a good husband to you. Now I am.

I bet you're shaking your head with disgust right now. I get it. I'm not asking you to forgive me just yet. All I'm asking is for you to take one little risk, get on a plane, and meet me here. You will love it—I promise. And even if you fly back to the

States certain you never want to see my face again, you'll at least have seen Paris.

Please, Annie. I love you. I never stopped loving you. I just lost my way a little, and I'm ready to spend the rest of my life proving to you that it will never happen again.

Love,
Jon

TWENTY-FIVE

September 3

"Oh dear," said Viola when she opened the door this morning. "Are you ill?"

"No," I said, though what I was thinking was, *yes, I have an incurable heart condition.* I barely slept last night after reading Jon's email. (Of course I read it the minute I saw it, just as he must have known I would.) Finally, I have an explanation about why he left. And shockingly, it almost makes sense—not that I would have ever made that choice, were I in his shoes. Still. It means I may be wrong about him not returning. I may be wrong about a whole lot, in fact.

"What is it, then?" she said, motioning for me to come inside. "I've not seen you like this before."

"I'm just having a bad day," I said, walking into the kitchen.

"Leave it," she said after I set down my bucket and vacuum, and she sounded serious enough that I felt I had no choice but to abandon my supplies and follow her into the living room. She patted her most comfortable chair, indicating I was to sit, then she sat across from me on the sofa. "Well, my dear, I've known you since you were no higher than my knee. This is more than a bad day."

The hollows of her eyes were dark, as my own must be, and she looked especially frail; I felt guilty that I was causing her to worry. "It's Jon," I admitted.

"I had a feeling. He's still in France, then?"

"Yes, but he emailed again to apologize, and asked me again if I would come visit him. He bought me a plane ticket and everything."

"And what do you think about that?"

"The timing's not great," I said.

"Why's that?"

"I can't just up and leave all my clients with no notice."

She tsked. "Annie Mercer, I do think we'll all be okay if we have to clean our own houses for a week or two. And I chatted with your mother just yesterday. She knows about Jon's little adventure, I assume?"

I nodded.

"Good. At any rate, she seems to be doing just fine."

"I guess she is," I admitted. Though my impending nuptials had provided her with newfound vigor, it hasn't dissipated since I told her Jon decided to stay in France. In fact, just yesterday she called Betty Smithers to make plans to join her at the prayer circle. So why do I feel so hesitant to leave her, even for one short week? "What would you do if you were me?" I asked Viola.

"I wouldn't blame you if you went—and I wouldn't blame you if you didn't." She coughed, then said, "But who cares what I think? All that's important is that you do what feels right."

"See, that's the thing. I have no idea what's right anymore." I feel like I couldn't identify a fact these days if it hit me in the head. And each time I think I've gotten a handle on something, everything changes.

I realized Viola was wheezing slightly, but it didn't seem to bother her. She smiled at me. "Just remember that life is to be lived. Do with that what you will."

"Thanks, Viola. I'll keep that in mind," I told her.

"I'm glad," she said, patting my back. "I'm a little tired today, so I'm going to go read in my study. You don't mind, do you?"

"Of course not," I assured her. And I didn't—except she's never not followed me around as I've cleaned. And though her house wasn't remotely dirty by anyone else's standards, the coffee grounds in the sink and dust bunnies in the corners of the foyer were as concerning as her wheezing.

As I began to clean her house, I kept wondering: *Aren't I already living life?* And wasn't my plan to make Jon come to *me?* Why should I be the one to do what he wants?

But there was a softness to his letter—an honesty that hints at the potential for a fresh start for us. I had no idea he'd lost his enthusiasm for teaching, nor that he felt nervous to tell me that. I can't help but think that losing my job—which is my version of losing my way—has given him the courage to open up about that. It might be the first and only good thing to come out of my resignation.

Viola had dozed off in her armchair, so before I left, I put a note on the counter telling her to call me if she needed anything. My mother was at the dining room table when I got home. As of this morning, blue file folders filled with old taxes had been strewn all over the surface. Though I had shown my mother the page on the IRS website where it clearly stated that with few exceptions, everyday citizens such as herself weren't required to keep a record of their income taxes longer than three years, she had insisted that she had to review each of her Reagan-era forms before allowing me to send them through the shredder and on to their final destination. At two o'clock, however, the folders had been replaced by no fewer than eight photo albums, all splayed open, and what appeared to be hundreds of loose photos that had been dumped out of the empty shoeboxes stacked next to the table.

"Ma," I said cautiously, "what are you doing?"

Her eyes were wet with tears when she looked up at me. "Hi, Annie," she said. "I was just taking a stroll down memory lane."

"Seems like a sad stroll," I said. "Why are you crying?"

"Oh, some of my tears are the happy kind. Look," she said, pointing at a photo in the album closest to her. I approached the table and saw that it was a picture of me. I was maybe four or five, standing in front of a frothing volcano I had made out of Play-Doh. Memory's a tricky thing, so I don't know if it was that exact creation that I was flashing back to, or another—but even all these years later, I could remember my father clapping as the vinegar and baking powder mix erupted from the dough mound's narrow opening. Acetic acid and sodium bicarbonate: my first successful chemistry experiment.

Then it hit me.

"You're looking at photos of my father, aren't you?" I asked her. I used to call him Dad, back when he was still around. And even after he left, that's how he signed his occasional postcards and letters, which always detailed his adventures and injuries—a finger lost but an elk won during a hunting trip; a beard singed off and scar tissue acquired during a fire on one of the oil rigs he worked on; a too-close brush with a grizzly (though obviously not so close that he didn't live to embellish the tale). He had so many stories to tell, but never an apology for unceremoniously exiting my life.

I'm sorry. How strange, the power of those two little words. Maybe that's why I haven't reached out to Leesa.

Maybe that's why I'm seriously considering Jon's offer.

Instead of answering me, my mother turned the page of the album in front of her. There was my grandmother, who died when I was young, standing behind my mother and father with a hand on each of their shoulders. My grandmother was immaculately groomed as always, and she was beaming proudly. My mother was thinner than she is now, and sporting a live-wire perm. But she was smiling. Beside her, my father was wearing a dress shirt and a tie. Maybe it was the tie. Maybe it was the guilt of knowing that he would soon swap his suburban home and all that went with it for the thrills of the Alaskan wilderness. Whatever the reason, he looked miserable—which is not how I remember him in my mind. Maybe he, like Jon, had been putting on an act when I was around.

"Grandma Tilly loved Andrew an awful lot," she said quietly, referring to my father. "She thought the world of him."

"Was she upset when he left?"

My mother nodded. "Wouldn't say his name ever again. It was like he never existed." She looked up at me. "I need to tell you something, Annie."

"I'm listening."

"No, sit down," she said, pulling out a chair. I saw then that the tax folders had been piled on the seats of the chairs. Which made sense in a strange way. Sometimes I suspect my mother is secretly an organized person; it's just that her systems don't match everyone else's. I moved the stack to the next chair and sat.

"It's my fault your father didn't stay."

"This isn't your fault," I told her. (It occurs to me now that this is exactly what Harper had said to me the other night at her house.)

"It is. I had a chance and I didn't take it."

"What do you mean?"

She winced, like she was causing at least one of us physical pain. "Your father came back."

"When?"

"When you were eleven."

Eleven—that pivotal point when impulse control develops, yet childhood dreams haven't disappeared yet. I remember being eleven. I still wanted my father to come home.

I didn't say anything. I couldn't.

"After almost five years of being gone, he wanted to come back," said my mother, who had turned toward the window now. "Said he was ready to put his wild ways behind him so we could be a family again.

I didn't want you to see him, not yet. So I sent him away and told him to return after you were asleep."

"And?"

"He did. He stayed with me until morning. It was one of the best days of my life, really. I never did stop loving him."

"What happened?"

"When the sun came up, I told him he had to leave."

"Why?" I asked, my voice cracking.

She gave me a sad smile. "Because I believed in my heart that he would eventually grow bored and leave us again. Not necessarily for Alaska. Maybe he'd go down to Texas or find work in the Pacific. Who knows. But I didn't want you to get your hopes up, only to have your heart broken again. Don't you remember the way you cried yourself to sleep for months after he left? Every time the doorbell rang, you went running to look for your father. Never mind that I didn't change the lock and he still had a key."

I shook my head; I must have blocked that out.

"I figured if he meant it, he'd come back. And he didn't." She closed one of the albums. "Have you heard from Jon?"

"Yes." I sighed. "He wants me to go to Paris to see him. He said he was sorry and wants to prove to me that he'll never do anything like that again."

"Paris," she said with a faraway look in her eyes. "I went to Paris once."

"You did? When was this?"

A smile surfaced on her lips. "Before your father. I went with the man I was dating. Grandma Tilly didn't approve of my traveling with a man who was not my husband, and I thought she would never forgive me. But I'm her only daughter. She got over it." She gave me a knowing look. "There's something about seeing that city that changes you."

"That's good to know," I said. But what I didn't say is that I'm not sure I want to be changed any more than I've already been forced to.

"I'm going to go to my room," I told my mother. "I've got a lot to think about."

"I understand," she said. "But Annie?"

"Yes, Ma?"

"Don't stay here because of me."

She's come such a long way, my mother—our conversation made me realize that. If she can survive the news that Jon isn't as dependable as she thought, then she can probably survive my being away for a week. I bent to kiss her cheek. "I won't," I promised.

Viola said life is to be lived, and so after I had closed my bedroom door behind me, I pulled out my phone. But instead of calling Air France, I gave in to a sudden impulse . . . and texted Mo.

—AEM

TWENTY-SIX

September 3

4:05 p.m. Hi, Mo. It's Annie. Do you want to get coffee or something sometime?

4:08 p.m. Annie Mercer? Sending *me* a text message?! 😃 To what do I owe this honor?

4:09 p.m. Don't give me a hard time.

4:11 p.m. But it's so much fun!

4:15 p.m. Ha. Is that a no?

4:16 p.m. It's a definitely. When?

5:05 p.m. Are you free tomorrow evening?

5:07 p.m. Yup.

5:10 p.m. Meet you at Community Cup at 6:30?

5:15 p.m. Perfect. See you soon. 😃

TWENTY-SEVEN

September 4

I was still feeling sheepish when I arrived at Community Cup this evening. Yes, I'd come to the realization that I'm lonely. But I couldn't help but wonder if my making plans with Mo was a subconscious attempt to fill my mind with minutiae instead of coming to a decision about Jon and Paris.

The café was crowded but I didn't see Mo, so I went back outside. It was a beautiful evening; the sun was already beginning to set, and the air hinted at cooler weather just around the corner. Fall has always been Jon's favorite season—he loves the rhythm of the school day, the way the colors change and the world submits to the tyranny of pumpkin spice. As I waited, I wondered if Jon thought fall in Paris was even better than here.

I wondered if I would, too.

I sat at a small table, watching people stream in and out of the coffee shop. About five minutes later Mo came running up to my table, breathless and flushed. "I am so sorry," he said, wiping his brow. "Did you see my text?"

I shook my head; my phone had been on silent.

"I was helping Aisha. My sister," he clarified. "It took longer than I planned."

"Everything okay?"

I could tell he was trying not to look aggravated about whatever had happened. "For now."

"Want to talk about it?"

"Yes, but let's get coffee first."

This time I insisted on treating him, though after I did he bought two chocolate chip cookies, one of which he handed to me.

"What if I'm on a diet?" I said.

He laughed. "Then I'd happily eat your cookie for you."

I laughed, too, then took a bite. The cookie was warm and had been sprinkled with coarse salt, which made the chocolate even more delectable—I bet there isn't a macaron in all of France that tasted half as good.

The table I'd been sitting at was taken, and no others were available, so we decided to take a walk. We turned off Main and headed down Grove, which I've always thought is the prettiest street in all of East Haven. The stately houses have sloping lawns and decades-old trees that canopy the sidewalks. "Is your sister okay?" I asked.

He nodded. "More or less. She goes to this fancy charter high school. You have to be really smart to get in—unless your parents donated a bunch of money to the school. Then you just have to be rich."

"Let me guess: she's having trouble with some of the rich kids."

"Yep."

"Let me guess again: they're giving her a hard time because of her ethnicity."

"You're good."

"At predicting disappointing human behavior, sure," I said. "Well, with the exception of my own disappointing behavior. But I recognize that most people are their own blind spots. What happened to Aisha?"

Mo told me that some of the popular kids were taunting her for wearing a hijab. They yanked on it in the hall, and a group of cheerleaders had paraded around her in the locker room with their heads wrapped, hijab-style, with towels.

His parents didn't make Aisha cover her hair, he explained; it was a personal choice. "Me, for example, I'm not big on religion," he said. "My mom and dad don't like that I'm not observant, but they left Lebanon because they were being persecuted for their beliefs, so it's important to them that I make up my own mind. I'm not sure if there's a God. I hope so. But I have a hard time with the concept of organized religion."

"Interesting. Why?"

"War, for starters. Religion is used to justify violence."

"And the oppression of marginalized groups," I added.

"Yep. Lots of good people, but still way too many hypocrites."

"So many hypocrites."

We grinned at each other, and then began to laugh. But just as abruptly, I stopped laughing—and not because my mother would have had a grand mal seizure if she heard me talking this way about Catholicism. Something had passed between us, and I'm not sure I'm ready to write about what it might have been. Even if I'm wrong, the fact that I felt it at all . . . well, I don't know what it means.

"I think there's much to be said for religion," I said, trying to move the conversation along. "My mother found peace in her faith after my father left, for example."

"Yeah, I can see that," said Mo. "Sorry to hear about your father, though."

"Thank you."

"The worst part is, I don't think these kids actually care about what Aisha believes. She's second in her class, and I think they're just trying to distract her so she won't do well on her exams."

"Is it working?"

"She's very focused, so it's hard to knock her down. But she called me today because she was so upset. It's starting to get to her."

"Imbeciles. What can you do?"

"I told her to keep her head high and try to kill 'em with kindness. All she has to do is get through this year. Then she's off to college."

Where she's sure to be faced with more half-wits determined to make her personal choices as publicly difficult as possible. I didn't say this to Mo, though—no reason to rain on his parade when the world's already sending in a storm. For the first time, his sunny demeanor made some sense to me. Maybe optimism is the only thing standing between him and giving up on the daily slog of human existence.

We had come to a park and walked over to a small bench next to the playground. "Want to sit?" asked Mo.

I nodded, and we each took the opposite ends of the bench.

"How did your wine date with Harper go?" he asked.

"Didn't you say I didn't have to report back?" I was teasing him—this occurs to me now—but the question made a line form in the center of his forehead. "What? Did something bad happen?"

"No, nothing like that," he said, looking down at his coffee cup for a minute before looking back at me. "I'm not working her case anymore, so you don't have to worry about saying something you shouldn't."

"I don't understand. You couldn't have possibly found out everything you needed to know already, could you?"

"My only job was to collect intel, which I did. Now that job is done."

"Wait—is this about whoever's hurting her? Did that person hire you?"

He shook his head. "I promise you, no one who's hurting Harper hired me to spy on her."

"How can you be so sure?"

He looked tired. I told him I was sorry, that I wasn't trying to be difficult.

He set his coffee cup beside him on the bench and touched my arm lightly. His fingers were warm on my skin, and though it was strange because he wasn't Jon, I didn't pull away. "I know you're not, but I need you to trust me on this, Annie. Maybe I haven't earned that trust yet, but I still hope you know I would never do something to hurt you."

"I have no reason to think you'd hurt me," I said. (Then again, I could have said this very thing of Jon just a few short weeks ago.) "However, I do have reason to think that you're a good person who knows that the right thing to do is stick with this until it's clear that Harper Brearley—or Ashley Sarah Jones, or whatever her name is—is safe."

"Let's not assume the worst."

"That's practically my job."

"Time to get a new job." He made an exaggerated grimace. "Sorry. Probably not the best thing to say under the circumstances."

"Only one year and ten months until I can practice chemistry again. Not that I'm counting."

"There's got to be something we can do about that."

"The non-compete I signed is legally binding. Jon thinks that there may be a loophole, since my boss sexually harassed me."

"So you spoke with Jon?"

I sighed. "He said that before he left. But we have been emailing. He wants me to come to Paris."

Mo did a double take.

"You don't think I should go?"

"I didn't say that. I'm just surprised. What do you want to do?"

"I kind of want to go," I admitted, "but I'm also afraid."

"Of what?"

Getting hurt. Risking being left behind again. For some reason, I couldn't admit either to Mo. "I don't know," I finally said.

He was quiet for a long time. Then he said, "If even a small part of you wants to give your relationship another chance, what do you have to lose by going for it?"

"That's a great question," I said. And it was—because what *do* I have to lose at this point? My career has collapsed; my future is murky and uncertain. I've considered and even accepted the possibility that my relationship with Jon is over. And though yes, I don't want to be abandoned yet again, it wouldn't be the first time. It may hurt like hell, but I would survive. "Thank you," I said to Mo.

"For what?" he said.

"Helping me think in a way I don't normally think." Because as we were talking, I'd decided that I was going to take a risk—one of the biggest of my life, in fact—and go to Paris.

Mo and I made small talk on the walk back, and in spite of the quicksilver shift from the conversation we'd just had, it was perfectly comfortable. There's something easy about him that I like. When we reached the parking lot, he looked at me, probably expecting to see if I was going to try to shake his hand and make a noncommittal comment about the next time we would see each other.

I stared at him for a moment. Maybe one moment too long. And then I did something reckless.

I leaned forward and hugged him.

He was broad and warm, and his arms made me feel safe. He didn't seem surprised that I had hugged him. If anything, he just looked . . . happy. "Thanks for reaching out," he said as we parted. "It was good to see you."

"Thanks for meeting me," I said, suddenly feeling shy and a little stupid.

He smiled at me. "Anytime, Annie Mercer. Anytime."

I waved goodbye and walked to my car. After I closed the door, I looked out the window and saw Mo still standing on the sidewalk. I wanted to soak up the wonderful feeling the evening had left me with. I wanted to tell myself that I had been wrong to swear off new people—and wasn't my friendship with Mo proof of that? But one thought kept rising over all that cheery clamor:

This won't end well.

—AEM

TWENTY-EIGHT

September 5
TO: Jon Nichols
FROM: Annie Mercer
SUBJECT: Paris

Dear Jon,

I've made up my mind: I'd like to join you in Paris. I can only come for a week, and it will have to be next week, as I feel obligated to give my clients some advance notice regarding my absence. Will it work for me to take an overnight flight on September 12 and arrive on September 13?

Love,
Annie

September 5
TO: Annie Mercer
FROM: Jon Nichols
SUBJECT: Re: Paris

Oh Annie. You don't know how happy you've just made me. Thank you, thank you, thank you for giving me another chance. I promise—I won't blow it.

The thirteenth is great—will you send me your flight info? I'll pick you up at the airport. Plan on customs taking at least an hour. Once you leave customs, there's a lounge area near the exit for the taxi stand. I'll meet you there. My phone is on, so call or text if you have any trouble. I can't wait to see you and show you Paris.

Love,
Jon

September 5
TO: Harper Brearley
FROM: Annie Mercer
SUBJECT: Help

Harper,

I feel kind of embarrassed to ask you this, but remember how you said you might be able to help me with my clothes and whatnot if I decided to go to Paris? Well, I'm going . . . wondering if the offer still stands?

Many thanks,
Annie

September 6
TO: Annie Mercer
FROM: Harper Brearley
SUBJECT: Re: Paris

Girl, thought you'd never ask. Of *course.* Hopping right on it. Give me two or three days to get everything in, and then let's make a date for your makeover!

xoxo,
Harper

TWENTY-NINE

September 9

When I went to Harper's this afternoon, she flung open the door and threw her arms around me (apparently hugging is my new thing). "You're going to *Paris*!" she said, still squeezing the air from my lungs. "I *knew* it!"

"Looks like it," I said when I could finally breathe again.

"What made you decide to go?" she asked.

Maybe it was because Harper had mistaken Mo for my boyfriend, but I felt silly admitting that he'd been the one to help me decide to take the risk. "Jon really wants me to, and it seems like the right thing to do," I said.

"I'm so happy for you," said Harper, taking my arm and marching me upstairs. "Because—well, because Paris."

We stopped in the same bedroom where I saw her singing that day when I was cleaning at Viola's. It had been transformed into a giant dressing room, with clothing racks and built-in shelves and a padded bench in front of an enormous shoe collection, just like a department store. She opened the door to an actual closet and began retrieving cardboard boxes, which she tossed on the floor next to the bench. "I took the liberty of ordering a few things," she said, head still in the closet.

I eyed what was quickly turning into a very high stack of boxes. "I probably should have mentioned that I'm on a bit of a budget."

She spun around. She hasn't been wearing sunglasses as much lately. Maybe it's the slightly cooler weather; maybe it's because she hasn't been around anyone who has a habit of mistaking her for a punching bag. Still, her eyes were shining with excitement. "I figured as much, but not to worry—nothing cost more than a hundred dollars, and you don't have to keep a single item you don't love. That's the magic of online shopping."

"You just . . . bought all this stuff for me." I didn't bother hiding how baffled I was. I'm not sure if I could have if I tried.

She flashed me a hundred-watt smile. "Pick what you like and I'll send you the bill. Everything else gets shipped back. I used to do this for my friends in New York all the time. I was like their personal stylist, but I don't charge. It's a passion of mine."

"Wow . . . thank you," I said.

"You're so welcome. Well," she said, throwing another box on the pile. "Let's get started."

"Do you think this will work for Paris?" I said as she handed me a gray sweater she had just pulled from one of the boxes. It was soft, even a bit fuzzy, with a deep V-neck. It was probably nicer than anything I currently own, and I couldn't imagine myself in it.

"I would never buy anything that you couldn't feel confident wearing in any situation or major city."

I thought of her purple caftan. While I couldn't have pulled it off poolside at a retirement community, I had a feeling she would have worn it with confidence whether in Duluth or Dubai. Still, that was not so much smart styling as atomic charisma.

"It's about dressing to please yourself," she said, seeming to read my mind. "It's about *attitude*."

"What pleases me is to be comfortable." I thought for a moment. "And to not draw attention."

"Oh, those days are over, love. It's time to start owning your space. But what's that about?"

"What's what about?"

"Why don't you want to draw attention to yourself? Do you think that asking for attention will automatically lead to the wrong kind? Because if so, that's not true. People make bad choices in spite of what you do—not because of it."

It was impossible not to relive the moment Todd grabbed my rear like he owned it. And really, that was just the culmination of months of predatory behavior. I suppose I have been blaming myself, at least for not being more vocal or suspicious—or even for not having the good sense to record some of the things he said to me when we were alone and report him. At least I have his emails. The man can boast all he wants about his Berkeley dual MBA/PhD, but he skipped Common Sense 101. "That's a lot to think about."

"I guess it is. I've spent years in therapy, so my mind just kind of goes there," she said with a shrug.

I slipped the sweater on over my T-shirt, then walked to the floor-to-ceiling mirror angled in the corner of the room. I never would have guessed it, but light gray is a good color for me. "For the sake of argument, let's assume I'm going to try to get used to attention. I'd still like to look nice without seeming like I care."

"Does that sweater fit the bill?" she said, smiling.

I glanced at my reflection again. "Yes."

"Perf! Because there's more where that came from."

I'll admit, Harper has a gift. She managed to choose items that were almost all in my size, most of which were flattering—though there was an off-the-shoulder T-shirt that I wouldn't have worn even to bed, and a torture device masquerading as a pair of faux-leather leggings. (Harper insisted that I keep them—"But your *butt!*" she kept saying— even though I swore I'd never wear them. In the end, she said they were her gift to me, so I felt my hands, or perhaps my legs, were tied.) I decided to keep nine pieces—four tops, four bottoms, and a blazer— even though I knew my savings account would take a hit. Moreover, I promised Harper I would order at least two new pairs of shoes online before I fly to France.

Just when I thought we were finished, Harper pulled out an enormous pink tackle box filled with makeup. She asked me to give her five more minutes, which I understood to be a minimum of fifteen, but I felt indebted because of the huge favor she had already done me. Honestly, even though I dislike the feel of a brush dabbing at my skin, it wasn't that bad.

"Look at you!" she said when she finished.

"Look at me," I said, peering into the mirror. I was wearing the gray sweater again, a pair of dark jeans, and at least four ounces of makeup. Because of this, I'd been expecting a stranger staring back at me. But Harper had managed to make me look like myself—only somehow better. I was particularly excited to see that all traces of my eczema had been replaced with what Harper referred to as a "fresh-faced glow." Indeed.

She had been placing the makeup she used into a pile. Now she scooped it all into a fabric bag and pressed the bag into my hands. "I have so much, don't feel bad," she said, heading off the protest that was about to pass through my lips. "There's not much we can do for your hair right now, but just—" She used her fingers to move my center part to one side and tuck it behind my ears. "Try that."

"It won't stay that way."

"If you go to the drugstore and buy a boar-bristle brush and a medium-hold hair spray—doesn't have to be pricey—then you're golden," she said. "Or just walk into a salon when you're in Paris."

"And make frantic hand gestures and pray for the best? Sounds like a foolproof plan."

"It's called Google Translate, love. But seriously, let them do what they want. A French hairdresser is *not* going to let you leave looking anything less than sexy."

Sexy is not exactly my aesthetic. Something tells me that even a French vacation is not about to change that.

"Annie," said Harper. She was staring at me intently.

"What is it?" I asked, wondering if I had smeared my lip gloss.

"Nothing, really. It's just that it's *so* good to see you excited for a change."

"Who said I'm excited?"

"Your face," she said, and I had to laugh. Then she hugged me again, and I hugged her back and thanked her. She smiled and told me not to mention it.

Anything, she said, for a friend.

I left Harper's house in possession of a new wardrobe, a bag full of face paint—and, yes, a fresh feeling of excitement. Was it the clothes? The prospect of Paris? Of seeing Jon after what has begun to feel like a very, very long time?

Or maybe it was just the fact that Harper had called me her friend.

I have to wonder why I've been fighting this so hard. Humans have had at least two hundred thousand years to settle into codependency—and that's discounting the time our more primal ancestors spent getting us ready to mingle. Though that number may be but a drop in the bucket of the universe at large, it's still breathtaking in scope. And yet I've been operating as though I—having leased space on planet Earth for a mere twenty-seven years—am somehow exempt from the behavioral inclinations my forebears fostered for millennia.

At any rate, I texted Mo again when I got back from Harper's to let him know I was going to Paris on Wednesday night, because after our last conversation, I felt like I should tell him what I'd decided. He said he was happy for me, and that the food alone was going to knock my socks off. Then he asked if I was interested in going on another job with him—this time to a dog park. I asked him if he even had a dog, as you can't really wander around a dog park without one. When he said no, I told him I'd see about borrowing Moppet for an hour or two.

So that means yes? he texted.

I'd be happy to, I responded.

Because Leesa was right—at least on one count. I *can* go it alone. But why would I want to?

—AEM

THIRTY

Date: September 11
To: Rick and Leslie Hammoud
From: Mo Beydoun
Subject Name: Max the Morkapoo [5.5 lb. Yorkie-Maltese-Poodle mix]
File Number: 159-B
Investigation Type: Domestic Services
Date Assigned: September 7

INVESTIGATIONS SUMMARY

On Tuesday, September 11, my investigation was initiated at the East Haven Dog Park. I was joined by an associate, identified here as AM, who was in possession of a legally obtained Shih Tzu (referred to as ST from here out). AM and ST were essential to this investigation.

Upon arrival at approximately 5:06 p.m., Stationary Surveillance was achieved, with a direct view of the Dog Park and its occupants, including the animal believed to be the Subject, and an unidentified male and female in possession of the Subject. The male and female, both Caucasian and approximately 25–30 years old, are suspected to have dognapped the Subject.

At approximately 5:12 p.m., AM, ST, and I entered the park from the south entrance and engaged ST in a game of fetch in close proximity (approximately 12 feet) from the Subject and the suspected dognappers. The Subject was well-groomed, appeared to be in good health, and was wearing a bright blue collar studded with red rhinestones. Like ST, the Subject did not show an interest in interacting with other dogs at the park. Instead, the suspected dognappers engaged the Subject in a game of fetch using a small red rubber toy. The suspected dognappers referred to the Subject as "Arlo." The Subject did not respond to this name.

According to the investigative plan, I had a dog waste bag in my hand. At approximately 5:17 p.m.—approximately one minute after ST relieved himself on a fence post—the Subject began to make a bowel movement. I moved toward the Subject, and as soon as it became obvious that he was about to finish his business, swooped in and scooped the waste using the bag in my hand.

The male suspect immediately became upset and tried to pull the untied dog waste bag from me, saying, "What the [obscenity] are you doing?" The female suspect joined him, saying, "We're good [obscenity] dog owners. You don't have to pick up our dog's [obscenity] for us."

The female suspect decided she, too, would try to pull the dog waste bag out of my hands. At this point, the bag opened and the Subject's waste went flying in the direction of the suspects.

Fortunately, AM was also in possession of a dog waste bag, and while the suspects were attempting to clean themselves off, she was able to bend down and retrieve a piece of waste. The suspects did not notice her doing so, though they did not attempt to clean the scattered waste, either.

As soon as AM tied her bag, I gave her our pre-discussed signal. She nodded, then yelled "Max!" as loud as possible twice in a row. These calls did not draw the attention of ST (because his name is not Max), who was on a leash in preparation for our exit. However, the Subject ran directly to AM. At this point, the suspected dognappers became extremely angry with both AM and the Subject.

"Arlo, come here right now," said the female suspect.

"I don't know what you're trying to do here, but you'd better knock it the [obscenity] off," the male suspect said to AM. The male suspect then picked up the Subject and began walking quickly to the Dog Park exit.

With the Subject in tow, male and female subjects hastily returned to their vehicle and drove north on 12 Mile Road at approximately 5:22 p.m. I am sorry to report that the Subject was unrestrained and was seated on the female suspect's lap.

In the interest of safety, I did not pursue the vehicle, which is a circa 2017 white Jeep Compass.

The vehicle's license plate is DMM 3891, and it is registered to a Derek Elliot, 28, a resident of East Haven, MI. As you can see in the attached document, social media photos of Derek Elliot match the image of the individual captured via Stationary Surveillance.

I have sent the Subject's fecal sample to Biometrics Labs of Michigan to be matched with the sample you provided me. As soon as I receive the results of that test, I will report back in a separate Investigations Summary.

Ten minutes and fourteen seconds of video was obtained during this investigation. Additionally, a fecal sample from the possible Subject, who is believed to be Max the Morkapoo, was obtained during this investigation.

Mo Beydoun, PI
PO Box 3487
East Haven, MI 48334

THIRTY-ONE

September 12

I'm on a plane headed to Paris, the City of Lights, said to be the most romantic destination in the world. In less than twelve hours, I will be face-to-face with Jon for the first time in two months (!!). And if what he says is to be believed, I will have the opportunity to assess his commitment to the entity known as Us, and potentially turn over a new leaf in our relationship.

Yet here I am—bunkered down in Comfort Plus (upgrade compliments of Jon's guilt), sipping a glass of free sparkling wine and listening to the flight attendant make an announcement in what I assume is flawless French. And instead of thinking about what's in front of me, I'm thinking about what I left behind.

Harper said she was happy to let me take Moppet to the park for a while—she claims the beast prefers me to her and will miss me while I'm in France—and handed him off with a portable carrier and an oversize tote filled with enough supplies for all 101 dalmatians. Soon after, Mo picked me up out front.

We had time to spare, so he drove Moppet and me to his office in order to brief me on the plan. I suppose I must have imagined him working out of a dimly lit storefront-type operation, because I was surprised to discover he rents a high-walled cubicle in an airy, shared workspace attached to a coffee bar. He showed me and Moppet around—turns out the workspace is dog friendly, if less welcoming to individuals with allergies—and then sat at his desk, where he pulled up an illustrated investigative plan on his computer.

We quickly decided I would be the one to see if the dog his clients believe to be theirs responded to its name, while he would be the one to secure the "sample" we planned to steal. (I was relieved to find that Harper's dog supply bag contained alcohol-based hand sanitizer that, thankfully, was *not* FastDry Sani-Foam. As Todd was fond of telling investors, a single gram of dog waste can contain up to twenty-five million fecal coliform bacteria.) It all seemed straightforward—rational, even—but when we got to the park and he set up his recording device on the dashboard of his car, I began to laugh.

Mo took one look at me and started laughing, too, even though he didn't know why I was cracking up. To be honest, I wasn't really sure myself. I guess it was just that the whole thing—stealing dog poop, me and Moppet working as accomplices, the very act of spying with the man who I caught spying in my backyard—struck me as so completely absurd. "You sure you can do this?" Mo asked, wiping tears from his eyes, and I managed to compose myself and assure him that I was ready to spring to action.

The mission itself took less than twenty minutes. It didn't exactly go according to plan—but I had anticipated that, and was able to put my own predetermined back-up plan in place and gather the sample.

"You're a quick thinker, Annie," said Mo after we'd gotten in the car. "I don't know that I would have thought to do that."

"Thank you," I said.

"No, thank you. That never would have worked without you and Moppet."

"Sure it would have," I said.

"You don't give yourself enough credit."

"I do. I'm way smarter than those dog-snatching doofuses," I said, thinking of the woman's horrified expression as Max/Arlo's poop when flying at her and the man she was with.

Mo kept both hands on the steering wheel and continued to look straight ahead, but he was smiling. "You're funny sometimes."

If by *funny* he means confused, that is certainly accurate. Because when he dropped me off, I wasn't really ready for the evening to end. I could make the logical argument that I was just trying to keep my pre-trip jitters at bay by distracting myself. But the truth was, I was enjoying myself in a way I had not in a long time—possibly even before Jon left. And maybe that's what I'm really trying to avoid thinking about. Were things between us growing stale, and I hadn't been paying attention? Is that why he really left? Even if Paris is amazing, it's not like we can re-create that when we return to Michigan. *If* he returns to Michigan, that is.

"You feeling good about your trip?" asked Mo once he pulled up in my mother's driveway.

But before I could respond, Harper came striding out of her door. "Uh-oh," I said.

"Worlds collide," said Mo.

"Just let me do the—" I said, but somehow Harper had crossed both of our lawns with stunning speed and was already standing next to the car. She was wearing a cream-colored V-neck sweater that nearly reached her knees, and black leggings that looked like the ones she had gifted me.

"Annie! Dog! How did it *go*?" she said as I pulled Moppet, who was in the carrier, from the floor in front of the backseat.

"Great!" I said, hoisting myself out of Mo's car. "One second."

I stuck my head back in the car to instruct Mo to stay put, but as I did so, he opened his door and got out. I walked Moppet around to where Mo and Harper were standing and stared at him until he looked at me, at which point I gave him a clenched-teeth smile to convey that he *was not supposed to be out of the car.*

Harper, oblivious to my distress, smiled sweetly at Mo as he handed her the tote full of Moppet's things. She placed the bag on the ground and extended a manicured hand. "I'm Harper," she said. "You must be . . ."

"Mo," he said, just as I said, "My friend!"

Mo smiled at me, clearly amused. That made one of us. He may not have been investigating her anymore, but that didn't mean they should be chatting each other up. Really, if the truth got out (which it inevitably will if they continue to interact), and Harper learned that I had been helping spy on her—and worse, had become *friends* with that spy . . .

Well, I don't know what she'll do. But if I were in her place, I would subtract myself from that equation faster than she can say Pythagorean theorem.

"Mo," said Harper, who had cocked her head like he was the most fascinating person in the world. "I'd like to say I've heard so much about you, but Annie hasn't told me a thing. How did you two meet?"

"On accident," I blurted.

"At a park," said Mo.

Technically both of these statements were true. They both sounded like lies to me.

Harper looked back and forth between us. "I see," she said slyly.

"Well, thanks again for lending Moppet to me," I said, pressing the carrier into her hands. I grabbed the dog supply bag that Mo had set down. "Let me help you bring the rest of the stuff inside."

"Sure," she said as I began pulling her toward her house. "Bye, Mo! *So* nice to meet you!" she called over her shoulder.

As we made our way across the lawn, she leaned her head close to mine, the way Leesa always did when she wanted to dish. "Is this about you know who and you know where?" she whispered.

"You mean Jon? And Paris? No, Mo knows I'm going. There's just . . . a lot of other stuff going on right now that I can't talk about."

She eyed me. "But you do know he's into you."ˎ

"Jon?"

Harper looked at me like I was an idiot, which I suppose was not unwarranted. "*Mo*, Annie. I'm talking about Mo."

My stomach did a little flip. What I knew was that Mo knew too many of her secrets, and once she found out, that would be the end of our tête-à-têtes. "I'm not so sure about that, but for the next seven days it doesn't matter."

She grinned at me like a maniac. "You've got angles, Annie! *Love* it!"

"I have no idea what that means, but thanks."

We had just reached her front door. She unzipped the carrier, and Moppet hopped out and scampered inside. Then she turned and hugged me. "It means go have a blast in Paris."

Harper's words were kind, but they landed heavily on me. If I'm to stay friends with her, I'll either have to fess up about how I know Mo, or continue to conceal the truth. Neither option is remotely appealing. If only I had just not bothered to talk to him when I had seen him in the car—or maybe even the day I fell on him—then I would never have learned that Harper had another name and a previous life that she feels the need to paint in opaque strokes.

But the idea of never having met Mo doesn't sound so appealing, either.

"Thank you," I said. "I'll send you a postcard."

"Or better yet, text me a photo of you in front of the Eiffel Tower!" she said, kicking one leg behind her. "See you so soon."

I wasn't sure if I should just say goodbye or hug her. So I sort of leaned in and lifted my hand toward her.

And damned if she didn't flinch.

I immediately retreated. "I'm sorry. I wasn't going to hit you."

"Oh, I know that, silly," she said with false cheer.

"But you flinched like I was going to," I said.

"It's nothing. I'm tired."

"That didn't look like tired to me. Is someone hurting you?"

"No, Annie," she said, sighing. "Whatever you're thinking is going on, it isn't. We'll talk when you get back."

"Are you in danger?"

"No, no. Not at all. I swear."

She looked so earnest, and Mo was waiting for me, and—well, I didn't know what I might accomplish by pushing the issue. Anyway, wasn't I telling Mo not to jump to conclusions? I hadn't seen anyone, male or female, come or go from her house in weeks. I had absolutely no evidence that anyone was hurting her currently, and if they had in the past, she wasn't under any obligation to tell me about it.

"Okay," I said. "But if you're not okay, please call me. No matter what time it is or what you want to tell me, all right?"

She swore that she would. Then she shot me a small smile and closed the door, and I walked away.

A day later, I'm pretty sure putting her comfort over the truth of whatever happened to her was a serious mistake.

When I got back to the car, Mo asked if everything was okay. I didn't want to pretend I was fine, but neither could I bring myself to explain what had just happened. Since there was so much he couldn't tell *me* about Harper, telling him what we'd discussed seemed like a betrayal. For all I know, he has a handle on exactly what's happening with her. Maybe he's even been in contact with whoever hurt her. I doubt it, but how can I be sure?

"Sorry," I said lamely. "I can't really talk about it."

He shoved his hands into the pockets of his jeans. "Don't be sorry," he said. But then he smiled and stepped forward, and then I stepped forward and hugged him like I might not see *him* for two months. He smelled like wood smoke, and his arms felt so safe, and . . .

Well, I suppose there's no use lying to myself. Pheromones have a way of taking over rational thought, and so in spite of the fact that Mo is the exact opposite of the man I love and am engaged to, I'm attracted to him. When I return from Paris, I will have to put some checks and balances in place in order to keep that attraction from blossoming into something that might jeopardize my relationship with Jon.

"No matter what happens, I hope you have a wonderful time," he said, and it was impossible not to notice that his voice was gruff.

"I'll email you to let you know how it goes," I said.

"Please do."

I stood on the lawn and waved goodbye until his car disappeared at the end of Willow Lane. Then I went into the house where my mother was waiting.

"That's a good-looking man," she said, still staring out the window.

"He's a bit short," I said.

"He's very handsome. He's your friend, you say?" she asked, turning to me with an eyebrow raised.

"Yes, Ma. I have two of those now." I meant this as a joke, but it struck me as kind of sad—because I do miss Leesa. I'm still upset with her, but not like before. I've even begun to think that what seemed sensible behavior on my part, at least at the time, was a bit of an over-reaction. But maybe time doesn't so much heal wounds as weaken one's convictions. "Anyway, you know I'm heading to Paris to see Jon."

"I know you are, Annie. And I'm glad." She gave me an indecipherable smile. "I'm already looking forward to hearing about how it goes."

Regardless of "how it goes," I now find myself at an impasse. I don't regret having chucked my vow, but it was a mistake to open my life to two new people who I must keep separate at all times. At least I'm currently thirty thousand feet over the Atlantic. Though I'm still struggling to understand why Jon ran, I'm starting to understand the allure of leaving one's troubles behind.

—AEM

THIRTY-TWO

September 13

Two months and one day. If someone had told me that this brief period was long enough for my fiancé to morph into a stranger, I would have smiled and nodded, then mentally filed that person between Flat Earthers and Illuminati applicants.

But when Jon greeted me at the airport, I almost didn't recognize him.

It wasn't his appearance, though there was that. His hair, which he had always cropped close to his head, had grown longer and was tousled stylishly. He was wearing a pair of gray wool slacks, a crisp white shirt that was open at the collar, and a gray jacket—hardly the plaid button-down and khakis I was used to seeing him in. But something more fundamental than these trappings had changed, even if I don't know what that something is. Really, when I looked into his green eyes, which seemed brighter and clearer than I had remembered, it was like I was meeting him for the first time.

"Annie, you came! I can barely believe it," he said. My stomach did a flip when I saw that he was carrying flowers. He leaned in, then hesitated. "May I kiss you?"

"Of course," I said, though I was glad he asked—given what he's put me through, I don't want him to take anything, least of all my affection, for granted.

Then he pulled me close and kissed me. And even though we were in the middle of the Charles de Gaulle Airport, I felt like I'd finally come home.

"I've missed you so much," he said.

"I've missed you, too," I said as he pressed a bouquet of paper-wrapped mums and celosia into my hands. When I looked from the flowers back up at him, I realized Jon, who I've never seen shed a single tear, was *crying*.

A tingle went up my spine. I know some researchers believe so-called psychic happenings can be explained by science. They say the brain is more than a machine, and in fact can act as a prism by refracting and reflecting other phenomena in the atmosphere—in certain cases, shining a light on what is normally impossible to see (e.g., the future). But there isn't an explanation in all of academia that could make me feel less spooked by my own prescience. Hadn't I imagined this exact thing happening? Now it was unfolding before my eyes.

"I can't tell you how happy I am right now," said Jon, kissing me lightly again. Then he stepped back and took in the entirety of me. "You look fantastic."

"Thank you," I said, touching my hair self-consciously. I had gone to the effort of parting it the way Harper had shown me, and had even secured it with hair spray. I was wearing the gray sweater, too, and the leggings—mostly because they're as tight as compression socks, and I knew they'd reduce my risk of developing deep vein thrombosis during the flight.

"Really, you look wonderful," he said.

"So do you," I said.

"Thank you. Let's head out?"

I nodded.

People jostled me from every possible angle as I followed Jon through the throng and out to the taxi stand. How strange for such chic people to be so incredibly rude! The women looked like they'd been born with scarves around their necks, and the men appeared as fresh as they must have when they first stepped onto the planes they had just disembarked. Only the tourists—whose weary expressions and rumpled clothing made them easy to spot—seemed as ruffled as I was.

The taxi line was short, and soon Jon was at the front, speaking in rapid-fire French to the woman working the stand. Of course, I'd heard him speak French plenty of times before—but never to an actual French person. This was nothing like him humoring students or occasionally their parents, who believed their college-level courses had rendered them fluent. No, it was quite different—almost as though I were seeing a briefly caged animal let loose in its natural habitat. As I watched him, I remembered what he'd said in his email, and realized I was witnessing what he had been working toward his entire life.

And at once, any anger I'd been holding on to evaporated. How happy he looked as he greeted the taxi driver and told him where we were heading. "Where are we going?" I asked as we sped away from the airport.

"To my apartment in Montmartre." Our eyes met. "There's a second bedroom if you need some space."

I wasn't sure how to react to this. I've spent the night at Jon's countless times over the past five years. And yet some small part of me—perhaps the last shred of self-protection I have left—thought, *Yes, space is good.* "We can figure that out later," I told him.

We sped through the gritty Parisian suburbs and the equally gritty city perimeter, finally emerging into the sort of place I had imagined Paris to be. Wide, tree-lined boulevards flanked stately pastel and cream-colored buildings, and countless cafés were filled with patrons, even at eleven in the morning. I stared out the window as Jon nervously yammered on about the neighborhood he was living in—how wonderful it was, and how I was going to love it. I wondered if he was as nervous as I was.

The taxi pulled onto a narrow street, and then turned onto another and another, and at once I felt every bit as jet lagged as I was. But then we stopped abruptly in front of an apartment building on *rue des Martyrs*, which appears to be residential but also sprinkled with cafés and bakeries and grocery stores. Jon paid the driver and took my suitcase from the trunk.

Then it was just the two of us, alone among millions of people.

"This," said Jon, gesturing to the apartment building we were standing before, "is where I've been staying." It was a pale stone structure with two windowless doors painted a color somewhere between peacock and cornflower—a shade I've begun to think of as Parisian blue. Each door was as high as the entire first floor and had a large, ornate door pull in its center. Jon punched in a code on a pad on the wall and let us in to a bright, covered stone courtyard. Just past the courtyard was another door leading to a marble-floored entryway and a beautiful, winding marble staircase with a worn wood rail. "Isn't it charming?" said Jon proudly.

It was, if less so five flights later. Though Jon took my suitcase, I was huffing and puffing when he unlocked the door to his apartment on the top floor. "You'll get used to it," he said.

He was referring to the climb, but as I walked into the apartment, I thought: *No, I will never get used to this.*

Because in front of me was an entire wall of ten-foot windows overlooking the city. Beyond rooftops that extended for miles, the Eiffel Tower stood proudly in the distance, declaring that this—this was Paris.

At once, I knew why Jon had been so enchanted. And I was incredibly glad I had let down my guard and actually joined him.

Jon appeared beside me. "I thought you might understand if you came," he said quietly.

"I think I do," I said. "Or at least, I'm beginning to."

Just beneath the glass panes were window boxes planted with lavender, rosemary, and the occasional pansy. Across the courtyard were more apartments with windows much like the ones I was looking through. A few floors down, a woman sat at a small desk. Below her, a man was cooking something in his kitchen. He appeared to be singing, which made me think of Harper, and I sent a silent request to the universe for her to be okay.

"I'm sorry—" Jon began, but I held up a hand.

"Not yet," I said. "I know there's a lot we need to talk about. But I'm a bit dazed and I'd like to get my bearings first."

"Of course," he said. "Are you hungry?"

Starving, in fact. I nodded.

"Let me give you a quick tour, and then why don't we grab a bite to eat? I'll take you to my favorite bakery."

"Is it far?"

"Five flights down and across the street," he said with that boyish smile that's melted me since the first time I saw it years ago. And there I was, melting all over again. Though this may be the least Annie-like thing I've ever said, maybe one day we'll be able to look back on this time as the best thing that ever happened to us.

The apartment is larger than I was expecting, and as charming as the building itself, at least if you find a shabby-chic vibe appealing (as it turns out I do). The floors are worn wood laid in a chevron pattern, and most of the furniture appears to have been passed down through generations. There are numerous shelves jammed with the only kind of collection I approve of—books. The ceilings are vaulted, and there are skylights in the living room, the second bedroom, and the bathroom— the one with an actual bath, that is. The toilet is in a small closet-sized space, and then there's another room with a claw-foot tub and sink, which is typical of Parisian apartments, Jon said.

The kitchen is by far my favorite space in the apartment. It's small, at least by American standards, with terra-cotta tiles on the floor and similar tiles on the counter, and a ceramic farmhouse sink (it's remarkable, really, the way HGTV has bloated my vocabulary). Above the sink is another set of tall windows that look out at yet more of Paris. Pots and pans hang above the stove, and spices are stored in a rack over a small table—as there is no space to hide things, and no room for real clutter. A place for everything, and everything in its lovely French place.

After he had shown me around, we went downstairs to the bakery across the street. I had anticipated croissants, but he ordered us a pair of small quiches: one with beautiful silken mushrooms that I already know I'll never come across in ShopMore, and another with some sort of meat and bits of chard. He also bought a loaf of something that looked like the sort of gluten-free health brick that Leesa is fond of, but was in fact cocoa-flavored bread with bits of chocolate melted within. After trying it, I wondered aloud if it was possible to have a conversion experience from a single bite of food. Jon threw his head back and laughed, seemingly relaxed for the first time since my arrival. "I knew you'd like it."

"You were right," I said. We were seated at a tiny table on the sidewalk in front of the bakery, and our eyes met. I did not look away, and Jon put his hand on mine.

"Annie, it is so good to see you."

I looked at him—his perfectly sculpted nose, his strong chin, those beguiling green eyes. His was a face I have loved since nearly the moment I saw it; and in that moment, finally, it was no longer the face of a stranger. "I love you, Jon," I said quietly. "I wasn't sure about coming here, but I'm glad I did."

"I know. I'm sorry," he said.

"You don't have to keep apologizing," I said. "In fact, I'd prefer you didn't. I just needed to say that to you."

"Okay." He looked down at his coffee. "Thank you."

When we returned from our meal, I told him I wanted to lie down for a while. I do need a brief nap, and I plan on taking one shortly. But before that, I want to capture the day before I forget it.

Because Jon is right. Paris *is* wonderful. And I almost understand why he did what he did. Because if I spoke French the way he does, and had found that I fit in among the French the way he appears to, I might have been tempted to spend a few months here, too.

Except it never would have occurred to me not to bring Jon. I've always felt I thought more clearly with him—whereas the fact remains that he needed to be without me in order to clear his thoughts.

And maybe that's why, when I went to take a nap, I took the second bedroom.

—AEM

THIRTY-THREE

September 14

After my nap yesterday, Jon and I toured his neighborhood, making our way through the narrow, café-lined corridors, up one sloping street to the next, until we had reached the Sacré-Cœur Basilica. The immense church towers over the entire area, which is already the highest point in the city. We climbed the stairs to the lawn surrounding the Basilica and were rewarded with a panoramic view of Paris.

"What do you think?" asked Jon, putting his arm around my shoulders as we regarded the slate-gray roofs that comprise most of the cityscape.

"It's amazing," I said.

We had done some catching up as we walked, but we still hadn't discussed what had happened between us. "I mean about us, Annie," he said quietly.

I looked up at him. "I think I'm not ready to talk about it yet."

He frowned, and I kind of understood why. It's not like me to repeatedly defer an opportunity to find out what I'm working with so I can make a decision. And yet I just wanted to enjoy being with Jon again. I didn't want to *think* (which is nothing if not proof that too much time away from the sciences is softening my prefrontal cortex) or have the moment be ruined by some slip of the tongue on either of our parts.

We had dinner at a touristy little restaurant carved into a hill, and it was actually really fun. Over wine and one French dish after another, Jon told me about his English students and the old man who lived on the ground floor of his apartment and kept mistaking Jon for someone else; each time, the man would insist he come into his flat and fix the sink.

"You do seem different," I admitted when I was done laughing. "French, almost."

"I don't know about that," he scoffed. A lock of hair had fallen over his eye, and he pushed it away and smiled. "But so do you. Maybe that's why you're here?"

"What do you mean?" I asked.

"It's just that . . . I honestly didn't think you'd come."

"Though that would have been a waste of a perfectly good plane ticket, neither did I."

"What made you decide otherwise?"

"Let's just say a conversation with a friend helped me change my mind."

"Well, thank your friend for me. Don't take this the wrong way, but this means more to me than you can know. I almost feel like you being here is proof you really love me, even though I screwed up."

It was my turn to frown. "Since when do you need proof of my love?"

"I didn't mean it like that," he said quickly. "It's just that you're so logical, and this is the opposite of that."

"Well, love isn't logical," I pointed out, even though it was the first time that had occurred to me.

"I guess you're right about that," he said, reaching across the table for my hand. "Regardless, thank you."

"You're welcome," I said.

But when we got back to the apartment, I couldn't bring myself to join him in his bedroom. Sharing a bed seemed like a privilege he hadn't earned yet. It was more than that, though. After such a promising start to our trip, I didn't want to open the door to potential disappointment. Now that I was in Paris, I *needed* this trip to go well. "Maybe tomorrow," I said, standing in the doorway. "It's been a long day."

"Of course," he said, sitting on the edge of his bed. "I'm just glad you're here."

"Me, too," I told him.

The sunlight streaming through the skylight in my bedroom woke me this morning, and I got dressed and made coffee and read the news on my computer. I'd been up for over an hour when Jon emerged from the other bedroom. He was only wearing his boxers and a T-shirt. I must have looked surprised to see him in so little clothing, because he took one look at my face and went back to his room to put on a pair of slacks. When he reemerged fully dressed, we grinned at each other, and then he kissed me good morning, and . . . well, it was a lot like any other time I spent the night at his place, except we were in France and I hadn't woken up beside him.

After I got ready, we grabbed another loaf of chocolate bread at the bakery, which was one of the few open shops on an otherwise shuttered street, then hopped on the Metro and headed to the Louvre. I took one look at the line snaking out the museum's entrance and told Jon that *Mona Lisa* and I would have to meet in another lifetime. He just smiled. Then he guided me through the garden and over to a set of sculptures. Through these sculptures and up a small set of stairs was a door. I assumed it would be locked, but I was wrong; the next thing I knew, a security guard had checked my bag and waved us inside. After Jon had paid our entry fee, he gestured for me to follow him.

I thought perhaps we were at a side exhibit in a separate building, but we passed numerous marble and stone sculptures, and soon we were walking through a long corridor where dozens of regal-looking Italians stared at us with beady oil-painted eyes, making it clear that this was, indeed, the *real* Louvre.

"How did you know how to skip the line?" I asked Jon.

He smiled slyly, pleased with himself. Admittedly, I was, too. "Let's go see the least interesting thing here, so I can show you the ancient Egypt exhibit," he said.

So we did. The *Mona Lisa* was underwhelming, though maybe it was just that so many museumgoers trying to snap selfies with her in the frame made the painting (which was surprisingly small) difficult to see. But we quickly moved on to the rooms filled with Egyptian artifacts, which were magnificent, even if nary a statue in all of antiquity seems to have survived with its nose intact. We saw a dizzying array of impressionist paintings, and three rooms' worth of jewelry from before Christ's time. Much of it looked like something Harper would wear. How odd to think that we live in a world filled with drones and iPhones, and yet women still adorn their ears with the same gold hoops our distant ancestors found fashionable.

With so much food at every turn, I'd begun to think I'd never be hungry again. But maybe I've discounted the effect of walking everywhere, because after we emerged from the jewelry rooms, I was ravenous. Jon and I ordered lunch from the cafeteria and stood side by side at a counter facing the wall, eating our small ham-and-cheese sandwiches and drinking plastic carafes of rosé (which even *I* knew was far superior to the pink stuff I brought to Harper's).

I was still standing there, contentedly sipping my wine and thinking about how well Jon and I were getting along, when he said, "So are we ever going to talk about this?"

"I thought we did that last night. Remember? I've shown you I loved you, even if that wasn't my intention, and you apologized in your email." I was being evasive; I knew this. But I didn't want to ruin our trip.

"I really am sorry," he said again.

"I really do know that," I said. "And I forgive you."

"But what happens when we go back?" he said.

I examined the thick lip of my plastic cup. I wasn't ready to talk about what happens next. Not when I still had questions about what got us here in the first place. "What do Charles and Carolyn think about your Parisian Rumspringa?" I asked.

"They're not pleased, but they haven't cut off funds."

"They never will, lucky for you."

"Probably not," he admitted. He drained his wine, then looked at me. "They're glad I've been in touch again and that I'm taking time off of teaching. My dad sent me a bunch of e-books about entrepreneurship that he wants me to read."

Suddenly my mind was abuzz with questions, and I finally felt ready to talk. "I think I get why you didn't want to speak to them while you were away," I said, because I do—Jon wants to be close to his parents, but their impossibly high standards have always made that difficult. "But why didn't you want *me* to contact you, either? Just feeling like you didn't have the same career drive I do isn't a very good explanation."

He rubbed his forehead for a few seconds, then sighed. "I thought you'd talk me out of going if I told you before I was already on my way. And I didn't want you to do that, or try to convince me to come home before I was ready."

I could feel anger beginning to boil up from deep within me. "Which is exactly what I did."

"I don't blame you. I probably would have done the same thing if our roles were reversed."

"And yet you went anyway."

"Haven't you ever wanted something so badly you were afraid of it?"

I stared at him, unsure of what he was trying to say. "Afraid of what?"

"Of it not being what you dreamed of. Or worse, being exactly what you dreamed of. Because then what do you have to hope for?"

I was about to say no, but then I thought about MIT, which I had wanted to attend since around the time I learned I could keep going to school after the twelfth grade. I had been accepted there for undergraduate but went to Michigan instead, because I didn't want to leave my mother. And then—after years of studying and testing and preparation—just when I was ready to send in my application for graduate school, I accepted the job at SCI . . .

The realization was a slap in the face: I accepted the job because I had been afraid.

If I were accepted to MIT, I would have had to choose between school and my mother—not to mention my relationship with Jon. But if I were rejected, that would mean what I really wanted most would never be mine.

"Yes, I do know what you mean. But I still don't understand why you needed to go live your dream without me." My voice was rising, but I couldn't seem to lower it. "Surely my speaking English wouldn't *really* keep you from living out your French fantasy."

"That's not it. I felt like you'd think it was stupid. And I wanted to do this because I wanted to do it—not because it was the sensible thing to do."

"Great. Sounds like a terrific decision-making process," I said.

"I didn't say it was my process. It was a onetime thing."

"Two times," I practically spat. "Which means it may happen again. I'm half expecting that the real reason I'm here is so you can tell me you're moving to France."

He winced, then muttered, "I'm at least glad to see you angry."

"And why's that, Jon?"

"When's the last time you were angry with me and actually told me?"

"You're arguing that it's healthy?" I could tell from the way my pulse was racing and my chest hurt that it was anything but.

"Maybe."

"I couldn't disagree more."

A couple next to us, who I was pretty sure was American, was doing a poor job of pretending not to eavesdrop. But I had just finished my wine, and my sandwich was long gone. "Let's walk," I said.

We walked, but we did not discuss it any further. In fact, we spent another hour in the Louvre very much not talking. What was the point? On the one hand, Jon appeared to be deeply contrite. On the other, was that really proof that he wasn't going to pull another surprise on me? Was there even such a thing as "proof"?

By the time we hopped on the Metro, we were back to stringing a few words together to form the occasional directive. At the apartment, we decided to take naps in our separate bedrooms, which was just as well—as exhausted as I was, I don't think I could have fallen asleep beside him when we hadn't finished our conversation.

When we woke up, Jon opened a bottle of Chardonnay, which he had purchased at the grocery store down the street. For six euros, it was awfully good—at least by my low but quickly elevating standards—and we each had a glass while lounging in the living room, reading. In spite of our argument, things between us seemed . . . well, normal. I watched his eyes darting across the pages of his John le Carré novel and wondered if I would spend the night in the second bedroom again. Part of me wanted to—it seemed safer, somehow, to limit our intimacy until I believed he was to be trusted. Part of me was tempted to walk over to him and make love to him right then and there. And yet the latter impulse wasn't so strong that I acted on it.

Around eight, we went out in search of dinner and ended up at a restaurant that only served dishes that contained duck (oh, France). Over wine-glazed duck legs and tomatoes stuffed with foie gras, we talked about SCI and Todd, and Jon's colleagues, too, who all shared my concern that his leave of absence would be permanent. Though I feel like Leesa saying this, the "vibe" between us stayed light during dinner and on the walk home, too. The sky was dark when Jon unlocked the door, but we hadn't drawn the shutters before leaving. Paris twinkled at us through the windows, lighting up his face. "Annie," he said quietly.

I was trembling with anticipation as he stepped toward me and put his hands on my waist. It had been so long. What if something between us—something fundamental—had changed?

Still, I was the one to inch even closer and put my mouth on his, because I was done waiting for him to make the right move. I swear he seemed to taste different somehow—though maybe it was just dinner. But we soon found our rhythm and before I knew it, we were tugging our clothes off and making love on the floor in the middle of the living room.

It was over quickly, which I suppose is what happens when you go two months without touching the person you love. Afterward, we were both lying there panting. And I looked over at him, and though I'm still not sure why I felt compelled to ask, I said, "Was that okay?"

"Okay? It was great," he said, grinning at me. "We haven't made love like that in months, maybe even the better part of the year."

"I suppose we haven't," I admitted. I mean, we *had* been sleeping together at least once every week or two, but our lovemaking hadn't had any sense of urgency in a long time. How is it that wedding planning depletes romance rather than adding it?

Yet I can't help but think that it was not the wedding at all, but a drop in the barometric pressure of our relationship, a forewarning of the storm that was soon to hit.

I turned toward the windows, because I suddenly felt like weeping, then excused myself a moment later.

Now I'm back at my computer. While I'm not weeping, I have shed a few tears. Because I'm wondering how it is that I still feel lonely when I've just been reunited with the man with whom I plan to spend the rest of my life.

—AEM

THIRTY-FOUR

September 15
TO: Harper Brearley
FROM: Annie Mercer
SUBJECT: Bonjour!

Dear Harper,

As promised, here's a photo of *moi* in front of the *La tour Eiffel*, snapped today. As you can see from my smile—and yes, the new scarf around my neck (which I bought—doesn't it match the navy blazer you picked out perfectly?)—I'm actually enjoying myself.

Now, I did not enjoy the Eiffel Tower. It took hours to get through the line and up into the bowels of the beast, even though we were part of a so-called accelerated tour. And though I know it defies the laws of physics, I could not shake the sensation that the iron structure was swaying in the wind, and I was about to slide right off of it, along with what seemed to be thousands of my fellow tourists (none of whom understood the concept of personal space).

However, the Louvre was lovely, the Latin Quarter was steeped in literary history, and I was utterly charmed by the Jardins des Champs-Élysées. Montmartre, the neighborhood I'm staying in, is absolutely delightful, and you will not be surprised to hear that I have yet to have a bad meal—though I regret to inform you that the leggings you gifted me are now sausage casing.

Meanwhile, things with Jon are going relatively well; I'd say a 7 on a scale of 1 to 10. We've had a few tough conversations about why he left, and while I'm glad we have, his answers haven't been as satisfying as I would have liked. He claims he went a month without speaking to me because he was worried I would have talked him out of being here, which—well, even if I had, isn't he a grown man with the ability to make up his own mind?

And yet it's been wonderful to see him again. I've never thought of Jon as tense, per se, but in France, he's markedly more mellow and yet somehow more engaging than before. And since I know you're wondering, yes, we've been intimate again, and that was perfectly nice.

Most of all, it's been so good to have someone to chat with, especially in the evenings (which seem to stretch endlessly when I'm at home; my mother isn't much of a night owl, and so I'm often alone).

But . . . Harper, every time we pass a real estate office, he pauses to look at the listings. If he has a chance to have a long conversation in French, he spends the following hour grinning like he's just discovered the antidote to climate change. He claims he's ready to spend the rest of our lives showing me he'll never hurt me again. I know he truly believes that. But I can't help but wonder if he's wrong, and just hasn't realized it yet.

I hope things are going well for you in Michigan, and that you're staying safe. Give Moppet a dog treat for me, and tell him I'd be happy to take him to the dog park again when I return.

My best,
Annie

September 15
TO: Annie Mercer
FROM: Harper Brearley
SUBJECT: Re: Bonjour!

Annie, LOVED the photo—thank you so much for sending! I'm so happy you're having fun. But can we please talk about your use of the term "perfectly nice"? Sweetie, we're talking about the man you plan to spend the rest of your life with. Shouldn't you be seeing fireworks? Feeling the *joie de vivre* via his lips? I'm not saying that's not going to happen for you two, but you might want to throw yourself into it to make sure your flame didn't blow out while he was parading around Paris for the past two months. (Sorry if that's too much, except—have we met? You know I want great things for you, so I'm going to have to be a smidge blunt.)

All that said, you look amazing, and that blazer is *so* good on you, especially with the new scarf! Send more photos if you have time, or swing by and show me when you get back.

xoxox, H

p.s. I am totally, completely, 100% fine. Like I said, don't worry about me.

p.p.s. You didn't mention your "friend." ;) Does he have anything to do with why your nookie with Jon is "nice"? (You don't have to answer that. Just throwing it out there as food for thought! xo)

THIRTY-FIVE

September 16

I'm sure Harper didn't mean much of anything by her comment about Mo. Okay, maybe she did, but it doesn't have to mean anything to *me*. I know I'm ever so slightly attracted to him, but humans put far too much stock into basic physiology (which is why Mo has so many adultery cases). And while yes, I enjoy his company, it's Jon who I adore; it's Jon who I have five years of history and memories and companionship with. Really, in spite of his confession that he feels it's my own fault he couldn't warn me he was leaving or communicate with me once he arrived, the past few days reminded me of how easy it is for us to spend extended periods of time together—and I can't think of anything that bodes better for a long and content marriage.

Yesterday, we visited Le Marais, which is a beautiful neighborhood, if a bit ritzy for my taste—even in the blazer Harper chose for me, I felt underdressed. We walked for a while before dining at a small café, where I ordered yet another charcuterie plate and the most wonderful four-dollar glass of wine (I thought for sure I was misunderstanding the prices, but no—it seems that the old rumor about wine being cheaper than bottled water in France is true). After dinner, we walked and discussed what Jon might do other than teach, and how interesting it is that we both find ourselves professionally unmoored at the same point in time. While I intend to keep my cleaning business open, Jon says he doesn't know what he'll do, and I'm not sure what to tell him—as I haven't had a chance to research useful applications for a dual degree in French and teaching that don't involve, well, teaching. Still, I assured him it will all be fine, and he said that assurance alone made him feel better because I'm not in the business of making predictions that don't have a high probability of panning out.

(I really hope I'm not wrong.)

This morning we had a leisurely breakfast of café au lait and croissants, then hopped on the Metro, which deposited us not far from the Seine. The river and the public park that runs its length are really something to behold—though I'm positive my pocket would have been picked had it contained anything worth stealing. Then we crossed the vast bridge onto Île Saint-Louis. The island itself is teeming with tourists, but there's a jewel at its center: Glacier Berthillon, the famed ice cream shop. I ordered a scoop of chocolate orange (French women may not get fat, but this American fully intends to try), while Jon had black sesame, which was surprisingly delicious. Then we crossed the river again to the Île de la Cité, to take in the Notre-Dame in all its gothic glory, before wandering over to Shakespeare and Company. We spent a good hour there, and I splurged and bought a copy of Stefan Klein's *We Are All Stardust*, which I've been meaning to read, and a book on French style icons for Harper.

Then we got home, and Jon gave me a look that I know very well, and I gestured for him to follow me into his bedroom, which I've been sharing with him since the night we first made love (while keeping the second bedroom as my office and dressing room; I do like having my own space).

"When was the last time we made love in the middle of the day?" I asked as I undressed. Harper's comment was still on my mind, and though I knew she was right—I really needed to throw myself into it—my thoughts were an unstoppable stream rushing from my mind to my mouth.

"I'm not sure," he said, pulling me down on top of him on the bed.

"I think it was at least a year ago," I said.

"It doesn't matter now, does it?" he said, kissing my neck.

"I'm just wondering why we always wait until it's dark. I'm not hung up about my body, and neither are you, so—"

"Shhh," he said.

"Do not shush me! This is important," I told him.

"Is it?" he said, flipping me over onto my back.

Well, I did my damnedest to not think about what Harper had said as we got down to it. But in the end, that only made it *more* difficult to enjoy myself. I don't think Jon noticed, though. We were still tangled up in the sheets when he relocated his linguistic capability and said, "I've been thinking about SCI."

"Is that right? Because I've been trying not to."

"I think you should go scorched-earth on them. Go find a lawyer who specializes in employment law and sue the crap out of them for wrongful termination. With the emails you mentioned, you have a strong case. I remember you saying they have cameras everywhere. Well, I bet they even have video footage of what he did to you. You could probably access it with a subpoena. And after you win, you can casually mention to any reporter who interviews you that you have serious concerns about some of the additives in SCI's new product."

His eyes were gleaming, which made me laugh. It wasn't a bad plan. In fact, Todd and Bethanne probably thought I was already contemplating it.

"That said, I wouldn't put it past them to be dirty about how they fight back. You'll have to be careful," he added. Then he leaned over and kissed me. "What am I even saying? You're always careful."

"Yes, I am," I said.

But now I'm wondering if that's true. I've done an awful lot of un-Annie-like things lately—from shoving Todd to befriending the guy spying on my neighbor to going against my own resolve by hopping on a flight to be with the man who left me behind. Yet here I am: free of a predatory employer, eating my face off in Paris, and finding a new and perhaps better relationship with the man I love.

Maybe careful is overrated, and I'm just now seeing that for the first time.

—AEM

THIRTY-SIX

September 18

All through breakfast yesterday morning, Jon was wearing a goofy grin. I only had to ask once before he broke down and admitted he had planned a special day for us—a boat tour along the Seine, and a food-and-wine pairing for dinner.

With several hours to spare, we set off for the Gustave Moreau museum, which is a short walk from the apartment. Afterward, we stopped at a charming Belgian restaurant for a quick lunch of crêpes before getting on the Metro. When we emerged from the station, the sun had hidden behind an ominous cluster of clouds, and the wind chafed my cheeks. Seeing me shiver, Jon put his arm around me, and in that warm formation we began to walk down the path along the river. "It's so good to have you here, Annie," he said, and I smiled up at him, woozy from the sense of déjà vu that had just washed over me. Our setting was new, but we were back to being Annie and Jon again, and that feeling of security and love was more than enough for me.

We walked for a while before reaching the dock and boarding the boat, which had high panels to shield us from the wind. Jon ordered us two glasses of champagne from the bar and sat next to me on the bench. He lifted his flute. "To us."

See, Harper? I thought as I leaned in and kissed him. *This has nothing to do with Mo.* "To us," I said.

After the Eiffel Tower tour I wasn't expecting much, but I found myself enthralled by the picturesque riverbanks and the deep, rushing waters of the Seine. When the boat ride was over, we took a taxi back to the apartment so we could change into "something nice," per Jon's response to my inquiry as to what to wear. Thankfully, I had packed a smart black shift dress that I wore to meetings at SCI; with my red scarf draped around my neck and my new black shoes, I was almost stylish. Then it was back into a taxi and across town. The restaurant, which was in a large, ivy-covered hotel near the Champs-Élysées, was at once grand and intimate, with dim lighting, burgundy velvet chairs, and a mirrored bar that recalled a different time. Jon and I were seated at a circular table toward one side of the room. Service in France has been glacial at best, but I had barely sat down when our waiter arrived at the table with two glasses of champagne. Jon spoke with him in quiet French, and soon our meal began to appear.

We had baby greens with shaved truffles and a glass of white Burgundy; an airy cheese soufflé with a light red wine, the name of which I couldn't pronounce even if I could recall it; and then a glass of Bordeaux and an elegant spin on Jon's favorite French dish, coq au vin. Between each delight, our waiter surprised us with petite treats—a small shot glass of chilled cucumber soup, a slice of a wildly stinky yet delicious cheese, and a puff pastry adorned with some sort of tart berry I had never seen before. Dessert was a spot of muscat and a crème brûlée that put to shame every imitation that dares call itself the same.

It was the most wonderful meal of my life. But even with so much food, the wine had worked a number on me, and the room was beginning to tilt ever so slightly. I looked at Jon, who was grinning like a fool. And why wouldn't he? Not only had I come to Paris, but here we were, savoring the best the city had to offer (I shudder to think of the percentage of his trust fund that meal must have dissolved) while pleasantly discussing the merits of the French educational system. Really, the two of us were getting on as well as ever.

It was almost like he had never left me.

At once, I became quite cross. But it was the week, not the wine, that had hit me. "Jon," I said—and I'll admit, I might have been slurring just a bit—"are you planning to extend your tour de France?"

His eyes widened; this was not the direction our conversation was supposed to be heading. "My rental is only until September thirtieth," he said.

"And then you plan to come back to Michigan?" I cocked my head.

"Of course, Annie," he said, like it was a dumb question.

"But if you had the ability to stay, you would," I pressed.

"Well, yeah, but that's literally not an option. I don't have a work visa. And I know you don't want to live here."

I shook my head. "No, I don't."

He frowned. "You seem upset, but I'm not sure why. I thought we'd worked through this."

I examined the longest of my many forks. I thought we had, too, but he was right—I *was* still upset. "I guess I'm not done working through how you could go a whole month without talking to me. Weren't you worried about me?"

"A little, but I knew you were okay."

"Okay? How is checking my inbox fourteen times a day okay?"

He winced. "Your cleaning business was keeping you busy, and you were making new friends. It seemed like you were doing okay."

I stared at him.

"What?" he said, reaching up to his mouth. "Do I have something on my face?"

I kept staring, even as I tried to come up with a vaguely plausible explanation for what he had just said. "New friends," I finally whispered.

"What?"

"New friends," I repeated. "How did you know that? I haven't mentioned meeting anyone to you."

Fear flashed in Jon's eyes. Instead of answering me, he motioned for our waiter, who quickly appeared. Jon said something to him, handed him a credit card, and then looked at me again.

"You were looking at my computer," I said. My cheeks were on fire, and not just with embarrassment; I was angry. If Jon had read what I had written, it meant he had stolen access to a part of my life that I never intended to share with him.

"No," he said quickly. "It's not that at all. I'll explain everything after we leave."

"Are you afraid I'll make a scene?" I asked, loudly enough that I was already doing so. "Ruin our dinner and our wonderful week by requesting you tell me the ugly truth?"

He leaned back in his chair, seemingly resigned to the inevitable, whatever that was. "Fine. I hired him."

"Hired who?" I said, because I didn't understand what I was hearing. Or maybe I just didn't want to.

"Mo," said Jon. His expression was half grimace, half frown. "I hired him to investigate you because I wanted to make sure you were okay."

"You're confused," I said, shaking my head. "Mo was spying on Harper."

"No, he wasn't. Maybe he looked up information on her after I told him you had a new neighbor, but she wasn't his, uh, target. You shouldn't be mad at him, though, Annie. The minute the two of you became friends, he contacted me and told me he couldn't keep working for me."

And when was that? When I got in the car with him? The first time he asked me to go on a job with him? "At what point did that happen?" I asked.

"After you saw him outside of your neighbor's house. I asked him if he could at least let me know if anything really bad happened, but he said he couldn't. He wouldn't even let me pay him—it was against his policy."

This should have come as a relief to me. But it wasn't. Because Mo had listened to me spill my guts about Jon and never said a word.

I held up my hand. "I'd prefer not to hear any more."

"Fine. But needless to say—"

"Anything needless to say does not need to be said!"

Now our fellow diners were certainly looking at us. Ah, *les Americans.* So thoughtless; so loud.

So careless with matters of the heart.

On the taxi ride home, Jon made a few more attempts to apologize. I vaguely recall some other mumbled sentiments about wanting to do the right thing and having his plans backfire, but that stretch of time, as well as my hasty retreat to the second bedroom when we got home, is a blur.

I do recall that I'd been in bed, covers pulled up to my chin, for almost an hour when he knocked on my door and asked if he could come in. I must have said yes, because he let himself in and sat on the end of the bed. He had changed into a gold-and-black Mizzou T-shirt and a pair of sweatpants, which was every bit as startling as seeing him dressed up at the airport.

He looked at me for a long time before speaking. "I'm sorry I told you that. I never meant to, and I didn't mean to ruin your friendship, either."

I shook my head. "I knew something was amiss, but I ignored my instincts. Anyway, Mo's just someone I hung out with a few times."

Jon gave me a funny look. "Most people refer to that kind of person as a friend."

"I guess it doesn't matter either way now." Through the window, the moon was low and full. "You know what bothers me the most, Jon?" I said.

Instead of answering, he waited for me to continue.

"Why would you go to the trouble of *hiring* someone to check on me instead of just picking up the damn phone and calling me to ask yourself? Or even just sending me an email? Or was this all just a way to clear your conscience without having the woman you claim you want to spend the rest of your life with muddying up your thoughts?"

"It was a mistake."

"You've been making a lot of those lately."

"Ouch. I'm not perfect, Annie. I told you—I was in a bad place. I'm doing better now."

I sighed. "Because you're in France. What's going to happen when you come home? What happens the next time you need to clear your head?"

He reached forward and put his hand on my leg, which was under the duvet. "Don't you love me, Annie? Isn't that enough?"

"Yes," I said. "I do. But I also love plans. I love certainty. I love knowing that if I say, *I do* to spending the rest of my life with you, you won't let me down."

He let go of my leg. "I'm not going to leave you, Annie. I'm sorry I wasn't thinking about how this would dredge up what happened with your father. You never talk about it. I should have made the connection between you living with your mother so long and your fear of being left."

"Pardon me?" I said sharply. "I do not have a fear of being left. Otherwise I would have freaked out on you when you called me on your way to the airport. As you'll recall, I gave you permission to go. And once you wrote to say you were staying, I did *not* cancel our wedding, even though a wiser woman might have. You're not the only one who hasn't been thinking straight over the past few months." I sighed, suddenly as tired as I'd ever been. "I think I need to be alone for a while," I told him.

Even in the moonlight, I could tell he was pained. "Okay. I understand. But, Annie, please don't leave because of this."

"I'm not in the habit of taking off when the going gets tough," I said pointedly.

He hung his head. "You're right. I hope we can talk about this in the morning."

"I'm sure we will," I said. "Goodnight."

"Goodnight."

As exhausted as I was, I had a feeling I would not be sleeping anytime soon. After Jon had gone, I rose and went to the window. I put my forehead to the cool glass and let my tears spill onto the sill.

Maybe my mother was right—maybe Paris does change you. Because if I'd learned about Mo even a week or two ago, I probably would have considered decamping to a one-woman island with only a volleyball to call my friend. I would have sworn off new people yet again—and perhaps not so new ones, too.

But as I stared at the Eiffel Tower glittering in the night sky, I suddenly understood that what had gotten me here wasn't going to get me where I need to go next. Though what Mo had done stung so much that I'm not sure I can resume our friendship when I return, I could not deny that the past two months would have been far worse if I really had gone through them alone. The price of self-protection may, in fact, be higher than the cost of vulnerability.

In spite of everything, I'm not actually angry with Jon. He's an idiot, but he's an idiot whose heart was in the right place. I wasn't ready to slip beneath the covers beside him just yet, though. I considered reaching out to Leesa, but she and I needed to have a face-to-face conversation—and perhaps come to a mutual understanding as to which topics are off-limits, including but not limited to which life-changing crystals I should invest in—before I spill everything to her.

But there was one person I could still turn to. And so I picked up my phone and texted Harper.

—AEM

THIRTY-SEVEN

September 18

10:59 p.m. Harper—I'm so sorry to bother you, but I need help. Are you around?

5:00 p.m. Annie, hi! Of course! I'm curating my Insta feed (read: deleting so-so pictures of me) and don't have to leave for spin class for another half an hour

11:01 p.m. Oh, good. Thank you. So, there's no easy way to say this.

5:01 p.m. Ah, the "I'm typing" dots of doom! Spit it out, I'm dying over here!

11:03 p.m. The thing is, I lied to you.

5:04 p.m. Oh no—you hate the leggings, don't you?

11:04 p.m. Ha! I wish that's what it was (and no, for the record, they're actually pretty great). But . . . you know Mo?

5:05 p.m. Obvs

11:07 p.m. Turns out he's been spying on me. He's a private investigator, which I knew. What I didn't know is that Jon hired him because he was worried about me.

5:08 p.m. Ew? But kind of sweet?

11:09 p.m. Pretty sure that's just ew. But that's not the worst part. Mo apparently fired Jon once he and I became friends, but he never told me the truth. Jon wasn't going to, either. He slipped up at dinner tonight and I figured it out.

5:09 p.m. Right—and now you feel totally betrayed, because now both the men you care for did something hurtful

11:10 p.m. Wow. I guess I wasn't thinking about it like that, but . . . yes. I feel pretty terrible.

5:11 p.m. I'm so sorry. I would, too. But don't feel bad for not telling me. That's yours to share if and when you want!

11:12 p.m. No, that's not even it. The thing is, Harper, Mo told me he was investigating *you*.

5:12 p.m. WEIRD. Was he?

11:14 p.m. No—he lied to me. But he looked up things about you after Jon told him I had a new neighbor.

5:16 p.m. Let me guess . . . he told you my old name

11:16 p.m. Yes.

5:18 p.m. What else?

11:19 p.m. Well, he knew the guy who came to visit you was your brother.

5:19 p.m. David?

11:20 p.m. Yes.

5:21 p.m. That was *not* David. He won't get on a plane and he's definitely not going to drive from Fresno to Michigan. I'll explain it to you later

11:22 p.m. Oh. Okay. But listen—I'm so, so sorry I didn't tell you the truth right away. I didn't expect us to become friends.

5:22 p.m. Girl, that makes two of us!

11:23 p.m. I know. I don't blame you if you don't want anything to do with me. I should have told you as soon as we started hanging out, but I didn't want to hurt you. Then it just got so messy. I'm really sorry.

5:23 p.m. Oh Annie. For such a smart person, sometimes I wonder about you. You made a mistake. You just apologized. I forgive you. We have a lot to talk about, obvs, but we'll do that when you come back

11:24 p.m. Wow. Thank you x ∞

5:24 p.m. I've never seen that emoji before!

11:24 p.m. It's an infinity symbol. :D

5:25 p.m. How are things with Jon, anyway?

11:25 p.m. They were going great until the accidental reveal tonight. I feel like we'll work past it . . . maybe? I don't know anymore.

5:25 p.m. Well, we can definitely talk through it when you get back

11:27 p.m. Thank you.

5:27 p.m. You are so welcome. Listen, I have to run but I'll be back in two hours if you need me. Did you read the Nutter Gazette (i.e. neighborhood Listserv) yesterday?

11:29 p.m. I haven't checked it this week—why?

5:30 p.m. Your client? Viola?

11:32 p.m. What about her??

5:33 p.m. She's in the hospital—sounds like she's not doing well

5:34 p.m. Annie? Are you still there?

11:33 p.m. I'm sorry—I dropped my phone. This is terrible. Thank you for telling me.

5:34 p.m. You're welcome x ∞. Keep me posted and see you soon? xo

THIRTY-EIGHT

September 17
TO: Annie Mercer
FROM: Oak Grove Neighborhood Association
SUBJECT: Abridged summary of OakGroveMI-NeighborhoodAssociation@googlegroups.com—8 updates in 2 topics

Today's Topic Summary
View all topics

- Ambulance on Willow Lane—6 Updates
- UNSUBSCRIBE ME NOW—2 Updates

Ambulance on Willow Lane
LarryNBessRogers@yahoo.com 8:43 a.m.
Friends,

I don't mean to be nosy but I was very concerned to see an ambulance in the middle of Willow Lane last night around 9 p.m. Does anyone know what happened?

Smiles,
Bess

thadskipperjohnson3@gmail.com 8:59 a.m.
Bess and all,

The ambulance was at Viola Moore's house. I spoke with a paramedic who said he couldn't disclose her medical status but said it was "serious" and that she would be taken to Beaumont Hospital. Does anyone have contact information for her family members?

-Skipper

LarryNBessRogers@yahoo.com 10:43 a.m.
Thank you for the update, Skipper.

Friends, I've just been to Beaumont. Viola is in the ICU, so I wasn't permitted to see her. I reached out to her sister, who is in London, but I haven't heard back yet. I'll let you know when I hear more.

Smiles,
Bess

jossjossjoss82@gmail.com 1:48 p.m.
I'm very sorry to hear about our neighbor, but is it possible to opt out of this thread? My great-grandmother died in an ambulance on the way to

the hospital and I'm finding these messages quite triggering.

Cheers,
Joss

NFlynn782@gmail.com 1:50 p.m.
Joss,

No, you cannot "opt out" of a thread on email. You are welcome to opt out of this Listserv, however, at any time.

Regards,
Nathan Flynn
442 Oak Grove Lane

LarryNBessRogers@yahoo.com 6:00 p.m.
Friends,

An update: I just got off the phone with Leticia Bachman, Viola Moore's sister. Viola took a serious fall after she suffered a stroke and is currently unconscious. Please keep this information close to your vest, and keep Viola and her family in your thoughts and prayers during this difficult time.

Bess

UNSUBSCRIBE ME NOW
DieHardTigersFan4EVR@gmail.com 2:01 p.m.

It turns out the tenth circle of hell is an endless email chain that I can't leave, no matter how many times I mark it as spam. —Mike, who hasn't lived in East Haven in almost A FULL YEAR and still gets these ridiculous updates from people who would rather tell other people what to do with their dog crap or complain about "unsuitable" (*cough*, not white) music—I'm looking at you, Margie—than be productive members of society.

MargieSueLinden@aol.com 9:45 p.m.
Sheesh, Mike. If you wanted to leave the Listserv, why didn't you just say so? I'll unsubscribe you now.

Namaste,
Margie
PS I resent your comment. Some of my best friends are black.

THIRTY-NINE

September 19

Jon was looking at me like I'd called off our wedding. "You're really going to go? Just like that?"

A minute earlier, I'd rushed out of the bedroom, told him what I'd read on the Listserv, and explained that I needed to get back to the US to see Viola immediately. The ticket-change fee would be a small fortune, but I would willingly pay it. Strokes could be deadly for anyone, but especially for an eighty-two-year-old woman. I had to see Viola before it was too late.

"I really do," I told him. "It's only two days earlier than I planned to fly home. She might die."

"Anyone could die at any point," he said, not unkindly. Still, I could tell by his befuddled expression that he felt I was overreacting.

"Exactly," I said. "Viola is like a mother to me. You know that."

He was pacing the length of the living room. "You're sure this isn't about what happened tonight?" he said, referring to our fight at the restaurant.

"I swear it," I told him. "That doesn't mean I'm over it yet. But this is a hundred percent about her having a stroke."

He rubbed his eyes and sighed. "Okay," he said. "But if you're going, I'm coming with you."

"No," I said quickly. "Absolutely not. I can do this by myself. You only have a little more time in France."

He frowned. He genuinely wanted to go with me—but was it out of concern, or because he wanted to make sure I knew he was serious about his renewed commitment to our relationship? Either way, I didn't want to be the reason he left early. "You need to say goodbye to Paris, don't you?" I added.

"Don't *you?*"

"It's not the same. I think we both know that, and it's okay," I said gently.

"Annie," he said, putting his arms around me. He kissed the top of my head. "Why are you so good to me?"

"Because I love you."

"I love you, too. When will you go?"

"As soon as Air France can get me on a flight. I'm going to call now."

He buried his face in my hair and sighed. "I'm going to miss you so much."

I had to resist the urge to pull away and look up at him. I'm sure he was just talking about the twelve days before he flew home. But a tiny part of me wondered if he meant something far longer. What will it take for me to get over that fear? Months of being shown that he means it? Years? Some other act of commitment that I have yet to identify?

There was a seat on the 6:00 a.m. flight, which meant I'd need to head to the airport well before dawn. Jon made me a cup of coffee and helped me pack, then called me a cab. After I swore for the seventh time that I was really okay to get to the airport without him, he kissed me tenderly and made me promise to call him the minute I touched down.

Oh, how things have changed.

Hours later, I'm midflight over the Atlantic, praying that Viola isn't teetering on the precipice of existence, as I fear—I called my mother but she didn't pick up, and I'm still waiting to hear back from Bess so I can get Viola's sister's contact information.

And now I am alone with my computer, my thoughts, and my seatmate, who's peeking at my laptop to figure out what's making me cringe. (Dear stranger, the answer is my life.) As heavily as Viola weighs on my mind, I keep returning to the events of last night.

Part of me is touched that Jon went so far as to hire a private investigator to check on me. The other part of me wants to donate my living body to science to see if some enterprising yet ethically compromised researcher might wipe my memory so I can unlearn what I now know. I hate the idea that Mo was investigating me, because it changes everything about the time we spent together. I think he's great. Or at least I did. But do I really want someone who lies—or at the very least, conceals the truth with such ease—in my life?

I'm not sure that I do.

And yet didn't I do something very similar to Harper? She took the news in stride and readily accepted my apology. In my experience, that level of benevolence and insight doesn't come naturally to most people (e.g., me). It makes me wonder yet again what Harper has lived through to act with such grace when it certainly isn't warranted, and if she'll ever share that with me.

But for now, I must try to get some rest. I have a long day ahead of me.

—AEM

FORTY

September 20

I don't know why people love to repeat the old aphorism about death and taxes. As many a Swiss banking client can attest, taxes can be avoided with the right loophole or three. The only true inevitability is that at some point, our cosmic ride must come to an end.

Knowing that as I do, it should be easier to accept that one day every person I have ever cared about will cease to exist, as will I. But when I walked into Viola's hospital room and saw her lying there, so small beneath the thin cotton blanket that she could have been a child, logic did little to soothe me. I did not need a medical degree to know that even if Viola made it out of that stale room, her days were numbered.

She was sleeping; an oxygen mask was over her face, and her arm was tethered by an IV. I sat on one side of the bed and carefully took one of her hands in mine. I was exhausted, and probably should have driven directly home from the airport. Jet lag and fatigue and all that had transpired over the past several months seemed to fall upon me at once, and so I let myself cry quietly a little. Then I wiped my eyes and watched Viola's chest heave in an alarmingly irregular pattern, and then I cried some more.

I'd been there awhile—long enough to run out of tears—when Viola awoke. Her eyes darted this way and that with confusion before settling on me. She let go of my hand and pulled off her oxygen mask. One side of her beautiful face was drooping, and I realized that the arm she had not used was lifeless beside her. "Annie." Her words were slurred. "You're home early."

I tried to smile. "Paris isn't nearly as important as you."

"You sweet girl. Did you enjoy it?"

"It was wonderful. I can't believe I ever questioned going."

"So glad. And Jon?"

"He's still figuring some things out, like what he wants to do with his career. That's going to be a process, especially since his parents are continuing to push him into finance. But the two of us . . ." I thought about our lingering kiss before I got in the car. "I still love him, and I know he loves me. I think we're on the same page now?"

In the background, machines beeped and whirled. "But?" she pressed.

Now I didn't have to force a smile. "You know me so well."

She patted my hand, waiting for me to respond. It took me nearly a minute to find the words. "It's just that it didn't seem real, in a way," I finally said. "He's a different person in Paris—almost like a better version of himself. He's got more energy, and he's at ease in his own skin. He seems . . ." I blinked back new tears. "He seems at home there. I know he can't just pick up and move to France, but I could see it happening at some point, and that scares me. As much as I liked Paris, I certainly don't want to *live* there. And if we don't want the same life, then how can we be together?" I shook my head. "In a way, I don't know any more than I did before I left."

"Maybe you do. Now . . ." She said something more, but I couldn't understand her.

"Oh Viola," I said, taking her hand again. "I'm so sorry this has happened to you."

She squeezed my fingers. "S'okay. I'm ready."

"Please don't say that," I told her.

A smile formed on half of her mouth. "Dear girl, I'm not afraid. I'm going to see Ned. And my mother, and my daughter."

I've known Viola all my life and had never heard her mention having had a child.

"Lost her at birth," she said, answering my unasked question. "My one and only."

Here came another tear, and another. Her having a child wasn't why she had been so caring and good to me all these years; that's simply the person she is. And yet it hurt my heart to know she hadn't had the opportunity to raise her daughter, and that her daughter had not had a chance to know the wonderful, caring soul that was her mother. "I'm so sorry," I said, wiping my face with a tissue.

"It's okay. When I close my eyes one last time, I'm counting on us all being together again." Each word was slow and labored, but she continued. "It's the only way I know how to keep on living without the people I can't live without."

Now I was really crying, because I wished I believed that, too. As much as I tried not to think about my father being gone, I can't always avoid it. Granted, I gave up on the idea of having a healthy relationship with him a long time ago—mostly. A small part of me, however, had always wondered if instead of sending cards or calling, he would actually show up and see the woman I'd become. Maybe then he'd want to be a part of my life, after all.

And his death had taken that hope from me forever.

Maybe Jon wasn't wrong about my fear of being left behind. I've worked so hard to toughen my self-protective shell. But as I recently learned, the truth has a way of finding its way into the light. No matter how much I tried to act as though I was okay with him taking off without me, I never really was.

But that vulnerability wasn't something to be ashamed of. I realize that now. Admitting it hurts doesn't make it any worse; in fact, given the frank conversations Jon and I had when I was in Paris, I think it might actually make it better.

Regardless, I had to get through it either way—and I did. In fact, I daresay I grew more than I would have if he'd never left. Not that I want him to pull the same thing again. But even if he does, I'll get through that, too.

Maybe that's what Viola meant when she said that maybe I did know more than I had before the trip.

She was wheezing, and she pulled her mask back on for a moment before removing it and speaking again. "Tell me more about your trip."

She fell asleep before I had even gotten to the Eiffel Tower. I was growing increasingly woozy myself, and so I left shortly after that with a whispered promise to return as soon as possible.

On the drive back to my mother's house, I thought more about my father, and the grief I'd been pushing down all this time. I told myself I was being strong for my mother, and I had to keep being strong and caring for her. Wasn't that why I'd ended up living with her for two years?

But when I pulled into the driveway and saw her standing in the doorway waiting for me, I began to cry, because I finally understood why I had made that choice. After my father's death, my mother's initial grief was like a riptide, and it had nearly drowned her. She had managed to resurface, though. She would probably always struggle with depression. It was unlikely she'd ever be a good housekeeper. Yet it wasn't her I was worried about when I chose to stay on as long as I had.

It was me.

After losing one parent, as lousy as he was, I was terrified to lose the one who had stayed and had done her best.

I dropped my bags and wrapped my arms around her.

"Oh Annie," she said, hugging me. "Did you not have a nice time?"

"It was terrific." I wiped my eyes on my sleeve, even though I was probably transmitting some antibiotic-resistant superbug I'd picked up at the hospital. "I'm just happy to see you."

"I'm happy to see you, too." She held me at arm's length. I thought she was going to ask about Jon, but instead she said, "I bet you're hungry."

"Like you wouldn't believe."

"Good. I made a frittata."

"You made a what?" I said, setting my bag on the ground and following her into the kitchen. Something was different. Actually, a lot of things were different. The waffle maker and George Foreman Grill remained untouched on the counter, but I couldn't spot a single clipped coupon or discarded food wrapper. There were crumbs on the floor, but unless my eyes were playing tricks on me, the top of the fridge had been completely decluttered. The only thing on the stove was a cast-iron skillet with a fresh frittata in it.

"Did we get robbed?" I said.

"Ha ha. I wanted to straighten up before you got home."

"I—I don't know what to say."

She reached for a plate in the cupboard. I was almost relieved to see that there were still pill bottles and random items shoved in among the dishes. My mother must have noticed me looking, because she said, "I've still got a lot of work cut out for me. But I figured I'd make a good effort. You're leaving soon, after all."

"You didn't even ask how things went with Jon," I said.

"I figured you'd tell me when you were good and ready. But either way, you're not going to stay on here forever, are you?" She smiled. "I know your job situation isn't all that great, but you're the smartest girl I know. You'll figure something out soon, and I bet it won't involve a vacuum."

She put a piece of frittata on a plate, which she handed to me. Then she poured me a glass of water and sat across from me at the kitchen table. "Now, how's Viola?"

I told her about my visit, and what the nurse had told me. If all went well, Viola would be out of the hospital after a few more days of testing, but then she would go to rehab. Then she would need to seek out an assisted-living facility. It went unsaid, but it sounded as though she would never be going home again.

"That must have been hard for you," said my mother. "I know the two of you have been so close. I owe Viola a lot for the way she looked after you when you were young."

"That makes two of us," I said with a sad smile. Then I looked at her. It occurred to me that she was wearing mascara, and possibly blush, too, and her hair was pinned back neatly. "You look nice, Ma."

"I'm going to prayer circle with Betty this afternoon."

I smiled at her. "That's great. I bet you'll really like that."

"I bet I will, too."

"Just be careful, or soon you'll be going to Mass three times a weekend."

"Wouldn't that be something. I know you've been worried, but I'm doing much better, moodwise."

"I know, Ma. The wedding really seemed to get you excited."

She shook her head. "I'm happy for you, but it's not just that. I don't think it's just that medication, either," she said, referring to the new antidepressant she'd started taking a few months earlier. "I just think I finally turned a corner. I feel at peace about your father. Do you, Annie?"

I looked down at my plate. "I think I'm only beginning to deal with it now. But at least it's a start, right?"

"That's all you need," she said, nodding.

"Ma, don't take this the wrong way, but I think you didn't need me living here all this time."

She gave me a wry smile. "That never occurred to me."

"The thing is, I feel like maybe I was afraid to lose you, after what happened to Dad." I blinked hard—just *calling* him that had a powerful impact on me.

My mother, too, looked to be on the verge of tears. She stood and walked around the table to hug me. "I'm not going anywhere, Annie," she whispered. "Of all the things you worry about, don't let that be one of them. I know only God can say when it's my time. But I think I have some good years ahead of me."

"I hope so," I said.

"I've loved having you. You're great company, Annie, and a wonderful help to me in all kinds of ways—and I'm not just talking about housekeeping," she said. "You're always welcome here. But I want you to feel free to go off and live your own life."

"Because life is to be lived," I agreed, recalling what Viola had said to me.

And I believe that. But after years of focusing on what I *thought* I needed to focus on, now I have to figure out what I really want.

—AEM

FORTY-ONE

September 20
TO: Annie Mercer
FROM: Mo Beydoun
SUBJECT: Please read

Dear Annie,

Jon emailed yesterday and told me you know that I was really investigating you. I'm so, so sorry. I had a feeling you'd find out while you were in Paris—but on the off chance that you wouldn't, I didn't want to wreck your trip or influence your decision about whether to get back together with Jon by telling you myself first. This might sound weird, but he was trying to do the right thing by hiring me. All he wanted to know was if you were okay, which is the only reason I took the job in the first place. He's a good guy, Annie, and even good guys sometimes make the wrong choice for the right reason.

Obviously, I should have fessed up that day you got in my car in front of Margie's house—or at least not have asked you to go to dinner with me, even if I *had* already decided to fire Jon as a client. Instead, I doubled down on my stupid lie about investigating Harper. I broke all of my own rules, so I won't try to make excuses for what I did. There isn't one.

Annie, I love spending time with you. For someone who claims to look on the dark side of things, you make my life a whole lot brighter. It was selfish of me not to tell you why I was really poking around your backyard. But I was having such a great time with you that I kept telling myself that it was okay to wait to ruin everything. Now I realize I already ruined everything the minute I lied to you. But I'm still glad I got a chance to know you—I just wish I hadn't caused you pain.

I don't blame you if you don't want to see me again. If I were you I wouldn't want to, either. But I'll miss you. I hope everything that comes your way is better than what has gone.

Mo

FORTY-TWO

September 22

One of the many things I miss about lab work is the all-consuming nature of it. When I was doing volumetric analysis or assays, there really was no opportunity to think about much of anything—even Todd's latest ridiculousness—besides the task at hand. When I went to work this morning, I was reminded that cleaning just can't hold a candle to that. Bess and Larry Rogers' house had morphed into an enormous hair ball (their words, not mine) while I was away, so when they asked me to put in a few hours this weekend, of course I said yes. But as I scoured and scrubbed the singular grime that is dead skin cells and soap from their tub while Puma Thurman meowed at me from the bathroom sink, all I could think about was Mo's email.

Make life brighter! I thought, rubbing borax into the porcelain. In nearly thirty years of life, I cannot recall anyone—not my mother, not Leesa, not even Jon—telling me I make life brighter. I may shine a spotlight on things, but they're usually the things most people prefer not to see.

I should forgive him. I know that. But who am I even *forgiving*? As far as I know, the man Mo presented himself as was a construct. Every time I think about the conversations we had about Harper, and even the ones we had about Jon, my chest tightens and my cheeks become so inflamed that I look like a "before" ad for eczema cream.

Mostly, I just wish I didn't miss him.

The hours were slow, but I managed to get through them with the help of the Rogers' cats, who I've become quite fond of (between them and Moppet, I don't know what's come over me!). I was hauling my bucket of cleaning supplies home when I saw Harper waving to me from her front door. She was barefoot and in jeans—not the kind with artfully deliberate holes in the knees, just a regular dark-wash pair, and a plain gray sweatshirt. Her hair was neither curled stylishly nor flat ironed into submission. Instead, it hung around her bare face. Without her usual makeup and accoutrements, she could have passed for a high school student—in fact, at first I mistook her for a stranger, perhaps a younger cousin who had come to visit.

"So sorry I missed you yesterday. I saw your note, but when I went to your house, your mom said you were at the hospital," she said when I got to her door.

"No worries," I said, setting my stuff on her porch. "I was just checking on Viola."

"How is she?"

"Hanging in there. She's got a long road ahead of her." She's still slurring—she may always, the doctor said—but she hasn't had another stroke, and she's regained a little movement in a few of her right fingers. "I have a present for you," I told Harper, because I hadn't wanted to leave the book in her mailbox when I'd stopped by yesterday. "I'll have to run home and get it, though."

"The present can wait—I want to hear about your trip! Can you come in for a few?"

I could. In fact, I had more than half a day to fill, and aside from calling Jon back, few ideas as to how to fill it. I left my things on the porch and followed her into the kitchen.

"Sooo," she said, perching on one of the island stools, "tell me everything."

I leaned on the counter. "Where to even start? You know about the Mo situation. I'm really sorry—"

"No more apologizing!" she interjected. "I forgive you."

"Thank you," I said, looking down at my hands; my fingers were still a bit pruned from cleaning. "I don't know how you managed to be that gracious about it, but it means a lot to me."

"What can I say? I like being friends with you. I didn't think there would be anything good for me in this weird town, but I was wrong. What else did he tell you about me, anyway?" Her eyes were the size of saucers—I forgot the colossal amount of dopamine released at the mere suggestion of a secret.

"He didn't tell me much other than your name, and that the guy who came to visit was your brother—although you said that wasn't right."

"Yeah, I can see why Mo might have thought that. They sort of look alike, and I think they're about the same height. But David wouldn't be caught dead in a suit. He wears ratty T-shirts and shorts year-round. I don't know if he even owns a pair of pants."

"I thought your family was wealthy?"

She laughed. "Middle class at best."

"Then how did you buy an entire house at twenty-three? Did your ex buy it for you?"

She glanced out the window. The temperature had dropped while I was in Paris, and though another heat surge has been predicted, she'd already covered the pool.

"Harper," I said gently. "Is Wells hurting you?"

"It's not like that," she said quickly.

"So why do you flinch if someone puts their hand near your face? And who gave you the black eye?"

"It was an accident," she said.

"That's an awfully big accident."

After a few moments, she sighed and met my gaze again. "Does Northridge High School mean anything to you?"

I frowned.

"Northridge High," she repeated. "Maybe you haven't heard of it. There have been so many since then."

"So many what?"

"School shootings."

Suddenly I could barely breathe, because I knew exactly what she was talking about. At the time it was the largest mass school shooting in American history. But there had been so many similar incidents in the following years that it had probably faded in most people's memories. Including, apparently, mine.

"You were there," I said.

She nodded.

"And Wells was, too?"

"Yes. Wells' name used to be Joseph Michael Wells. Now he's Wells Michaels—we both legally changed our names. We grew up together and went to the same school, but he's a few years older than me."

"When you said he saved your life, you meant it," I said.

"He helped me and three other students hide in the walk-in freezer in the kitchen." When she shivered, I had a feeling it wasn't just from the memory of being cold. "He was going back for more people when he was shot in the back and left to die. But somehow he survived, and we've been together ever since. My parents were against it from the very beginning—they said he was too old for me, and they wanted me to move on from that part of my life. And now . . ."

"Now he hurts you sometimes."

"Only twice," she said firmly. "Both times he had just woken up from a bad dream. I've been telling him to get treatment for more than a year, but after the second time it happened . . . I didn't even have to ask him. We both knew he needed help."

"Treatment?"

"Wells has PTSD." Her tone was suddenly matter-of-fact. "He's at an inpatient facility in New Jersey that specializes in it. His therapist told me that ninety percent of people who live through trauma come out just fine. Or at least, as fine as a person can. But a small number . . ." Her shoulders slumped. "They get PTSD. And some of those people end up like Wells. Fine most of the time."

"But sometimes not," I said.

She nodded sadly.

"I'm so sorry," I told her. "It sounds like an impossible situation. I still don't get why you changed your names, though."

Now she lifted her chin proudly. "More reasons than you might imagine—but mostly we wanted a clean slate. We were tired of being known as 'those kids from Northridge.'"

"How did people know that?"

"There was a settlement. Did you know that there's a lawyer who does this for a living? It's the same guy who decided how much 9/11 victims and their families would get during the government payout. He does school shootings, too. We all got something. Several hundred thousand if you lived—a little more if you were in direct contact with the shooter, a little less if you weren't. If you died, your family got over a million. Like it even matters at that point."

"That's how you bought this house at twenty-three."

She laughed bitterly. "*I* didn't buy anything. My parents did."

"Wait, the money is theirs?"

"No, it's in a trust until I turn twenty-five. Until then, they can do what they think is best. And they thought getting me as far away as possible from Wells was best."

"And you said he agreed."

"We want to spend the rest of our lives together. He wants to make sure he's okay before we do that."

"That sounds wise to me. Why East Haven, though?"

She looked around at the kitchen. "Did you know Bob and Linda when they lived here?"

"Not well, but yes."

"Bob's my great-uncle on my mother's side. My parents thought it would be good for me to be somewhere 'calm' and 'normal,'" she said, making air quotes. "They hated that I liked to wear nice clothes and travel and have experiences that they never even considered—I think they thought it made me even more of a target or something. Michigan was the last place I wanted to be—no offense—but I'd just graduated, and I had two years before I finally could make my own choices. Anyway, I didn't want to be anywhere near New York. Everyone at college made a big deal out of me attending there; they held me as this example of resilience. Resilience my butt." She laughed bitterly. "For four whole years, people acted like I was made of glass. The only time I was free was when I pretended to be someone else. When I graduated in May, Wells and I sat down and had a big talk. And we decided to do what that madman tried to do eight years ago."

"I don't follow."

"We got rid of Joe and Ashley and became Wells and Harper. Life is too short to be living the story someone else has told about you."

I nodded, thinking of Jon. Even though he didn't go into finance like his father expected him to, that expectation had continued to hang over his head. He may have decided to become a French teacher, but Paris had been where he accepted that he had other dreams.

"We decided we were going to start over the way we wanted to, but he argued that I should follow my parents' plan so I didn't lose my trust. We fought about it, but finally Wells realized it was a good chance for me to settle into my new life as Harper. Everything was going great, but when he came here, he freaked out."

"Is that when he hurt you?"

"Yes. We were sleeping, and he woke up from a terrible dream and—I don't know, maybe the new environment spooked him, but he accidentally hit me." She started to cry, and I walked over and hugged her.

"I'm so sorry, Harper."

"Me, too," she sniffed. "He was really doing great for a long time. It had been more than six months since the last incident."

I started running the numbers in my head. "Wait . . . it's been eight years since the shooting, right?"

She nodded.

"So why is he having so much trouble after all this time? Or has he been struggling all along?"

"Eight years isn't that long. I mean, I close my eyes and I'm right there again. But about a year and a half ago, Wells was at a concert and a couple guys got into a fight. One of them shot the other in the middle of the concert hall and something in him just snapped."

"Oh, my gosh. How terrible."

"I know. As if he hasn't already been through enough." She bit her lip. After a minute, she said, "I'll be twenty-five in less than two years. That's when we're going to buy a house together and really start over."

"Harper," I said, maybe a little sharper than I would have liked. I softened my tone. "Hopefully Wells will be better then. But what happens if he's not? What if he keeps hurting you?"

When she frowned at me, I could imagine exactly what she looked like as a little girl—back before she had come face-to-face with the ugliest side of existence. "You don't just give up on someone you love."

"Still. If you're not safe, then nothing else matters."

"Well, Annie," she said, wiping her eyes with the sleeve of her sweatshirt, "I guess we're just going to have to do what good friends do."

"And what's that?"

She managed a small smile. "Agree to disagree."

I thought of Leesa, and decided I would call her later on. "That's a good plan."

Moppet, who'd been dozing on his bed in the corner, woke suddenly and came rushing over to me. I scooped him up and let him lick my face, because as it happens, dogs' tongues are actually quite sanitary.

"Annie," said Harper, "I know you came home early for Viola, but how are you and Jon doing?"

"Good, I think." As I told her, we've talked every day since I've come home, and wedding planning is back in full swing—in the next month alone, we have a cake tasting, a registry appointment, and favors to pick out. That's not even including my dress fitting.

"But are you two in love?" she pressed.

"I love him. I've always loved him." It's true. I think the minute he began speaking to me on the plane all those years earlier, I felt somehow that we would end up together.

"Now that you're apart again, though, is he all you can think about? Or"—she winked—"are things still just 'nice'?"

"Ohhh," I said. "Well, no. I think Paris was really good for us."

"I'm glad," she said, smiling at me. "You deserve to be happy."

But the fact is, I haven't been thinking about Jon all that much. It's almost like since the moment I realized I would survive if he left me again, all of my worries evaporated. Maybe that's normal. It's possible obsession is the byproduct of conflict, and that's why I keep thinking about Mo.

Regardless, now I finally know how Harper became Harper—and my neighbor. And while I want her to be happy, too (and yes, safe), I'm still preemptively sad knowing that she plans to move away from East Haven in less than two years.

And yet just this morning, I went on MIT's website and downloaded the application package. I don't know if I'll apply this year; I have to take the GRE again first, anyway. But it's good to have something to think about—something productive and within my control.

—AEM

FORTY-THREE

September 23

I was packing up my room this morning—the last time Jon and I spoke, we made plans to go apartment hunting as soon as he returns—when I came across the wig Mo had given me. I looked at it for a while, then stood in front of the mirror and put it on. It wasn't quite the same without the eyeglasses, but he was right: I look good with a bob. *Funny*, I thought; Leesa had always told me I would.

I'd been putting off texting her, in part because . . . well, I was ashamed of the way I behaved. But I was also scared she was going to double down on LITEWEIGHT junk being legit (or worse, continue to push it on me). Harper said good friends can agree to disagree. But is that really true when the truth itself is at stake? What if mutual respect isn't enough to reseal our bond?

No wonder I've been avoiding Leesa; in the back of my mind the possibility that we were one argument away from ending our friendship has always been there. But I would never really know until I stopped speculating and risked that conversation. I grabbed my phone from the desk and texted her.

Hi, it's Annie. Are you free sometime soon?

She wrote back right away.

I could meet today if you're free.

I am—what time works for you?

If you don't mind the kids being there, 3 would be good.

I'd love to see them. East Haven Park?

Perfect . . . thank you for reaching out, Annie.

You're welcome, I started to write. But then I erased it and wrote,

Thank you for responding.

When I went to leave, my mother glanced up at me from the sofa, where she had been reading a book about healing from the inside out.

"I'll be back in an hour or two," I told her.

"Where are you heading?"

I hesitated. "To see Leesa and the twins."

She smiled at me, then stood. "One second." She dashed into the kitchen and returned with a couple of lollipops, which she pressed into my hand. "Give these to the kids for me."

I slipped the lollipops into my coat pocket. "Thanks, Ma. You're the best."

"I'm glad you and Leesa are making time for each other. Friends like that just don't come along very often."

"No, they don't," I admitted. "I'll tell her you say hello."

My stomach was aflutter as I drove across town. Yes, Leesa had made mistakes—but I had not been fair to her. I wouldn't fault her if she held that against me. As she said, all of her other friends support her.

Children were running around the playground and lawn when I got to the park. I didn't see Leesa, but somewhat illogically, I glanced at the bench where Mo and I had sat the last time we were there, half expecting to spot him. Of course, he was nowhere to be seen, but Leesa, Ollie, and Molly came scrambling over the hill.

"Aunt Annie!" squealed Molly and Ollie, wrapping themselves around my legs.

As I squatted to hug them, I wasn't sure my heart wouldn't burst right then and there. Who needs to have your own children when you can spend time with your best friend's adorable twins?

If she's still your best friend, a little voice chided me.

"We never see you anymore," said Molly, pouting at me.

"Yeah! Where have you been?" said Ollie.

I smiled at them. "Actually, I was in Paris."

"Paris!" said Leesa. "Here I thought Florida was exciting!"

I looked up at her. There were bags under her eyes, which I'd never noticed before. She looked tired. "I went to see Jon," I told her.

She frowned. "I'm glad to hear that, though I didn't realize he was still in France."

"We've got a lot to catch up on—that is, if you want to catch up." I turned back to the kids. "The thing is, you two, Aunt Annie was kind of mean to your mom. And that's not okay, right?"

Molly shook her head. "That's not okay."

"That's right," I said. Then I stood and, still addressing the twins, met Leesa's gaze. "I think your mom and I may not agree on everything, but I shouldn't have pushed her away just because of that."

"Pushing is bad!" said Ollie. "We use our words!"

I laughed. "Yes, we do. And I should have told her I was feeling left out when she was hanging out with your friends' mommies."

Leesa tilted her chin up and looked at me through narrowed eyes. But just as my heart was sinking, her arms were around me and she was hugging me so tight I might have heard a rib crack. "Of course, I forgive you, you numbskull. Thank you for apologizing. Do you forgive *me*?"

Just hearing her say that—well, it made me all kinds of joyful. We didn't have to be on the same page about everything to love each other. I grinned at her. "You know I do."

I remembered the lollipops my mother had given me. "Can the kids have these?" I asked, showing them to Leesa behind my hand. "They're from my mom."

"Sure. Guys, why don't you go into the field while you have those?" she said to the twins as I handed them the treats. "Aunt Annie and I have some more talking to do." As they ran off, she looped her arm through mine and smiled at me. "Now, tell me everything."

So I did. I told her about Jon and Paris, and Harper—minus the confidential stuff, of course—and my mom and Viola, and even Mo. When I was done, she just gave me another too-tight hug. "I'm sorry you've been through so much over the past couple months. I wish I could have been there for you."

"That makes two of us, but I only have myself to blame for that."

"No, I shouldn't have tried to get you to buy the LiteWeight stuff. I wanted to tell you how angry I was with Jon. I mean, part of me felt like you should have told him the wedding was off."

"Really?" We'd gone to sit on the bench, and I looked across at her with surprise.

She nodded. "I know you think you're tough, but sometimes I think you're too kind. Regardless of his motivation or who he hired to try to make himself feel better, what Jon did made me wonder if he's really ready for marriage. I mean, trust me, it's rough even when you know what you want out of life." She touched my arm lightly. "I'm sorry—it's hard for me to say that, so I'm sure it's hard to hear."

"It's okay," I said, watching Ollie scramble up the slide—good thing he'd already finished his lollipop. I turned back to her. "That's a fair point. More than fair."

"And what happened with SCI . . ." She pursed her lips. "Annie, I won't tell you your business, especially when it makes so little sense to me. I can see why you'd just want to walk away. But something tells me you're not quite done there."

"You mean I should go ask for my job back?" I asked, incredulous.

She shook her head. "No, nothing like that. But you're a facts kind of person. I know that's why LiteWeight bugs you so much."

I didn't try to correct her. "I respect that you need to make money. I'm really sorry I wasn't more understanding about that. I guess I didn't try to see it from your point of view, which is a hundred percent on me."

Molly was running toward us, screaming her adorable head off, with Ollie hot on her heels. Leesa, who was pretending she hadn't seen them yet, said, "Thank you. I'm actually thinking about trying something different, but that's a subject for when my kids aren't seven seconds from melting down. You want to get together again sometime soon?"

"I don't know," I said. "How busy are you?"

She grinned. "For you? Not busy at all. What I was going to say," she said, raising her voice as Molly began bawling into her shirt and hollering about how Ollie had poked her, "is that I know you. I've known you your whole life. And that's why I find it hard to believe you'd let SCI get away with lying, especially at the expense of something that's so important."

I looked at her for a minute. Then I smiled. "You're right. I guess sometimes it takes another perspective to help you see what you've been missing."

Leesa winked at me—and I'll admit, her eyelashes did look phenomenal. "That's the whole point of having people in your life who love you, Annie."

I'm inclined to agree.

—AEM

FORTY-FOUR

September 24
TO: SCI BOARD (all)
CC: Bethanne Wynn
FROM: Annie Mercer
SUBJECT: Meeting regarding my resignation
and claims against Todd Bizer

Dear Board Members,

I'm writing to request a meeting between myself and all board members regarding the circumstances leading to my resignation, as well as Todd Bizer's alleged claim that I assaulted him.

As you may or may not be aware, I resigned on July 5, following an incident between myself and Todd. During this incident, which took place on July 3, he insisted I come into the lab during an office holiday, then groped me. I pushed him away from me, which resulted in several thousand dollars' worth of damage to laboratory equipment. This incident followed approximately six months of harassment on Todd's part. After attempting to explain what had happened to Bethanne Wynn and being told I was responsible for the incident, I handed in my resignation.

Given Bethanne's response to my disclosure and our subsequent email communication, I am not confident that she has passed any or all of this information on to you. While I trust that you have access to footage from the surveillance cameras throughout the SCI offices, including footage taken on July 3, I would like you to have my full account of the incident and aftermath before we meet. As such, I've attached my email correspondence with Bethanne below, as well as a series of emails from Todd Bizer to me, which I believe provide ample evidence of Todd's escalating pattern of sexual harassment toward me.

While I would like my professional reputation redeemed, as well as back pay for the months I have been unable to work because of my resignation—which, again, was entirely due to my inability to continue working in an unsafe environment—my primary objective is to ensure that Todd Bizer's predatory behavior is stopped. Because if I've learned one thing during my time at SCI, it's not a matter of if; it's when. And I can promise you that most women are (to use Todd's adjective for me) far less "naïve" than I. When Todd strikes again, rather than a pleasantly worded letter to the board, you will no doubt be looking at a lawsuit with multiple plaintiffs.

I would like to meet October 1 between 9 a.m.
and 12 p.m. ET. Please advise.

All best,
Annie E. Mercer

September 25
TO: Ann Mercer
FROM: Todd Bizer, PhD, MBA
SUBJECT: Your position

Dear Annie,

I'm writing to see how you're doing, and to
tell you that I'm very sorry about what transpired
this summer. I have deeply regretted firing you ever
since I did so—and have continued to feel regretful,
as the individual we hired to take over your position has not been the right fit for Sanity Chemical
Innovation. Would you be interested in discussing
the possibility of returning to SCI? Bethanne tells
me you've been in contact with the board, which
suggests to me you're interested in continuing your
work on bacterium imaging with spatial resolution.
Naturally, your rehire would come with a significant
bump in compensation and a promotion to senior
scientist. Please contact me at your earliest possible convenience.

All best and best,
Todd

September 25
TO: Todd Bizer, PhD, MBA
CC: SCI BOARD (all)
FROM: Annie Mercer
SUBJECT: Re: Your position

Todd,

I would love nothing more than to accept your offer, but I'm afraid that in order to do so, you'll have to first stick your right hand in a vat of hydrochloric acid; remove 1,4-dioxane from FastDry Sani-Foam and disclose that the batch that's out may be harmful to anyone with a liver or even one kidney; then resign from SCI. If I were you, I'd move fast on those last two.

For the record, no matter how you attempt to spin it, you did not fire me. I quit. Do not contact me again.

All best and best and best—
Annie

September 25
TO: Ann Mercer
FROM: SCI BOARD (all)
SUBJECT: Re: Meeting regarding my resignation and claims against Todd Bizer

Dear Annie,

Thank you for reaching out to the board. We would be pleased to meet with you, and would like to invite you to attend a meeting with us on October 1, at 9 a.m. in boardroom A at SCI headquarters.

Todd Bizer will not be in attendance, or in the building or area that day. Bethanne Wynn is no longer an SCI employee, so please think of me as your primary contact at SCI until we meet.

Continued success,
Patricia Nelligan
President of the Board of Directors
Sanity Chemical Innovation

FORTY-FIVE

September 27

I called Jon yesterday morning to tell him about my meeting with SCI. We spoke at length—though he wishes I would have gone the lawyer route, he said he was proud of me, and he had a couple good ideas about what I might ask for (i.e., having my non-compete clause voided—it's a long shot, we both agreed, but it's one worth taking).

So imagine my surprise when I answered the front door this afternoon and found him standing there.

By the look of his rumpled button-down, he'd come straight from the plane. "Jon, what are you doing here?" He was smiling at me, but for some reason, he didn't actually seem happy. "Is everything okay?" I asked.

"Yes, of course." He leaned forward and kissed me. "I was hoping to surprise you."

"Mission accomplished," I said, gesturing for him to come in. "I thought you wouldn't be home until the first."

"I didn't want to wait any longer." He glanced around the living room. "This place is looking good. You've been working hard?"

"Ma and I have been working together, actually," I said, surveying the clutter-free credenza and the new shelving unit my mother had just built, where I'd stored many of the knickknacks that had been lying around.

He raised his eyebrows. "She's doing well."

"I'm doing great!" said my mother, emerging from her room. She'd traded her usual sweats for a sweater and a pair of slacks, and she was wearing makeup again. I was about to ask if she'd been expecting him when she put her arm around him and said, "I'm thrilled to see you, Jon, but Annie told me you wouldn't be home until the beginning of next month?"

"Change of plans, Fae. I just really missed Annie."

"That's wonderful. I'm sure you've just made Annie's week," she said, beaming at him. "I'm about to run to the grocery store, but would you like to join us for dinner? We could even go out if you'd prefer. I feel like I haven't seen you in years. And we have some wedding planning details to go over."

Jon looked at me. "I'd love that," he said. "Annie, does that work for you?"

I'd already cleaned Donna Guinness' this morning, and though I'm going to Harper's for wine tomorrow, the evening was wide open. "Works great," I said.

My mother excused herself, and then it was just Jon and me, standing in the middle of the living room staring at each other. "It's kind of weird to see you here," I admitted. "I know we just saw each other last week, but that almost feels like a lifetime ago. I feel bad that you left France early to come back to . . ." I glanced out the window. The leaves were just starting to turn. It was lovely, but not in the same elegant way the Parisian cityscape was. "Well, here."

"I love fall in Michigan. You know that. And we have to get moving on wedding planning. And like I said, I really wanted to see you. Aren't you happy to see *me*?"

"Of course I am. I just wish you hadn't given up your last four days in France." It was a sweet gesture, so I wasn't sure why it bothered me. Maybe because it didn't make sense. We have the rest of our lives to be together, but who knows the next time he'll be in Paris?

"I like that you worry about me, but I promise you, this was absolutely what I wanted to do. I should probably go drop my stuff at home and shower. I just wanted to say hi first," he said, shoving his hands in his pockets.

"I'm glad you did. How about we go out tonight?"

"Sure. Where to?"

I immediately thought of the restaurant I had gone to with Mo. "I know a good Mexican place that I bet my mother would like. Not sure if that sounds appealing after two and a half months of French cuisine," I added. "And I have to warn you, their margaritas are the worst."

"Mexican is great. Meet you back here at five or so?"

"Perfect."

He kissed me again, this time pulling me close to him. "Hey," he said quietly. "Are we okay? We never did finish the conversation we were in the middle of before you left."

"We're fine," I said, but my voice was stiff. I didn't want to talk about Mo with Jon again—ever. For starters, I didn't want to tell him that Mo had apologized to me, and that for reasons that have evaded capture in my mind, I haven't responded to him. "I feel okay about everything, and don't really want to revisit it."

"Well, that's all I need to know. Thank you for being so great about . . ." He smiled at me. "About everything."

"Of course," I said.

He was looking at me so intently that I felt a little unnerved. "I want you to know that I'm okay not having kids," he finally said. "My parents are going to be weird about it, but you and I have agreed from the get-go that parenthood wasn't in the cards for us."

"Wow. Okay," I said. "Thanks for that, I think."

He frowned. "You think?"

"I mean, as long as you're not just saying it to make me happy."

"I would never."

I got on my tiptoes and kissed him. "Then thank you—period. That means a lot to me."

It wasn't until after he was gone that I wondered why he hadn't asked me to come with him back to his apartment. He was so eager to see me that he'd returned four days early. We could have chatted in the car, then made love at his apartment and showered together—or maybe even made love in the shower, not that we had actually ever done that before—and then headed back to East Haven for dinner.

And yet I hadn't suggested coming over, either.

Stop it, I ordered myself. It was almost like I was picking a fight in my head. I resolved to let it go, and by dinnertime, I nearly had.

I may have looked around the restaurant a few times to see if anyone I knew was there. And yes, I did think of Mo as I drank my spectacularly bad margarita, and may or may not have looked to see who was coming through the front door every time the cowbell attached to it rang. Thankfully, my mother's hundred questions were as much of a social lubricant as the tequila—I don't think I've ever been so grateful for her yammering.

When we were done eating, we said goodbye to my mother, who had driven separately.

"Do you want me to spend the night?" I asked Jon when we got in the car.

He rubbed his head. "I'm zonked, Annie," he said. "Can we make a date for tomorrow?"

"I have plans with Harper tomorrow," I said.

"Okay, so maybe Saturday night then."

"Great."

He kissed me in the car when he pulled up in front of my mother's house and told me he'd call me in the morning. I told him that was a good plan.

Maybe a good night's sleep is all we need. And of course, he'll need time to transition from his Parisian fantasy to real life.

Yet I keep thinking that Jon just left his real life behind and doesn't know it yet.

—AEM

FORTY-SIX

October 1

Patricia Nelligan may have promised that Todd would be nowhere near SCI, but I had the shivers as I pulled up to the building. I wanted to believe I was a rational, reasonable person who, to quote Leesa's twins, "uses her words."

But a different side of me had emerged when I shoved Todd into the lab table. It was a side I didn't like one bit. What if I overreact again—even if he never puts a finger on me? That's a pattern. And it's one I don't want any part of.

"You've got this," said Leesa from the backseat.

"We'll be right there if you need anything," said Harper, who was beside me in the passenger seat.

They'd offered to come with me for moral support, even though they wouldn't be allowed in the actual meeting. Harper had even shown up at my front door at seven thirty this morning to help me select an outfit (my new blazer, a pair of navy trouser pants, and a cream blouse she lent me) and to do my makeup. I think they both expected me to say no—I wasn't bringing Jon or my mother, who I'd recently filled in about why I'd really left SCI. But I told both women I'd be thrilled to have them at my side—a decision that was already proving to be wise.

"We'll walk you right into the building," soothed Leesa as I stared out at the asphalt parking lot.

"Okay," I said, taking a deep breath. But when I got out of the car, there was a white sports car exactly like the one Todd drove parked several rows over.

Todd isn't here today, I reassured myself. Maybe he'd left it there while he was traveling, or someone else had an identical car.

"Don't worry," said Harper, hooking her arm through mine.

"Let's march in there like you own the place," said Leesa, taking my other arm.

Babs, the longtime SCI receptionist, did a double take when she saw me on the other side of the glass double doors. "Missed your face, Annie Mercer," she said, and for the first time that day, I managed a real smile.

"I missed you, too, Babs. The board should be expecting me."

"I have your name down, but no one else," she said, pointing to Leesa and Harper.

"I know. It's going to be a tough meeting—I need backup," I explained.

"Well, it's against policy, but"—she winked—"I hear a certain boss around here doesn't follow policy, either. Go on in."

"Thanks, Babs."

"Don't mention it, kid. Go get 'em."

When I reached the boardroom, Patricia Nelligan was waiting for me. With her hair helmet and black suit, she looked every bit the board president. "Welcome, Annie," she said warmly as I walked up to her.

"Thank you for having me," I said. Peering through the doorway, I was reminded that aside from Patricia, every other board member was male.

"Wish me luck," I whispered to Leesa and Harper.

Leesa patted my back. "Forget luck, Annie. Just go tell them the truth as loud as you can."

"I'll try," I said as I stepped into the room.

Patricia Nelligan motioned for me to sit at one end of the table across from her. Before I took my seat, I retrieved my folder from my carryall and went around the table depositing a stack of stapled documents in front of each person.

"What are these?" said one man.

"In addition to copies of the materials I sent Patricia when I requested this meeting, I've also included an extensive timeline and written account of every occasion that I can recall when Todd Bizer acted inappropriately toward me. Of course, I'm sure I've overlooked at least a few instances. Even wildly inappropriate behavior can start to seem normal if it's left unchecked long enough."

The board members glanced at each other.

"Annie," said Patricia, "we were not aware we'd be receiving additional documents. I thought you were here to provide a statement."

I smiled sweetly at her. "As the board president of a scientific corporation, Patricia, surely you believe more information is always a good thing. And I'm sure that we can all agree that the end goal here is truth and justice, so that we can continue our work as scientists, researchers, and agents of public health."

"Right," said Patricia, sounding less sure of herself. "Shall we begin?"

"I believe we already have," said one of the men.

The more I spoke, the less the board did, which was perhaps the most satisfying inverse equation I've ever had the pleasure of working on. Patricia made it clear that they believed me—they really had no choice not to, given the paperwork I provided. Then she asked me what reparation might be appropriate if the board concluded I had been wrongfully terminated.

"Well," I said, "I want back pay. I want my non-compete agreement rendered null and void—today. I want Todd fired; as you probably know, the work can be done without him. In fact, it already is being done without him. But more than anything, I want you to immediately tweak the formula for FastDry Sani-Foam so that it doesn't include 1,4-dioxane or any other substance known to be harmful to humans."

"We can't just do that," said one man, who had yet to identify himself.

I channeled Harper's confidence and winning smile. "You can do anything you want, and so can I. That's why I have the names of several of the best employment lawyers in the state, and am fully prepared to provide copies of the documents I gave you today to the press. I'll expect to hear from you by the end of the workday."

"You'll need to sign a non-disparagement clause," called one of the men as I stood up to leave.

I swiveled around. "What I'll need," I said, "is your response by five o'clock."

The whole thing was over in less than twenty minutes. "That was fast," said Leesa when I emerged. "How did it go?"

"Did you tell them what you wanted?" said Harper.

I nodded, feeling pleased. I wasn't sure what the board would decide, but there was no question that they understood the gravity of the situation. Maybe that's why, as I recounted the meeting to Harper and Leesa, I didn't immediately realize that the person slinking down the hall was one Todd Bizer, PhD, MBA.

"Hello, Annie," he said smoothly.

The tiny hairs on the back of my neck were standing at attention. My blue blazer was unbuttoned, and maybe he could see through my blouse. I shook my head, righting my thoughts. "I thought you weren't allowed to be here today," I said.

He was too close to me, and his breath smelled like stale coffee and soul rot. "I'm here to meet with the board. I have a right to defend myself."

Behind me, Harper snorted. "So did Annie. You should be thanking her for not doing worse to you."

"I apologized for any misunderstanding," he said, sounding not even remotely contrite.

I sighed. I'd been so worried about how I would respond to him if I saw him again. Maybe, at an earlier point in time, I would have acted badly. But now I knew I had nothing to worry about. He didn't have power over me—not anymore. "Oh, Todd."

"Ann—" he began.

"Stop talking," I said. "You've had your chance. I don't know why you secretly feel like a little man, or why you decided to hurt others to feel big. But I hope everything that comes your way is better than what has gone before. Because having a bunch of degrees, starting a successful company, driving a fancy car—well, none of that can make up for the fact that you're a total creep."

I smiled at him as I turned away and walked out of SCI for the last time, arm in arm with two dear friends. It was a brisk, biting day for early October, but the sun warmed me as I made my way through the parking lot. I don't know what happens next, but I believe I can handle it. And I'm beginning to think that's practically as good as a fact.

—AEM

FORTY-SEVEN

The Detroit Tribune

Sanity Chemical Innovation CEO Todd Bizer Out After Sexual Harassment Claims

By Charles Villegas and Leslie Hart

Sanity Chemical Innovation founder, CEO, and chief scientific officer Todd Bizer has left the company amid allegations of sexual harassment and sexual assault from colleagues, says Sanity Chemical Innovation board president Patricia Nelligan.

In an exclusive statement to the *Detroit Tribune*, Bizer confirmed his departure. "While I categorically and unequivocally deny all claims made against me—which are not reflective of who I am as a husband, father of daughters, scientist, or entrepreneur—I believe staying on at SCI will only serve as a distraction. I started this company twelve years ago with the intent of reducing infection and infection-related complications in health-care settings, and our team of scientists has done precisely that. Hospitals and clinics that use Sanity Chemical Innovation products have decreased the rate of both patient and clinician infection by an average of twelve and seventeen percent, respectively, and numerous lives have been saved in the process. I look forward to seeing how my successors carry on this critical mission."

Chief Financial Officer Dr. Linda Goodwell will serve as interim CEO while the company searches for Bizer's long-term replacement.

In a separate press release issued the evening of Monday, October 1, Nelligan announced that FastDry Sani-Foam, Sanity Chemical Innovation's newest product, will be removed from the market, effective immediately, while the company "reviews the product's safety and efficacy to ensure we're doing our absolute best to stop infection where it is most likely to start: people's hands," stated Nelligan. Sanity Chemical Innovation has frequently been cited as one of the biotech and health-care firms breathing new life into the Detroit-area economy. However, industry analysts say that this move, coupled with Bizer's departure, is likely to interfere with Sanity Chemical Innovation's reported sale to Johnson & Johnson.

Most former and current Sanity Chemical Innovation employees declined to comment on Bizer's departure. However, one scientist who left the company earlier this year, who spoke on the condition of anonymity, said she welcomed the news. "It can seem impossible to change the status quo, especially if you're not in a position of power. But as I've recently learned, you're only as alone as you think you are. I'm glad several people came together to ensure that one person's actions did not contaminate an entire body of scientific research."

FORTY-EIGHT

October 4

I'm free.

I can get a job in any chemistry-related field—I could even work for one of SCI's direct competitors if I wanted to. I can apply to graduate school, and Patricia Nelligan herself will write me a letter of recommendation. (She called me at 4:55 p.m. Monday to say SCI had fired Todd and would meet all of my other requests.) The only thing I *can't* do is speak ill of the company—on record, at least, as the one condition of all of the above was my signing a non-disparagement agreement.

It's been glorious, imagining the many possibilities that I opened back up by speaking out. Or at least it *was* glorious. I was driving back from the hospital after seeing Viola when I had an unsettling realization.

Over the past two days, I've been imagining strolling along the Charles River. I've pictured creating a 3-D nanoscale bacteria map using the equipment in one of MIT's state-of-the-art labs. I've envisioned my mother coming to visit me, and me coming back to Michigan to see her, and maybe Viola, too. I've mentally planned vacations with Harper and Leesa, and attending chemistry conferences all over the world, including Paris. Really, the events of the past couple months must have fertilized my parched mind, because I've even thought of getting a little pup like Moppet. But something has been missing from these fantasies.

Or should I say someone—Jon.

And someone else has been occupying the mental space where he should have been.

When I got home, my mother had just brewed a fresh pot of coffee. "Want a cup?" she asked.

"I'd love one," I said, hoping she didn't pick up on my psychic angst. What did it mean that my own fiancé wasn't a part of the future I was dreaming of? It's one thing not to be worked up about the wedding, as I tried to explain to Leesa when she insisted on knowing why I didn't want a big wedding shower. It's entirely another to not be thinking about the person I intend to marry. Jon and I have seen each other every few days since he returned. I've enjoyed helping him research new career possibilities. (He's eyeing a position at one of the airlines, with the hopes of getting flight benefits so he can jet back and forth to France. No surprise, Charles thinks he should open a hedge fund in France; I think this excites Jon more than he lets on.) We've figured out most of the remaining wedding details (e.g., where to seat his dreadful uncle) with a certainty and speed that have both of our mothers second-guessing every decision we make. If I never have to hear, "Are you *sure?*" again, it will be far too soon.

But our lovemaking . . . truth be told, it's been rote, when it happens at all. And when we're not together, I don't really think about where he is or what he's doing. Some of it is him—there's absolutely no way to pretend he hasn't lost the spark he had in Paris. He's simply not as happy here.

Some of it is me, though, and the nagging thoughts I can't seem to let go of.

I suspect there's a third factor at play, too. Which is that Jon and I don't want the same life anymore. I believe he secretly wants children, and even more than that, he's itching to find a way to live in France. If we don't want the same things at the start of our marriage, what hope is there for the middle or the end?

"How's Viola?" my mother asked, handing me a mug and the container of cream.

I poured the cream and watched clouds form in my coffee. "She's hanging in there, but I don't know that she wants to go on this way." Viola hasn't suffered any additional setbacks, but she seems weaker and less engaged every time I go to see her; it's as though she, too, has lost her spark. It's difficult to see her that way, but—this may sound strange—she seems at peace, and that makes me feel as though I should try to be at peace with her situation, too.

"It'll be hard to lose her."

"Yes," I said, blinking back tears. "It will be. But I'm glad to have had this time with her."

My mother smiled kindly. "Me, too. Are you still planning on seeing Jon later today?"

I nodded.

"How are things going between you two?"

I hesitated. "I think it says a lot that he came back . . ."

"Sure, but how are things actually *going*?" she said.

I sat on one of the many stools my mother has collected over the years. "Really well. Which is why I'm confused about what I'm feeling."

"About that man you'd been seeing?"

I startled. It wasn't as though my mother could see inside my head. So how had she known I'd been thinking about him? "Pardon?"

"The one with the silver car. Have you had a fight?"

If only it were that easy. A fight can be fixed with little more than a sincere apology. But what had happened with Mo . . . well, that was something else entirely. "It's a little more complicated than that," I told her.

She pursed her lips and regarded me for a moment. "You know from complicated. But I bet you also know the right thing to do, don't you?"

I took a long swig of my coffee. My mother had poured it into my old MIT mug, the one I had bought myself, when I flew to Cambridge to tour the campus back when I was still in high school. I'd thrown it out after deciding to attend the University of Michigan, but my mother had fished it out and saved it. It might be the one time I was grateful for her tendency to "curate" trash. Then I sighed. "Oh, Ma. This is such a mess."

"Emotions can be messy, Annie, but that doesn't mean you should run from them." She put her arm around my shoulders. "It's okay to change your mind, you know. In fact, now is the best time, before you've said your vows."

I could barely process what she was saying. Change my mind? What had been the point of going to Paris, then? Why had I gone to the trouble of cutting Mo out of my life? But nearly as soon as I asked myself these questions, I knew their answers.

Fact: Even being friends with Mo is at direct odds with rekindling my relationship with Jon.

Fact: That's because I like him entirely too much. And *that* is what I've been running from. I was so stunned at this revelation, you'd think I'd just figured out the theory of relativity.

"I thought you wanted me to marry Jon?" I said.

"Sweetheart, it doesn't matter what I want, unless we're talking about the fact that I want you to be happy. Better not to marry the wrong person than to marry the right one for the wrong reasons."

I sat there, digesting what she had said, as well as what I had just figured out. After a moment, I stood and hugged her. "Thanks, Ma."

"Be strong, my girl."

"I'll try."

I walked back to my car and, as if on autopilot, got in and began to drive. What would I say? How would I approach this?

It had been raining all day, and the roads were slick; the drive took longer than it should have. There was plenty of opportunity for a ruminator like me to do some mental damage, but as I gripped the steering wheel and concentrated on the road, the only thing I could think about was his face.

All operating systems switched back on the minute I parked. What was I *doing*? This was the opposite of logical. This was the opposite of practical. Even after his transgression, Jon checked all my boxes. He was a great conversationalist! He consulted *Consumer Reports* before making a major purchase! He loved my mother and endured my many quirks! I could have gone on and on.

But I did not. Instead, I parked my car and got out. I'd barely taken two steps across the asphalt when I heard a voice from behind me.

"Annie!"

I spun around and saw Mo running through the parking lot of his office building.

He was wearing a black T-shirt and a pair of jeans. When he reached me, his brown eyes were twinkling again—but this time I could not say with what. "I wasn't expecting to see you here. Or at all, I guess," he said, slightly out of breath. "But then I was looking out the window and there you were."

"Yeah," I said, feeling sheepish. "I wasn't actually expecting to come, and then something came over me."

"Something, huh?" he said, grinning.

How could I not smile back at him? "No, that's not entirely true. I'm sorry. I *wanted* to see you. I've been wanting to see you since the minute I got on the plane to France."

"I don't hate hearing that. But what about Jon?"

"I haven't broken off our engagement yet, but I plan to today, actually," I said. Just saying this out loud was an incredible weight off my chest. I love Jon. He's a good person, and he's good for me—in theory.

But I don't want to risk my heart for someone who only works in theory. If I'm going to take the chance that I'll be abandoned or crushed by another man, I want to at least be *in* love with him. I want to constantly think about him when I'm not with him—and to feel like I'm living life to the fullest when I am.

Which is how I feel when I'm with Mo.

"You're not angry with me?" he said.

"I know I should be."

He put his arms around my waist. "You're not nearly the pessimist you pretend to be, are you, Annie?"

"I'm as pessimistic as you are optimistic," I protested, but mostly I was thinking about how good it felt for him to be holding me.

"Every silver lining has its cloud." He was still grinning like a fool. "I'm crazy about you. You know that, don't you?"

"I may or may not feel the same way," I said.

Instead of responding, he took my face in his hands and kissed me, and suddenly I knew exactly what Harper was talking about when she said *joie de vivre*.

"I've wanted to do that since the day I met you," he said when we finally parted. "I'm sorry I lied and messed everything up—I wasn't thinking straight. But honestly, Annie, I don't know if I'll ever be able to think straight when you're around."

"Me, neither," I admitted. "Your story didn't add up, and I probably could have figured that out right away if I'd really wanted to. But I didn't. I just wanted to be around you. There's something about you—about us—that defies logic. And I love that." Then I kissed him again.

It was a bittersweet day, because after I left Mo (who I'll see again this evening; I can hardly wait), I had to drive to Jon's and tell him that I was so very sorry, but I had to return his ring and end our relationship.

And yet our parting was more sweet than bitter. There were tears in Jon's eyes as I delivered the news—but there was relief there, too. Without him even having to say it, I knew I'd just given him permission to go live the life he truly wanted. Then we held each other and we cried. But before I left, we agreed that if any couple can make the transition to friendship, it had to be us—if only because we believe it's possible.

It turns out I was wrong about all endings being inherently unhappy. As a few friends have recently helped me understand, if you're willing to look for joy and open yourself to new possibilities, the end is not an ending at all.

It's a beginning.

—AEM

EPILOGUE

September 2
TO: Jon Nichols
FROM: Annie Mercer
SUBJECT: Fwd: We've Moved!

We've Moved!
    Annie E. Mercer, Mo Beydoun & Moppet
    23 Flagg Street, #2
    Cambridge, MA 02138

Dear Jon,

    Just a quick note to follow up on our moving announcement—isn't it mind-boggling how much has changed in less than a year? Mo and I are getting settled in, and things are good. Actually, they're great. Maybe I'm being preemptive, but MIT is . . . well, it's everything I thought it would be—but better. I just met with my new research supervisor to discuss my long-range research interests (just typing "long-range research interests" makes me giddy), and she's amazing! She's done groundbreaking work in bio-organic chemistry and chemical biology, including imaging studies that closely align with my work at SCI. I can hardly wait to see what the next eight years will hold.

Mo found a work-share space in Somerville, and though he will be handling a lot of his cases remotely, he's already had two new dognapping clients. On the subject of animals, Moppet seems to like the apartment; he's partial to the bay window, which has a seat where he perches much of the day and watches the passersby. I'm still astounded Harper entrusted me with her dog—which I suppose is my dog now—but she swears he's happiest with me, and it was an ideal solution after she decided to rent out the Novaks' place and spend some time traveling. Leesa's taken on most of Harper's clients in the interim, and they're talking about making her a co-president of Pseudonym Style when Harper comes back to the States in a few months.

Anyway, it was so nice to video chat with you and Genevieve last week. Please tell her I say hello, that I hope her pregnancy is still going well, and that Mo and I are looking forward to meeting her in person over the holidays. I'm really happy for you, Jon—I know it took a lot of courage to decide to return to France last year, especially with your parents being so hesitant about it. But I'm sure meeting their half-French grandchild later this year will smooth any remaining rough edges.

Even more than that, I'm proud of you—of us, really. Your seemingly bad decision turned out to be one of the very best things that could have happened to either of us, and that's because we made the most of it. Don't worry, I haven't had a personality transplant. I'm still roughly 78% certain I won't have children, because (no offense) I still can't bear the thought of bringing new life to a planet that's highly likely to implode during the next one to two centuries. And don't even get me started on the water quality here in Massachusetts. As a member of my cohort said to me the other day, it's best to close your eyes and pretend it's straight from one of our many melting glaciers, because if anyone actually tested for the micropolymers and pharmaceutical runoffs contained in a single sip—well, we'd all die of dehydration in short order. (I think I may have made a new friend!)

But as clichéd as it may sound, Viola's passing reminded me that every day really is a gift if we're willing to make it so. Sometimes I think you already knew that last July when you said goodbye.

Send my best to Paris.

Love always,
Annie

ACKNOWLEDGMENTS

My deep gratitude to: Shannon Callahan, Laurel Lambert, and JP Pagán for reading early versions of this novel; Jodi Warshaw for seeing the potential in this story and helping me shape it; Tiffany Yates Martin for providing invaluable editorial guidance yet again; Elisabeth Weed, for being a stellar agent, big thinker, cheerleader, and so much more than I can mention in such a small space; Danielle Marshall, Gabriella Dumpit, and the entire Lake Union team for making publishing a rewarding and collaborative process; Michelle Weiner at CAA for being a tireless champion of my work; Kathleen Carter and Ashley Vanicek for helping my books find the right readers; my friends and family (especially Indira and Xavi) for cheering me on as I write; and my fellow Tall Poppy Writers for your continued support.

And to every reader who has taken the time to read this or any of my novels, thank you. You are why I write.

ABOUT THE AUTHOR

Photo © 2017 Myra Klarman

Camille Pagán is the Amazon Charts and *Washington Post* bestselling author of six novels, including *I'm Fine and Neither Are You*, *Woman Last Seen in Her Thirties*, and *Life and Other Near-Death Experiences*, which has been optioned for film. Pagán's books have been translated into more than a dozen languages. She has written for the *New York Times*; *O, The Oprah Magazine*; *Parade*; *Real Simple*; *Time*; and many other publications. Pagán lives in Ann Arbor, Michigan, with her family. Learn more about her novels at www.camillepagan.com.